Letters, Lovers & Lies

The Lindsey Lark Series

Book Two

Cricket Rohman

Cover design & interior formatting by
Sweet 'N Spicy Designs

Author photos by Curtis Ryan

ISBN: 9780989697156

Novels by
Cricket Rohman

THE LINDSEY LARK SERIES
Wanted: An Honest Man, Book 1
Letters, Lovers, & Lies, Book 2
Hit the Road, Jake!, Book 3

Saving Madeline

THE FANTASY MAKER SERIES
Forever Island
Winter's Blush

THE MCALLISTER BROTHERS SERIES
Colorado Takedown
Montana Countdown

For Muffin, Tweed, Clark, and Charlie …
Until we meet again.

Acknowledgments

I would like to thank:

My talented feedback readers Jerry Gallegos, Carol Anfinson, Pat Vreeland, and Cindy Butierez

My brother, Richard Rohmann, for his helpful hints.

My friends and colleagues in the Saguaro Romance Writers group.

The firefighters at Station 16.

CINDERELLA
AT WORK

ONE

Lindsey

What had I gotten myself into? I really didn't know, and that was the part about my new career that kept me up at night. However, this morning, in spite of all the nervous twinges that had visited me in the darkness recently, excitement filled my body with butterflies, delightful butterflies—the kind that whispers tunes, flutters and glides. All those wings had me floating on air. And, in a couple of hours, I'd be on a plane flying to Denver, Colorado to make my first professional presentation.

Saying good-bye to Jake at the security checkpoint was far more difficult than I ever could have imagined. He was so sweet, making a big effort to look happy. I knew that deep down he didn't want me to go, and if I were being honest with myself, a part of me didn't want to go either. But the rest of me couldn't wait to get this show on the road.

The corners of his mouth turned up in a small smile, but his sad eyes betrayed him. "I guess this is it," he said, his voice slightly husky. "You're on your way, Lindsey. Someday soon the whole world will know Lindsey Sommerfield. You'll be a household word."

I chuckled, wanting to keep the mood light. "Well, I don't know about the whole world," I replied, "but a roomful of teachers in Colorado might remember me for a couple of days."

He nodded, then he touched my cheek with his fingertips. "Be careful, okay? Sure wish I could go with you this first time."

"I'll be back in six days, Jake." Holding my smile presented a challenge, but I had to try. "We can do this. Besides, Wendell and Malcolm need you here."

Maybe, if we'd been together longer, this departure might have been easier. But we were fairly new at being a couple, and I had to admit that leaving like this didn't feel quite right. We gave each other one last hug and a long, delicious kiss, then I made my way through the metal detector and on toward the gate. Glancing over my shoulder, I saw Jake wave, and I waved back. I knew his eyes would watch me until I was completely out of sight. Such a melancholy moment.

The plane's door shut mere seconds after I'd buckled my seatbelt, and though I sat, my body wanted to run up and down the aisle. I wasn't afraid of flying, though my airborne experiences were limited, but for some reason I suddenly felt anxious. The powerful roar of the engines, preparing themselves to lift the mass of metal into the sky, made me clutch the armrests as if I were about to have a root canal.

I knew it wasn't only the plane and the hurdling through the air high above the ground that triggered my distress. The truth was, I was more than a little nervous about my new title as the National Innovative Teacher of the Year. Oh, I loved the title and everything associated with it. I really did. After all, I'd earned it. I'd won it fair and square. But with the win came new responsibilities and a whole bunch of ... the unknown. That's what worried me the most. The only thing I knew for certain was that I was venturing far beyond the borders of my comfort zone.

I also felt a little odd about not being at school with my students, surrounded by the joyful noises that fill a kindergarten classroom: the laughing, the hugs, the questions, the singing ... But that job had a downside, too: long hours, frustrating meetings, constant strategic lesson planning. Even so, now that I was stepping away from that, albeit short term, my life almost seemed too easy.

I felt a little sad not knowing who my students would have been this year. They'd all been placed with a teacher on a temporary contract while I was on sabbatical, but I could vividly picture everyone of last year's kindergarteners and could imagine them as first graders: shy little Harley, brilliant Emma, funny Armando, spoiled but talented Joseph ... and then there was Willy. I said a little prayer for his new teacher.

We were still parked at the end of the runway, waiting to take off; a few planes must have been in line ahead of us. It would have been nice to have Jake by my side, holding my hand. Ever since he'd moved in with me, about four weeks ago, I'd felt different about myself. Instead of extracting energy from me, as Anthony, my former husband, had done, Jake, somehow, added to my strength. And just thinking about him made me smile. I should have known he was a great guy from the first night we met. After all, my mastiff, Wendell, took to him instantly. It had taken me almost a year to figure out what my dog knew in a split second. I should have trusted the dog.

The engines roared again, sounding like a pride of hungry lions, and my pulse quickened. What could I do to take my mind off the impending race down the runway? I closed my eyes, trying to recall the conversation I'd had with Jake the previous night, knowing it would be the perfect distraction. A peaceful feeling warmed me from head to toe at the memory, and I didn't need a mirror to know my face had brightened with a smile. I let my mind drift beyond the confines of the plane's thin walls and snuggled back into my comfy, cozy bed with Jake.

"You're not going to work anymore?" I'd asked him. "With your PhD on hold, won't you get bored? You can't just sit around the house. That scares me a little. I'll worry about you."

"Well, I gotta walk Wendell. Taking care of him and Malcolm was part of the reason we moved in together so quickly, right? And I plan to start writing any day now, so that'll keep me busy."

I grinned. "Oh, yes. I'd almost forgotten. You're now Jake the Detective Novel Writer."

As soon as I'd said those words I wished I hadn't, but I gave him a sweet, girlish grin to ease what could have turned into a tense moment. I hadn't belittle his dreams, just tease him a little.

"Hey, I hear from my colleagues that writing fiction is difficult work," he said, sounding slightly put off. Then he shrugged, back to his easy self. "And, okay, if you must know, I'll still be bartending at the Coyote Café for a while."

That was reassuring to hear because part of our deal required him to pay half of our living expenses. Besides, even if his writing took off, it could be years before that translated into actual dollars.

6

We bantered back and forth a bit more, each at ease saying whatever was on our mind, then concluded our evening with kisses, caresses, and hot, steamy—

"Ma'am, would you care for something to drink?" asked the flight attendant, bringing me back from thoughts of yesterday. My distraction had worked, and now we had reached a comfortable cruising altitude. The plane soared smoothly, and I began to relax.

I wasn't a seasoned traveler. I didn't have lightweight gadgets or trendy traveling clothes, so it had been necessary for me to pack two large bags. In my defense, only one bag contained clothing, the other had been filled with books, notes, copies of my presentation, and student work examples. Now, if I could just drag them from the conveyer belt without pulling a muscle … *Here they come.* I heaved them off one at a time, then turned, looking for a cart to carry my luggage to the ground transportation kiosk. After that, I'd be able to really relax. *Liar, liar.*

My eyes passed over the baggage claim area then stopped. The skin prickled at the back of my neck, and I had the distinct impression that I was being observed, not just casually watched or glanced at. Whoever it was must have been staring intently. Typically, I'm not a paranoid person, and while it's true that I'd always had a good imagination, I wasn't—wait!

The cause of my concern was a handsome man wearing a black suit standing on the opposite side of the colorful carousel of luggage. He held up a sign and continued to stare directly at me. Squinting my eyes, I noticed the sign had my name on it.

Lindsey *Lark.*

No one had used my maiden name in almost four years. I'd always liked the way it sounded, though, and I'd been thinking of dropping my married name for a while now. Maybe seeing it written there was some kind of omen. Anthony and I had been divorced for over six months. I didn't need to use his name anymore. Why should I?

Still, it was odd seeing Lindsey *Lark* written on the driver's sign. How did he know my maiden name? He walked toward me, expressionless.

"Ms. Lark?"

"Yes, that's me."

"This way, please." He snapped his fingers and a skycap appeared and grabbed my bags. We followed the man in black outside.

He was all business, as I supposed a driver should be, but as I followed, I began to feel a little uncomfortable. I had not expected to find myself sitting in the back seat of a Lincoln Town Car, being driven by a chauffeur. Especially not to an educational conference. In my humble experience, anything educational was synonymous with low budget.

"I had no idea Denver was so big," I said, watching out the window. "It's certainly taking a long time to get to the hotel."

"Airport's in Denver, hotel's in Boulder."

That was a surprise. "Is there a Wellington Hotel and Spa in Denver *and* in Boulder?"

"Yes."

Oops. In all the excitement, I must have misread the information packet. I'd have to call Jake when I was all checked in and let him know what I'd done. Slightly embarrassed at the mix-up, I stayed quiet and kept my eyes on the scenery. No more words were spoken for the duration of the drive. I didn't think the driver minded at all. He wore a wireless gadget in his right ear, and I imagined he was listening to his favorite tunes as he drove.

My jaw dropped when we entered the hotel's lobby. The place was incredible. No matter which way I looked I was treated to a spectacular outdoor view melding Colorado nature with the building itself. I felt as if I'd been submerged in a glorious garden of tranquility.

"Wow! I'll bet kings and queens and presidents stay here," I whispered.

He must have overheard. "Yes, they do."

I wasn't exactly sure what to say after that, and my thoughts turned to wondering how much I should tip him. Was I supposed to tip him at all? I stalled. "Thank you very much for picking me up at the airport," I said. "Will you be driving me back to the airport at the end of the conference?"

He didn't smile. "Ms. Lark, I am the advance man for this conference as well as for all of Ms. Meriwether's conferences. It is my job to keep the keynote speaker— which this year is you—informed, on schedule, and safe for the duration of the conference." He tilted his head to one side. "If you'd follow me, please, I will show you the hall where your keynote address will take place."

After his earlier silence, I'd expected no more than an obligatory 'yes' or 'no' in response to my question, so I was almost speechless after his brief lecture. Actually, it probably would have been better had I remained that way. Instead, I blurted out, "Oh, so you're not just the driver?"

He did not look impressed. "Correct."

I followed him, feeling bewildered. I'd just been picked up in a Lincoln Town Car by an efficient-looking man in an expensive black suit, I was being led through the most beautiful hotel lobby I'd ever seen, and now it appeared I had a personal assistant to watch over me throughout my experience here. He opened the door to the massive, sparkling hall where I'd be making my presentation, and I swallowed a hefty dose of reality. The wave of resultant anxiety almost knocked me over.

Memories of how this all started, how I ended up here, briefly flooded my thinking. Last spring, as the result of winning a contest, I was asked to share my Art Journal Lessons at a private conference in front of fifty friendly teachers. And, get this, it had taken place in a barn in Rugby, North Dakota At this Boulder conference, I would be speaking in front of almost 250 attendees. Those nervous twinges had returned.

My room—actually, my *suite*—was extraordinary. After I unpacked my bags, I had some time to unwind, so I ran steaming water into the Jacuzzi tub, which could easily have accommodated four people. With delight, I realized the only decision facing me at that moment was which fragrant bath oil I should choose from the shelf: Serenity, Tranquility, Apples and Oranges, Balsam Fir, Very Sexy, or Amber Rose? Since it was my first night in Colorado, I decided it was appropriate to go with Balsam Fir. Unfortunately, a mere fifteen minutes into my heavenly soak, an untimely knock sounded on the door.

"Just a minute," I said, trying not to whine. Still dripping but smelling like a fresh pine forest, I wrapped up in a towel the size of a tent and hurried to the door. The peephole was a few inches too high for me, so I opened the door against my better judgment.

It was the conference advance man—my *very own* advance man. I blushed, thinking again how silly it felt to actually say that and mean it. Who has an advance man besides the President?

"Ms. Lark," he said, "we have dinner reservations downstairs in twenty minutes. Will that give you adequate time to dress?"

My mind flashed with visions of applying make-up, styling my hair, dressing, then wondering how I could possibly do it all and meet the fast approaching deadline. "Um, yes, I believe so—"

He nodded. "I will wait for you in the sitting area."

He walked stiffly to the leather sofa, his movements almost robotic. All business. What could I say to a guy who walked and talked like that? This man, practically a stranger, now sat in *my* hotel suite while I prepared myself for … dinner.

TWO

Jake

"What do you mean there's no one by that name staying at the hotel? She *must* be there."

I had no patience whatsoever when it came to Lindsey's safety or well-being. The receptionist's calm, cool voice only ignited flashes of fear in my heart. I knew she heard my frustration, but there was nothing I could do about it. I was frustrated and worried.

"I'm sorry, Mr. Lee. Could she have checked in under a different name?"

My brain raced, looking for an answer. "I don't think so. Please check again. Lindsey is there for a teachers' conference."

Wendell stared at me while I was on hold. I swore the dog could read my mind—or at least my mood. He was too smart for his own good sometimes. "I'll find her, big buddy," I assured him. "I will."

The receptionist came back on. "Sorry, sir. No luck. And there are no conferences here until next week." I heard hesitation in her voice. "Can I put you on hold one more time? I just had an idea."

I gritted my teeth and began to pace. This idea had better be a good one because I was about to come unglued. I wanted to kick myself. I *knew* I should have gone with her on this first trip. Why hadn't I insisted?

"Mr. Lee? Mr. Lee?"

"It's Jake," I snapped thinking how I'd just been reduced to a bad '50s song. "Please call me Jake."

"Good news! The Wellington Hotel and Spa in Boulder is having a conference this weekend, and there is a Lindsey registered there—a Lindsey *Lark*, not *Sommerfield*, though. Could that be her?"

My whole body drooped with relief. "Yes. That's her. Thank you."

"And thank you, Mr. Lee," she said. I heard a smile in her voice.

"For …?"

"For solving our perplexing flower mystery."

"I'm sorry?"

"We all wondered why this beautiful flower arrangement had arrived for a woman who wasn't a guest at the hotel."

I let out a sigh of resignation, remembering how I'd arranged for the flower delivery several days ago. In the confusion of Lindsey's temporary disappearance, I'd completely spaced that out.

"What would you like me to do with them?" she asked.

"Enjoy them."

I hung up and turned to my compadres. "Okay, guys. We're back on track. Let's give her a call and wish her well. Malcolm, I expect you to say a few chirps and tweets, and Wendell, maybe a little dog-breath breathing into the phone? Or some tail thumping?"

We were poised and ready, but there was no answer. Lindsey didn't answer either the room phone or her cell phone. I wouldn't be able to write or rest until I could speak with her. I knew that about myself. In the meantime, with nothing else to do, I poured a glass of wine and put my feet up. Wendell curled up on the floor beside me with a long suffering sigh, and I smiled, remembering the special evening Lindsey and I had shared only twenty-four hours before. The memories would get me by ... for a while.

I'd been sitting on the couch in the living room when something had caught my eye. I looked up at the most beautiful sight I'd ever seen: an angel, *my* angel, standing on the stairs wearing only baby blue satin panties. She said nothing but curled one slender finger, motioning for me to come closer. I obliged, but not before removing most of my own clothing—leveling the playing field, so to speak. Hand in hand we climbed upstairs, and when I got to our door I saw she'd already lit candles around the bed. As usual, Wendell followed us.

"Hey, buddy," I whispered. "We need a little alone time. You go back to your own bed for now." He gave me one last, disappointed look, hoping for a reprieve, then he turned and plodded back down the stairs.

Having only three sexual notches in my belt to date—actually, make that two—and with Lindsey being such a sweet, feminine lady, we had some learning and experimenting yet to do. But, hey, a teacher and a researcher should be able to rise to that challenge.

Once the door was closed and we'd headed toward the bed, Lindsey began to talk about me, and what I would do while she was gone. She had a tendency to be chatty, but I loved that ... most of the time. Then, I wrapped my arms around her and took charge of this last night together before she winged her way to Denver. I explored every inch of her, first with my eyes, then gently with my hands. She moaned softly as I lowered my body over hers, and when the serious kissing began, we found the perfect tempo to ride our sexually charged wave of passion. High tide arrived right on schedule.

What a night. What a lady.

I tried calling again, and this time I left a message on her cell. It wasn't ten o'clock yet, so I assumed I'd just have to be patient. She was probably out with the other conference people. She'd call.

Ten o'clock came and went, and though Lindsey wasn't calling me, my laptop was. I decided I might as well take a stab at writing, it was time, and I wanted Lindsey to be proud of my efforts, as I was proud of hers.

We'd set up a home office, so I had a decent space in which to work, to be a writer. Now ... if only I had a clue as to how or where to begin.

I perused the pages of *How To Write Detective Stories*, skimming the table of contents and the first chapter. From what I'd read, it seemed all I needed in order to get started was for a crime to take place. The rest of the story would be about the mystery surrounding that crime and, of course, I'd solve the mystery in the end. Piece of cake, I told myself.

Convinced it would be easy, I got up and made some tea. Wendell gave me a look, so I gave in and took him for a short walk to the corner. When we got home I sat back down, staring miserably at my desk. No words, no thoughts, nothing surfaced. How could I have writer's block before I'd written a single word? Was that even possible? Wondering if there was another name or word for this unexpected dilemma, I did a quick search on the Internet, but didn't find an answer. On the other hand, I did download a contemporary, post-apocalyptic novel that looked fantastic. I read a few chapters, dozed off, and dreamed of Lindsey and me, lost and alone in a withering world. Needless to say, I didn't sleep well.

THREE

Lindsey

Awakened suddenly by the sound of pounding, my brain not yet up to speed, though my heart rate certainly was, I didn't recognize my surroundings. Where was I? An instant later I remembered, then flew out of bed. I'd overslept by thirty minutes and someone was knocking on my door.

There he was, Mr. Advance Man, appearing formal, serious, and polished. He'd surely pass any inspection. I, on the other hand, was a not-ready-for-prime-time, tousled version of myself. We sat together on the sofa, munching the breakfast he'd ordered: English muffins, scrambled eggs, and turkey bacon. He informed me of the day's schedule of events, which included the general session for all attendees, lunch, prep time for my keynote address the following day, and a debriefing dinner. Then he supplied the details pertaining to each individual event. A verbal version of the details came first, followed by a written file reiterating everything he'd just said. Nothing was left to chance. Nothing would go amiss on his watch.

"Any questions?"

It was my first chance to get a word in. I smiled brightly. "Yes. As a matter of fact I do have a question. What's your name? I don't think you ever told me."

"Lad. People call me Lad."

I blinked. "Lad?" I repeated bluntly, then I wished I hadn't thinking my terse response may have come across as rude. He only shrugged, glanced at his watch, then requested to look at my clothes. *What?* Before I could think of an intelligent reply, he and I stood staring into the closet.

"Here," he said, removing a plain but bright-colored sheath dress from my pathetic, teacher wardrobe. "Wear this. I'll meet you downstairs at 9:45."

And he was gone.

I spotted Lad the moment I stepped off the elevator, and he led me directly to the meeting hall. The place was already packed when we arrived, and the powerful energy in the room engulfed me. Lad escorted me to the front where a few other presenters were waiting for the event to begin, and I realized with relief that I wasn't nervous. Yes, a few friendly butterflies were flitting around my insides, but it was a good feeling. All I'd been asked to do this morning was tell the audience a little bit about my background, my experience, and anything personal I wished to share. That might even be fun.

Elisabeth Meriwether stood poised at the podium, and the buzz of chattering voices went silent. She had that effect on people. Without saying a word, she had everyone's attention.

"Thank you for coming to our conference, aptly named *Educational Excellence Through Teacher Innovations.* During the four days that you are here, you'll have the opportunity to meet and observe this year's National Innovative Teacher, Ms. Lindsey Lark, as well as several past award winners. Our hope is that you not only learn masterful teaching ideas that you can willingly take back and share with your own schools and districts, but that you also find this learning experience to be stress-free and infused with peace, joy, and tranquility. You all deserve that."

She had them in the palm of her hand; the audience was mesmerized. Oh, to have that kind of public speaking talent, I thought. A tough act to follow, for sure.

"And now I'd like to call to the podium, Ms. Lindsey Lark, this year's National Innovative Teacher."

I thanked her and stepped up to the microphone. Once I began to tell my story, my words flowed easily. I explained how my colleagues had tricked me last fall, sending me away from our monthly staff meeting so they could secretly fill out the application for the Arizona Innovative Teacher Award. And how I had been offended by the principal's quick dismissal of both me and my friend, Laura. But it had all been a well-orchestrated ploy to lead me astray. I had such good friends.

The next time I took a breath, I caught Lad's signal from the floor to wrap it up. Already? I guess it's true that time flies when you're having fun, and I'd definitely been having fun.

On the second morning, Lad's knock on my door came a little earlier than it had the day before, but this time I was prepared. He not only wheeled in the breakfast cart, he'd brought along several unidentifiable bags, and my curiosity danced ... alone. We ate egg whites, whole-wheat toast, and fruit, in total silence, until Lad suggested I skip the coffee. He explained that the caffeine might make my hands shake, *I knew that,* then added, "Anytime you need an energy boost, let me know. I've got something for that." The man thought of everything.

Afterward, he stood, walked to my closet, and took out my little black dress—the one I'd been saving in case an evening event sprang up. Then he opened one of the bags he'd brought, *Ah, ha! The mystery would unfold,* and plucked out a beautiful, turquoise silk scarf, which he draped expertly over the dress's neckline. The next bag contained a pair of black, high-heeled pumps with platform soles. I wouldn't be able to walk, but at least I'd be able to look out my peephole and see who was knocking on my door. Lad waited while I dressed, brushed my hair, then applied a little mascara and lip gloss.

Onstage, Elisabeth Meriwether introduced me, adding a few brief, anecdotal tidbits to what I'd shared yesterday. Her introduction was a flattering and pleasant surprise; she'd laid the groundwork for my success. As I stepped carefully to the center of the raised, portable stage, wary of my new shoes, I noticed a nod of approval pass between Elisabeth and Lad. They stood off to the side, leaning against the wall. Looking good and feeling fine, I was prepared and ready to be a successful, national presenter.

That was when I saw—*really* saw—more than two hundred and fifty pairs of eyes, all staring at me, waiting for me to be brilliant. The pressure was on. My knees weakened suddenly, and my mouth filled with imaginary cotton balls, inhibiting my ability to speak. The physical reaction caught me completely off guard, and I knew I was in trouble.

I glanced at Lad. Could he see the panic in my eyes? He motioned for me to take a drink from the glass on the podium, and as I took a sip, upbeat music began to play. The lights in the room dimmed slightly, and the words, "Everybody On Your Feet and Clap To The Beat" flashed across the giant screen behind me and to my left. The audience needed no other invitation. They participated enthusiastically, and we clapped together to the rhythm. Images of my students' Art Journal work flashed up on the screen next, and by the time the incredible, two-minute opening was over, my mouth and knees had returned to their normal state.

Having regained the power to both think and speak, I explained my Art Journaling process to the teachers in the audience. I said it consisted of a simple, guided drawing lesson conducted by the teacher followed by time for students to add detail to their drawings. Afterward, the students were given an appropriate writing assignment, which could be a caption, a label, a sentence, a list, a paragraph, a poem, or something else related to previous writing instruction to accompany their pictures. I'd brought samples of student work to illustrate each of my points.

"After all," I told the crowd, "a picture *is* worth a thousand words!"

I made eye contact with the audience whenever possible, and one time as I looked out, I noticed Lad standing at the back of the meeting hall, holding up something that resembled a credit card. When I looked again I thought it was perhaps an ultra slim camera. I guessed that would make sense, since they'd want photos of this event—except they'd hired an actual photographer, and I knew he was out there doing his job. So why was Lad taking photos, too? I decided that was another question I could ask the next time he said, "Any questions?"

I went a little over the ninety minutes allotted for my keynote address, but no 'wrap it up' signals came from Lad. Overall, I thought the presentation went well, but I also felt confident I'd get better with practice. Now it was time to move on to the luncheon, where participants would have the opportunity to ask questions about the information they'd just heard.

I knew I'd have some additional explaining and empowering to do, since any type of change or addition to a teacher's day can be a little frightening for some. No problem. I could handle that.

After an exhausting day, room service delivered a light snack—for two. Lad arrived moments later to partake in the delicious plate of fruits, vegetables, and cheese.

"I guess I should thank you," I said, grinning. "You really saved me today. Or was the intro music and the visuals already a part of the show?"

He gave me an expressionless stare. "If it was part of the show, I would have told you."

"Oh." I swallowed, feeling unaccountably as if I'd just been disciplined. All of a sudden, I was the one with few words.

He must have seen the dismay on my face because he relented a bit. "We always plan for the unexpected. I have multiple back-up plans for anything and everything. Any more questions?"

Something about his tone brought me shockingly close to tears, but I swallowed them back. "Yes. Will I have any time to myself while I'm here?"

"No."

I was determined to prove him wrong. As soon as he left, I filled my tub again. After a brief and frivolous consultation held within my own head, I selected the *Apples & Oranges* bath oil and learned from reading the label that the oil had the capability of producing intoxicating bubbles. I sank into the warmth, becoming one with the fragrant, bubbly water, and gave thanks for this rare opportunity to experience a little solitude. It seemed the Ladies Room and my hotel room's Jacuzzi tub were the only Lad-less locations in all of Boulder.

Apparently I had spoken too soon. I heard a knock, the lock clicked open, then "Hello, Lindsey?"

"I'm ... uh, I'm in the Jacuzzi, Lad."

That didn't stop him. He walked right in and sat on the edge of the tub as if that were a completely normal thing to do. I hugged my body, grateful for the thick blanket of *Apples & Oranges* bubbles, and I prayed those bubbles had staying power.

"We won't be dining together," he informed me. "Elisabeth called a last minute meeting. I've ordered dinner for you. It should arrive," he said, glancing at his watch, "in forty-five minutes. I'll be around later." Then he left. Fortunately, the bubbles had not failed me.

The next knock came exactly forty-five minutes later. Barefooted and still wrapped in the luxurious robe supplied by the hotel, I noticed my new, high-heeled, platform pumps placed right next to the door, and I grinned. Lad *did* think of everything! I stepped into them, instantly creating a taller me, and peeked out the peephole. Dinner had arrived.

With a plate of blackened sea bass in front of me, and three conference days behind me, I felt both relaxed and exhilarated. The past few days had been like a dream come true. I knew I was on my way to being a *little* famous—with the elementary school crowd—and I'd also be upping my financial situation, at least for this year. But, who knows? This experience could lead to even bigger things, bluer skies, greener pastures, and I smiled, musing over how the teachers had loved my Art Journal handouts. The actual published teacher guide would be complete and available for purchase in a few more months, and that was just the beginning of a product line I could easily expand upon. Yes, life was treating me well.

I took a sip of wine, smiling proudly. Now look who was being all business-like!

If I hadn't already assured the members of my little world that I'd severely cut back on my constant inclusion of fairy tale references, I'd be calling myself *Cinderella* right now. I held onto a vision of myself, standing at the podium in a pale blue gown, looking very much like a Disney princess, push-up bra and all. I started giggling then couldn't seem to stop. Yes. I was Cinderella. Cinderella with a job, a fairy godfather dressed in black and a handsome prince that would love me for—

I froze, horrified at what I'd done, or rather, what I had failed to do.

Jake! Oh, my God! Jake. Jake and Wendell and Malcolm! The three most precious figures in my life, and I hadn't even thought of them in almost three days. How was that possible? Poor Jake. I'd been so selfish—again. I hadn't even called him. Being busy was no excuse.

Where was my phone? I checked my purse, my pockets, my carry-on bag, the drawers in the desk, everywhere. When was the last time I'd used it? Finally, I pulled open the drawer of the nightstand by the bed and there it was. Strange, I didn't remember putting it there and wondered briefly if maybe housekeeping had done that for me. I also didn't remember turning it off.

I powered it up and the screen calmly informed me that Jake had called six times on Wednesday, three times on Thursday, and once yesterday, but there had been no call today. Had he given up on me? The disappointment in myself weighed heavy, and a substantial dose of guilt slithered through me—like the rattlesnakes in one of my kindergarten desert songs.

An envelope slid under the door. Curious, the sight of it distracted me from beating myself up, and delayed the overdue call to Jake. It couldn't be a bill because I wasn't paying for the room. It had to be a note, and I could only hope it was a message from Jake. Bouncing to the door and trying not to trip on the oversized robe, I stooped to retrieve the envelope.

With excited anticipation, I ripped it open, stared at the note within, then shook my head with confusion. The room swayed, moving in muddled slow motion, and I think I screamed, though I heard no sound. I fell to my knees by the door, shocked, and rocking in a numbing vacuum.

When I'd regained an inkling of awareness, I found myself on the sofa with Lad's comforting, strong arms around me. The note had been spread open on the coffee table, and I noticed the edge was stained with blood. A stinging sensation brought my fragile attention to the napkin wrapped around my finger and the pressure Lad was applying.

"Just a paper cut. You'll be fine."

My eyes were drawn back to the note. I stared at the words and my body trembled.

ANTHONY HAS LEFT THE PHYSICAL WORLD.
HIS FUNERAL IS TOMORROW
AT THE DESERT HOPE CEMETERY AT 3:00 P.M.

Lad had some tea sent up then began his questioning. "I take it you knew this man, Anthony."

Nodding and dabbing my eyes, I told him, "He was my husband. He was everything to me for a while."

"For a while?"

"Yes, until he began having an affair … with a stripper. He moved out of our house and in with her—*her*, that's a joke because the stripper ended up being a transsexual, a guy." My emotions bubbled up, and I wasn't sure whether my grief or my fury was stronger. "I was served with divorce papers a few months later. I loved him, and I hated him, but I never wanted him to die. In the end, he wanted me back, but I wouldn't give him the time of day."

Why did I suddenly feel so guilty, so devastatingly sad? Of course the sadness made some sense. It was normal to feel sad, even shocked when someone you knew, someone who had always been fit and healthy, passed away so unexpectedly. But what about the guilty part? Wasn't he the one who had hurt me? Destroyed our marriage? Treated me like dirt?

"I have to get back to Tucson," I managed to say before curling up around myself again. "I should go to the funeral."

"I'll get you there," he said softly.

Drained now of the small amount of energy that had lingered after this long day, and beaten down from the sudden surge of adrenaline, followed by dose of shock, I drifted off in Lad's strong arms. One last foggy thought tiptoed through my brain just before I fell asleep: *Mmmm. He smells good.*

Early the next morning I was in the back of the Lincoln Town Car, staring out the window. "We'll take the toll roads," Lad said. "They'll get us to the airport quicker."

I simply nodded. I wasn't in the mood to talk, even though I probably would have felt better if I'd voiced my thoughts and expressed my emotions. Lad and I never had a real, non-business conversation, so I didn't expect one now. It didn't matter. My eyes closed, and I let myself pray for a miracle. Maybe this was a mistake or a cruel joke. A welcomed numbness spread through me. The next thing I knew, we were at the security checkpoint. I turned to say good-bye and thank Lad, but he was busy showing the guard some kind of ID. To my surprise, they let him go right through and on to the gate with me.

I stared at him as we walked toward the departure lounge, but he only frowned. "Don't ask."

I ignored his demand. "Who *are* you?"

I could see he was thinking hard about the answer he might give. Would it be fact or fiction?

"Well, Ms. Lindsey Lark," he finally said, "I am the guy responsible for making sure the company's main investment is safe and sound. And informed. So don't worry about the events you'll miss at the conference. There are enough speakers to keep the participants busy today. I will contact you later about the final debriefing and product development meeting."

He'd chosen to tell me neither fact nor fiction. Instead, he'd completely avoided answering my question.

"Do you need my home phone number?"

"Got it right here," he said patting his upper left coat pocket and pulling out a card. He handed it to me just before I stepped through the final walkway toward the plane. "I will see you in Austin in a few weeks. You can call me anytime. For any reason."

I stared at the card, hoping to learn a bit more about my mystery man. It was a very simple card. Just L.A.D. and a phone number. He was, apparently, a man of few *written* words, too. When I glanced up, he was gone.

FOUR

Jake

I listened to the messages on my phone certain that one of them would be from Lindsey, but I was wrong. Instead, I received the incredibly shocking news that Anthony was dead.

Wendell yawned, giving a huge, wide-mouthed performance designed to distract me from my laptop screen. It didn't work. I had to make sense of the situation, but I couldn't. It didn't make sense. How could a young, healthy guy like Anthony turn up dead?

Did Lindsey know? We needed to talk now more than ever. She hadn't returned any of my other calls all week, so I doubted she'd answer, but it was worth a try.

"Sorry, sir. No one is answering. Would you care to leave a message?"

"Yeah. I guess so. Please tell Lindsey that it's Jake, and it's urgent. She needs to call me."

What about Shawna? Did I dare call her? After all, the last time we'd spoken she'd given me a black eye, a bloody lip, and a swollen face. I shook my head, remembering the pain. I'd learned my lesson; I'd call her shrink instead.

"Hi, Julie."

"Jake? Surely not my brother, Jake." She laughed. "What's up? Two calls in four months? That's some kind of record."

"Yeah, yeah. I know. Sorry about that. Listen, something odd has happened. Have you heard from Shawna recently?"

"Of course. We had our weekly, long-distance phone session last Monday. Why? What's going on?"

Hmmm. Maybe Shawna didn't know about it yet. "It's just that today is the funeral, and—"

"Whoa! Hold on. A funeral? Whose funeral?"

"Anthony's. There was a weird message on my phone when I woke up this morning."

"Anthony *died*? Holy crap!" She hesitated. "Oh, man. I'm not sure how Shawna will react to this news."

"Yeah," I mused. "She's a hard one to figure out."

"That's putting it mildly. On one hand, Anthony was the man she loved and wanted to marry as soon as her final surgery took place. On the other, he's the one who dumped her, said he hated her, called her a sick, psychotic, evil person. So she could be devastated *or* she could be delighted that he got what she felt he deserved."

"That's what I was thinking," I said. "Either way, a traumatic meltdown is in her future, and because we're all connected, it'll likely splatter into our lives, too." I blew out a breath, hating the thought of all the drama starting up again. It had been hard enough the first time around. "Anyway, I thought you could use a heads-up."

I agreed to call Julie back after the funeral, whether or not I saw Shawna there. I imagined I'd have a little more information by that time.

My next call would be to Laura, Lindsey's best friend. Maybe she'd heard from Linds.

"Hi, Jake. What a surprise. Getting lonely with your honey out of town?"

"Have you heard from her?" I asked.

"Lindsey? No, but I didn't really expect to," she said. "She's only gone for six days. Why do you ask?"

"Oh, I don't know," I replied, trying to sound as casual as she did. "Maybe because I haven't heard from her at all, or maybe because Anthony is dead and his funeral is this afternoon. How's that?"

Silence. "Oh, my God," she finally muttered. I could almost hear her thoughts traveling over the phone. "I can't believe it," she whispered. Then finding her full voice she said, "Pick me up on your way to the cemetery. I need a ride and someone to lean on. I hate funerals."

It was twenty minutes before three when Laura and I made our way across the short green grass and over to the tent which shaded the hole in the ground. About two dozen folding chairs stood at attention beneath it. A few other people had arrived, but the only one I recognized was Mrs. Madera, Anthony's assistant from his chiropractic office. Other than that, I saw two cemetery workers and a handful of strangers. That was it. I was sure more would arrive soon. Would Lindsey attend? Did she even know about the death, the funeral?

The desert air was hot and motionless, just like the mourners. I couldn't tell if Mrs. Madera was dabbing at tears or wiping away perspiration. Probably both. Laura and I stood with linked arms, taking in the stillness, the silence, waiting for the service to begin. We both looked over when a taxi pulled up and Lindsey stepped out. Before I even knew that my feet were moving, I was taking purposeful, angry steps to meet her.

"Where have you been? I called you every day. I called you multiple times last night trying to let you know about the funeral. "

Her face went dark with ... what? Shame? Embarrassment? I could see she hadn't slept. The lines under her eyes were dark with grief and exhaustion. "I'm sorry, Jake. I was in constant meetings with the conference staff. You have to understand: my time is not my own on these trips." She shrugged weakly, sounding tentative. "Maybe you called the wrong room. We never heard the phone ring."

I stared, knowing she wasn't telling me the whole truth. What had changed? Why did she feel the need to lie to me now? "The meeting was in your room, late at night?"

She started to cry, and I felt awful for being so abrupt. Or maybe she was crying for Anthony. Hell, it didn't matter. My girl was hurting, and I was being a selfish jerk. Today was not the day for questions. I wrapped my arms around her, holding her tight, and attempted to console her. She'd been through so much.

Her soft sobs eased, and she reached for my hand, giving me a pleading look. My heart broke, seeing her like that, and I kissed her gently, hoping to reassure her. Hand in hand, we walked closer toward the others, who we could hear speaking softly. From their questions and expressions, it appeared no one knew what had caused Anthony's demise. Everyone wanted to know more— everyone but a couple standing the farthest from the group. Their only contribution to the questioning was, "Who cares?"

I gave Mrs. Madera a *who-are-they?* look, but she just shrugged. Then Lindsey jabbed me in the ribs with her elbow, grabbing my attention. With her chin, she subtly pointed toward the approaching minister, with Shawna at his side. Were they together? Or had they merely arrived at the same time? I wondered.

She looked completely different from the last time we'd seen her. We stared, shocked at the sight of the obvious initial stages of her voluntary transformation, which included shorter, darker hair and flat shoes—a far cry from her long, bright strawberry blond locks and spike heels. She was still dressed as a woman, but now she looked like a conservative woman, not the flamboyant sex siren of the past.

The female cemetery worker asked us to gather in the shade of the tent. A few people sat, though most stood behind the chairs. The minister began; his eulogy canned and impersonal. A medley of short clips from the songs, "One Way or Another," "The Impossible Dream," and, finally, "Amazing Grace"—thank God, something appropriate—flowed quietly from a small CD player. Not exactly a typical requiem.

I was not paying attention to the service. I was not a good and reverent mourner. A tearful Lindsey noticed and didn't look entirely happy with me, but my brain was on overdrive.

"Where is the casket?" I whispered to the male cemetery worker who stood off to the side, looking bored.

"Oh, it's in there. It's just real small 'cause the guy was cremated."

"Kind of a big hole for such a small box," I added.

"Sure is."

That made no sense. My academic research disposition kicked in with a vengeance. Turning back was not an option for me, now that I clearly saw questions that needed answers. Somebody had to know something about Anthony's death. Either that, or for reasons yet to be determined, they were not willing to come forward with such information. My eyes went to Shawna, who looked neither happy nor sad. I couldn't read her, but that was nothing new.

A recording of taps began to play, and my brain relaxed briefly. The hollow, lamenting sound echoing from the bugle got to me, gave me chills. Death. I don't do well with death. When the minimal gravesite service was almost over, the mourners once again milled around, not certain of what they should do. Lindsey took a few steps closer to the burial site, and I moved toward Mrs. Madera.

"Do you know *when* he died?" I asked her.

She sniffed, looking up at me. "Not exactly, but …" She fumbled in her purse, pulled out a pocket calendar, flipped through the pages, then stopped and jabbed a finger at it. "Okay, here. During the last two weeks in August, things got a lot better. I saw him on August 27th when he told me he was going out of town for a three-day weekend. I never saw him after that." She blinked and a stream of fat tears rolled down her cheeks. She looked away. "I miss him. He was like my own son. I took care of him."

Whoa! I was completely baffled by her statement. "Really? He never seemed like a guy who needed to be taken care of."

"Oh, he was," she said quietly. "He certainly was."

I glanced around for Laura, thinking it was almost time to leave, but I saw no sign of her. She'd already gone. I guessed she'd found another ride.

Lindsey stood by the grave, her head bowed. It broke my heart, seeing her like that. I didn't want to interrupt her final words, so I stood a few respectful feet away.

"Anthony," she said softly. "What happened to you? You never said good-bye. Not when you left me and not before you departed the earth. Why? I hope you're at peace now. Goodbye." She reached over the open hole and gently dropped in a rose, then she knelt to pick up a handful of the soil. Without a word, she sprinkled it over the grave, then returned to my side.

Shawna went next. As she stepped up to the opening in the earth her stance seemed awkward and her expression inexplicable. Was she angry, sad, or just holding it all in. She said nothing when she threw a fist full of dirt into the hole, then walked away.

FIVE

Shawna

The bed still felt too large, too empty without Anthony in it. I suppose by now I should've gotten used to that, but while lots of things had changed, that one thing hadn't. I still wanted him there with me. It had been over three months since he'd walked—no—since he'd *run* out on me. That's not even right. He'd run *away* from me. Stupid man. He could have had his little fantasy world, but his feet got too damn cold, right at the brink of my perfection. He'd ruined everything for me, for him, and for us.

I refilled my wine glass to the brim and raised it in a toast to my dearly departed. "To Anthony," I sneered. "May you rest in peace, down deep in the dirt!"

My cell phone rang just as I was about to turn off the light. Didn't matter. I wouldn't be able to sleep anyway. If there was such a thing as pacing while lying down, I was doing it. My nervous energy had no outlet tonight.

"Shawna? It's Julie."

"Hi, Julie. I suppose you heard."

"I did. How are you? How are you feeling right now?"

Sometimes, Julie's voice was soothing. Sometimes, I liked the fact that she listened to me and helped me sort through all the confusing feelings that lived in my head. I wasn't sure how I felt about tonight's call, though.

"Weird, strange, awful, like I do most of the time. Only today's been worse than that. I'm really not in the mood to talk about it."

"That is a very normal way to feel right now, Shawna. Death of a loved one is difficult for anyone to cope with. Tell me about the funeral."

She was a stubborn woman, but really, I had nothing else to do but talk. I reclined, staring at the ceiling. "Let's see," I said. "A few people, a few words, a song, Taps, dirt in the hole. That's about it."

She followed up with her predictable question: "How did that make you feel?"

She asked that all the time. Over and over and over. She could be a real pain in the ass. But, Julie was also a talented psychiatrist; I'd give her that. She could manipulate my brain just enough that I'd lower my guard and begin to talk. *Really* talk.

"I felt very alone and sad at the funeral, and I wasn't sure why."

"What did you expect to feel?"

"I don't know. Something." I sighed. "The few people who were there kept to themselves. A hug or a handshake—hell, even eye contact would have been nice. I had no friends at the funeral, that's for sure."

"Strange vibes at a funeral are not unusual, Shawna. Probably not the best time or place to find friends."

Julie listened attentively as I spewed out my lingering anger toward Anthony. I guess that's what I'd paid her for. I was emotionally on edge—more than usual—for countless reasons, and my anger soon turned to self-pity.

That made me cry, and that made me angry all over again. Years ago—ever since that dark day back in Benson, when I'd been sitting across the kitchen table from my father as he shot himself in the head—I'd vowed I would never ever shed another tear as long as I lived. Well, look at me now. I was a blubbering idiot.

"This is all *your* fault," I told Julie between sobs.

She let me vent; she always did. So my ranting continued. "You think you're so smart. Thanks to your baby brother, you put the thought in my head that I had to "be a man" because I still have a dick. Well, if Anthony hadn't run out, I'd be the happiest, most beautiful *woman* in the world right now. But now it's all messed up and I don't know who the hell I am or what I want to be."

"You were born a male," she reminded me gently. "And your father distorted your childhood and put you through hell. That's all I'm saying, Shawna. That's all I've ever said. You came up with the rest."

I heard her words, but I wasn't really listening to them. Listening did not come naturally to me. I suppose my shrink would say I was too self-centered. Well, she wouldn't actually say that, she'd get *me* to say it. That was one of her tricks that drove me crazy. I do whatever it takes to survive. I always have, and I always will.

"You've ruined my life, Julie," I declared, my volume building with each word. "When I was Shawna and only Shawna, I had *fun*. I looked terrific and got lots of attention. Now I'm some kind of freak that doesn't know how to look, how to act, or how to feel."

Tonight I hated everything. Even my precious cell phone. I didn't want to just hang up on Julie, I wanted to slam down the receiver. Tapping a little spot on the screen with my finger didn't cut it. So I hurled the phone across the room and watched it crash spectacularly into the mirror.

How did I feel about *that*?

Damn good!

TUNNEL OF LOVE

SIX

Lindsey

Our relationship was at risk. I'd have to be blind not to notice. Was it worth fixing? Jake was in a fog. So was I, for that matter. It didn't help that I felt partly responsible for Jake's fogginess, though. The travel, the conference, and especially my total lack of attention toward him during my absence had been hard on him, though he tried not to show it. I thought about how I'd feel if the tables had been turned. Add to that Anthony's death, the funeral, and the oddness surrounding all of the recent events ... well, it was a lot. And Jake appeared almost obsessed with any topic associated with Anthony. Perhaps that was a coping mechanism for him.

This was to be a time for us to carefully build our relationship, making certain we were truly meant for each other. But so much had gotten in the way of that process. To make matters worse, way too often I caught myself thinking about Lad. No, not Lad! Anthony! I kept thinking way too much about *Anthony*. Ugh! The fog had thickened.

A whole week passed with little communication and no intimacy between Jake and me. That had to change. Deep down, I knew he loved me, but I needed his rock-solid disposition to resurface. If only I could count on him, lean on him again like I used to. I smiled, knowing exactly what to do. I'd take the lead and make the first move.

Jake sat at the desk, staring at his computer as he so often did these days. I walked quietly up behind him and covered his eyes with my hands. Keeping my voice playful, I asked, "Guess who?"

He didn't turn around. "Hey, Lindsey. Your perfume gave you away. Got plans for today?"

I didn't reply, and he didn't seem to notice. Drastic measures were called for. I moved around to his side, letting my fingertips tickle his neck as I changed position. Eventually, I placed myself between him and his computer, giving him an unobstructed view of me, then I leaned back against the desk and began to remove my clothing. Nothing. I *still* didn't have his full attention. He was in one of his working/writing modes—or so he said, but I could see no evidence that any writing had taken place. In fact, the computer seemed to be getting less attention than I was.

I leaned in. "Do I need to commit a crime to get your attention?"

Ah, ha! Those key words finally roused him from his oblivion. He looked at me, really *looked* at me, and I felt his full attention. He blinked slowly, his eyes roaming over my scantily clad body.

"What kind of crime did you have in mind, Ms. Lindsey?"

Donned only in my favorite pale peach panties and matching bra, I eased onto his lap and whispered something into his ear. He gave me a funny look. "I don't think that is a crime. Not in my book, anyway."

"Okay, Mr. Detective," I teased, "but … would it be a crime if we *didn't* do that?"

Well, that did it. We never got to the bedroom. We'd made it as far as the sofa in the living room and we were in the midst of making passionate love when we noticed Wendell sitting at attention just three feet away. He kept cocking his head from side to side, the way he does when he's trying to understand something, and our laughing began. Wendell took that as an invitation to join in, and he howled, which encouraged Malcolm to chirp. Then Wendell moved in close enough to lick our faces. So while it didn't end up being a hot, intense lovemaking session, we had a heck of a lot of fun.

Jake lay on his side, looking down at me. His fingers drew circles on my tummy before they skimmed over my lips. As much as I loved our passionate lovemaking, I still craved these tender moments and the pillow talk that almost always followed. "Thank you," he said. "I needed that. You are so sweet." He kissed me lightly. "And I love you so much."

"I love you, too," I said, meaning every word.

He touched a fingertip to my nose. "Hey, I know you've been slightly overwhelmed with your new job, but weren't you going to write a romance novel in *your* spare time?"

I laughed. "Spare time? I haven't had any spare time yet. Maybe next year. Besides, I'm not really in a romance state of mind right now."

"You could have fooled me."

His boyish grin brought a smile to my own satisfied lips. "Remember the night in the tent last June up in the Zuni Mountains?" I asked.

"Remember? It's forever embedded in my thoughts. Our first night alone together, except for being side by side with a dog and a bird. If there'd been a chapel down that dusty trail, I'd have married you right then and there."

I smiled because I felt exactly the same way. "Well, there was no chapel, so here we are, being wise and careful, making certain we're doing things the right way." I grinned. "Besides, I want a 'white' wedding."

He frowned, confused. "That's a reference to the color of your dress, right?"

"Um ... No. It's a reference to snow."

SEVEN

Lindsey

I had work to do. The ten neon-colored sticky notes, all lined up on the refrigerator door were an unmistakable reminder. Each named a "must do" task which had to be completed before I headed to the next conference in Austin, Texas. According to Lad, Elisabeth had requested that I create at least five new Art Journal Lesson Plans for each conference.

If accomplished, the Teacher's Guide would contain a total of twenty or more lessons by December. I agreed with her plan; it was doable. Finding the time to try them out with real students would be the challenging aspect of this assignment.

Elisabeth's second request, since I'd missed the product development meeting, was to come up with two of my own ideas for additional products for teachers. Idea #1: A Children's Art Book featuring art created during or after a guided art lesson. Idea #2: A Teachers' Guide for creating and implementing Primary Writing Centers. Her second request was both doable and, suddenly, done!

Elisabeth's third request had three parts to it. I found it a bit unusual, more difficult than the others, and downright surprising. First, I was to plan something wonderful to do for my family. I was curious to find out how she defined *my family.* Then she asked me to do something for *myself* that I've always wanted to do. Finally, she wanted me to write down what I thought my life would be like two years from now.

The first seven, colorful Post-It squares were gone by the end of the week. Mission almost accomplished. I gave myself three days to complete the final three requests, thinking I'd do one a day.

Jake seemed to need some solitude lately, so I'd been using the kitchen table as my desk much of the time. But now that I had most of my paperwork complete, some family time was in order. I decided to begin with Wendell who'd been trying to get me to shake hands with him for the past hour. He was in dire need of some dutiful dog work.

I decided that playing with Wendell and learning new agility tricks would be my 'plan something wonderful for my family' assignment—at least until I thought of something better.

"Okay, then," I said, addressing Wendell. "Look here. I have catalogs for K9 Training at Home and Agility Training Starter Kits."

Wendell cocked his head from side to side as I spoke to him—a trait he'd had since puppyhood. I liked to think he did that in order to understand my every word.

I flipped through the catalog. "Look, Wendell. It says we could purchase a platform hurdle for $649. Bargain? I don't think so. How about a catwalk for $580?" I nodded, looking at him. "I can see you liked the sound of that one, but we're not getting it. Here's an A-frame for only $325.

Huh. That's some pretty pricey fun, Wendell. Let's look at the agility equipment."

Ultimately, I made an online purchase of a single-jump and a fabric tunnel that would arrive via FedEx in two days. Today, a good walk was about all I could offer the dog. I ran upstairs to change into my comfortable walking shoes ... and discovered an adorable stuffed animal on the bed: a little green frog with a note tied around its neck. The note said:

Dear Princess,

I will clean the house and even pick up all the you-know-what in the backyard if you grant me a one wish.

Skipping down the stairs with the frog dangling from my hand, I stopped beside Jake and kissed him on the neck. "Sounds like your Frog Prince friend has proposed a good deal. Let me see if I understand. This frog wants a wish granted? Or is he asking for a wish on your behalf? Or ... are you now the frog?"

Jake scratched his head, searching for a reply, and I giggled. He'd told me recently that I was a master of making the simple, complex, and perhaps, in the name of fun, I'd done it again. On the other hand, Jake often thought too much.

"But I've got to tell you," I said, "I think I'm over all that fairy tale stuff. I don't need it for survival anymore." I looked directly into his kind, blue eyes and added, "Besides, I've got my Prince Charming."

Jake got up from his desk and held me in his arms, not speaking for several moments. "Okay," he finally said, "but I do still want my wish."

I giggled. "Of course, my prince. You can tell me all about your *wish* a little later. For now, Wendell and I are going for a walk. Do you want to come with us?"

He gave a little shrug, looking helpless, then sat back down. "I would, except I think I'm finally onto something. I'd better finish writing these thoughts down while they're fresh."

I had to admit: he did look like a writer, sitting with his laptop, tapping one rhythm with a pencil and another with his feet. At the same time, I couldn't help but notice that not a single word was visible on either the screen or his notepad.

"Okay. We won't be gone more than thirty minutes." At the door's edge, I turned and added, "Just don't become Jack Nicholson in *The Shining*. That would not be good."

FedEx had come and gone. Now Wendell watched attentively as I set up the single jump. I placed the cross bar at the lowest spot possible. It was no more than twelve inches above the ground—easy for a one hundred and sixty pound dog. I sat him about six feet from the bar, asked him to stay, then went around to the other side.

"Wendell, come! Here boy. Come!"

He approached the bar, sniffed it, licked it, then sat by it. Treats! I needed some treats. As it turned out, the treats did nothing to build his enthusiasm for the bar.

Plainly, he wanted nothing to do with this activity. Then another strategy came to mind. I attached his leash and tried to lead him over the bar—all he had to do was step over—he leaned back, planted his feet firmly in the grass, and would not budge. We were *not* having fun, and that had been our main purpose. We move on to the tunnel.

He did think the tunnel was interesting. He bounded all around it, nudged it with his nose, and even poked his huge head into one of the ends. I hurried to the opposite end to call him, hoping he'd wiggle his way through to me. With great determination, I inched my way to the mid-point of the tunnel and called him again. Oh, he came, all right, but not *through* the tunnel. He pounced on *top* of the tunnel, on top of me. I could only imagine what that looked like: me, the lump in the now thrashing, giant blue wormy-looking thing, wrestling with a large, leaping mastiff. The barking, screaming, laughing, and the occasional "Ouch!" even managed to rouse Jake from his "work."

"What's going on here? Lindsey?"

"Help!" I yelled, laughing, though I actually did need some assistance. The tunnel was a tangled blue blob with me in the middle.

"I'm coming in!" His shout was infused with laughter. Wendell kept on bounding and pouncing, and I'm sure he was laughing in dog language. Jake straightened out one end of the tunnel, crawled in like a marine, and soon we were head to head, face to face in a very small space. The tunnel lay still. Evidently, Wendell had taken a break.

Jake said, "Hi," his dreamy eyes looking bluer than usual, and then …

I highly recommend making out in a dog tunnel with someone you love.

EIGHT

Jake

*O*nce upon a time there was a crime.
No, that wouldn't work. Nothing was working.
A blank screen stared at me, taunted me, then I recalled an article I'd read somewhere that had advised writers to "write drunk, edit sober." As a result, I seriously considered getting a drink to aid the process—and I didn't mean water. I needed to be in writing mode, so I figured it was worth a try. This would be a scientific experiment, I told myself. Research. I already knew I was good at research, so with that in mind, my novel-writing comfort zone looked within reach.

By ten o'clock in the morning, I was already on my second glass of red wine. I'd begun to type the words, *I need to write, I need to write, I need to write.*

Oh, my God. Was I becoming that scary guy in *The Shining*? I was so not a drinker. But I *was* still a thinker. Thoughts began trickling in, but unfortunately they weren't really helping with the writing. They were thoughts like: I need to take better care of Lindsey, spend more time with her. I needed to write that detective novel, even if it proved to be unworthy of an audience. That way she wouldn't think her housemate—who would someday become her husband, I hoped—was nothing more than a dog-walking bartender.

The pathetic trickle of story ideas morphed into a powerful flood when my thoughts took a turn toward Anthony. I hadn't consciously tried to go there; it just happened. I couldn't get past the fact that no one at the funeral had known anything about his death or the funeral arrangements. That was just wrong. Someone had to know *something*.

Knowing I was just the man to figure it out, I began making some calls.

"Hi, Mrs. Madera. It's Jake. How are you doing today?"

"I'm all right." The heavy sigh betrayed her words. "I just don't know what I should be doing since I no longer have a job or an employer."

"Well, you have a tiny job today," I said, trying to sound chipper, "because I need your help."

"With what?"

"Would you mind telling me how you found out about the funeral?"

"Sure. That's easy. I received a card in the mail just the day before. It looked like an invitation to a party with balloons, party hats, smiling people, and the words *You're Invited* on the front." Her voice trembled with emotion just sharing this little piece of information. "So I open it up, but on the inside it said, *To Anthony Sommerfield's Funeral.* The only other words spelled out were the date, time, and place. I didn't believe it at first."

Not wanting to freak the poor woman out, I kept my rat-smelling thoughts to myself. But receiving a party invitation to a funeral? That was sick, suspicious, and downright disturbing. Who did crap like that?

"Wow," I replied. "That's bizarre. Do you still have the invitation?"

"I don't know. Maybe. It came to the office, and once I regained a little of my sanity, I began calling his favorite patients to let them know." She hesitated. "Jake, why are you asking these questions?"

"Because … I'm interested. Thanks, Mrs. Madera, You've been a big help. And if you do come across that invitation, call me right away, okay?"

"Sure."

"Oh, and …" I said, grasping at straws, thinking quickly. "I have one more quick question. Did you ever meet Anthony's parents?"

"No. I never had the pleasure of actually meeting Katie and Hank. I don't think they've ever been to Tucson."

"Okay. Thanks again, Mrs. Madera."

Moving on, though not without some trepidation, I called Shawna and asked the same question.

"Why, Jake? What difference does it make?"

"Don't you want to know what happened to Anthony?" I asked. "Don't you find the absence of facts to be a little odd?"

Angry exhales and grunts preceded her words. "I think you should drop the whole idea. Let him rest in peace." She was not impressed by my curiosity or my need for answers.

"I can't do that."

"Suit yourself," she said, letting out a long sigh. "But you know what happened to that cat?"

"What cat?"

"The curious one."

I repeated my original question one more time, hoping for a real answer.

She relented. "All right. I received a beautiful bouquet of flowers, and the funeral information was typed on the card. I thought that was a very nice way to give me the news." Apparently she had nothing more to say after that. She'd hung up before I could ask her who'd sent those flowers.

Still curious about their lack of attendance at Anthony's funeral, I googled Hank and Katie Sommerfield, his parents, hoping to find some contact information, but no luck. Nothing. My investigation barely limped along. And then there was my so-called novel. It didn't even have a leg to stand on. I slumped outside to find my girl.

"Hey, Linds?" I found her in the backyard, reading, Wendell by her side. I decided to ask my question *du jour,* and she explained about the envelope that had appeared under the door of her hotel room.

"The news of the death and the information about the funeral was typed on a plain sheet of paper, in a plain envelope. At the time I was too upset to give it any thought. But, really Jake, does it matter? He's gone. We can't bring him back."

"I think it does matter, Lindsey. You, Mrs. Madera, Shawna, and even I received odd communications about the funeral, but no information about his death. Who could have sent those messages? Who made the funeral arrangements?"

She shrugged. "His parents must know something. Or maybe he had a friend that none of us was aware of. There has to be a reasonable explanation."

"Exactly! That's my point, but so far, there doesn't seem to be one."

Then, just like that, she changed the topic and flashed a beautiful, bright smile at me. "Hey! How's your novel coming along?"

That was so unfair.

NINE

Lindsey

As a child who'd grown up in several foster homes, it was difficult to develop any lasting friendships. As an adult, I'd kept busy, too busy, working my way through college, then on to devoting twelve-hours a day to my teaching career. I let the job consume me. I realized that now.

I had only one true friend, and that was Laura. Ever since I'd taken the sabbatical, we hadn't seen each other, but today that changed. We hugged, we drank our fancy, high calorie coffees and attempted to catch up on each other's busy lives.

"Tell me about the kids," I begged. "I miss them so much."

"The temp-teacher filling in for you this year is okay. She's nice and gets along with the staff, but she's not you." She twisted her mouth to the side, thinking. "Let's just say that next year's first grade teachers will have a lot more work to do."

I didn't want to think badly of the teacher, but I couldn't help feeling a twinge of pride. I always made sure my students were well prepared. "Is Harley there? Did he return to our school this year?"

She nodded. "He's there, and boy, did he grow over the summer. Shot up like a weed. Still a sweet, quiet kid, though. Emma's mom put in a request to have her tested for the Gifted and Talented Program."

"That's appropriate. If she hadn't, we would have."

"Agreed." She grinned. "Oh, and get this. Armando is working on a stand-up comedy routine for the school talent show. His parents must have an old tape of Bob Newhart doing his one-sided phone conversation act because that's kind of what Armando is doing out in the courtyard every chance he gets. Could he have thought that up on his own?"

I could just imagine! Armando was such an entertaining little guy. "I don't know," I said, chuckled. "But I sure want to see that act. How's Joseph doing?"

She wiggled her eyebrows, smiling. "Our favorite show-off is in the after-school drama club."

"Really? How can that be? It's for second through fifth grade students."

"I think the parents put more than a little pressure on the principal. Don't know the details."

"And my little buddy, Willy?"

This time she let out a long sigh and shrugged. "Yeah, well, he's been suspended again. This time he launched his lunch tray at the lunch lady because he wanted 'little smokies' and the cafeteria had run out of them. But other than his occasional—okay, *daily*—outbursts, he's learning. He's making academic progress. This year's teacher doesn't have your magic touch, though, so the lucky boy gets to spend a lot of time with me. Far more than his IEP calls for." She took a sip of her coffee then smiled. "Your turn. How was Colorado? Tell me about your conference."

I explained the content of my busy days, then told her how I'd quite literally had no time to myself. I also mentioned that I had my very own ... what? Personal assistant? Dietician? Fashion consultant? What was he, exactly? Explaining Lad to Laura was a challenge, since I didn't understand him or his attentiveness. It seemed, well ... excessive.

She didn't see a problem. "I don't know. All that consideration and attention from a good-looking guy sounds heavenly." She grinned. "Like you're famous, almost part of the one percent."

"When did I say he was good-looking?"

"You didn't have to. It was written all over your face."

I needed to change the subject. "Any word about Bobby?" The little boy had been taken from his parents—and rightly so—by Child Protective Services the previous spring. "I still worry, wondering where he is, with whom, and if it's working out. And, when he'll wander back into our lives."

Laura leaned back in her chair and gave me a funny look. "There you go again."

"And just where do you think I'm going?"

"On one of your alliteration adventures. You are aware that you use alliteration a lot, right?"

I shrugged. "Hmm. Maybe." I could feel the smile creeping across my face. "So, Laura ... let's linger a little longer, have a luscious and lazy lunch while I listen and learn without linking the lot to literacy and lowercase letters."

We both laughed and ordered lunch, but Laura's face fell when she got around to sharing what she knew about Bobby. "I overheard a phone call in the office a few days ago. It was only Mrs. Wilson's side of the conversation, but I did get the impression that someone—the foster mom, the agency, the judge, someone—intended to get in touch with *you*. I take it you haven't heard from anyone yet."

"No."

I no longer felt chatty; I even became a little evasive with my friend. My life didn't feel quite right lately, but I couldn't put a finger on the exact cause. No, that was a lie. I could. I just didn't want to.

Laura narrowed her eyes. She knew me too well. "Come on, Lindsey. What's the matter? From where I sit, your life appears to be nearly perfect. So what's going on?"

"It's just that the past several weeks have been difficult for both me and Jake," I admitted softly. "Being away from home when we'd just begun to build our relationship, Anthony's death, the funeral... Now Jake is obsessed trying to figure out that whole *Anthony* situation. And *that* hasn't brought us any closer. In fact, the opposite is happening. The only fun I've had since returning to Tucson has been with Wendell."

I wasn't surprised by Laura's next comment. "Since Wendell is the bright spot in your life," she said, looking thoughtful, "how about participating in a reading program that involves a dog and its owner/trainer visiting schools, listening to struggling readers read."

Laura's idea lit a spark in me. A reading program sounded like fun, and it would serve several purposes. I could visit the students and be with Wendell at the same time. Wendell would probably prefer that to agility activities, anyway. So when Laura reached into her bag and brought out the information, I took it, planning to study the details later. I couldn't concentrate on it right now, though. Now that I'd started to open up, thoughts of Jake weighed heavily on my mind.

"I worry about Jake," I told her. "I'm afraid that when I'm gone he'll never leave the office, that he won't eat or sleep or pay enough attention to Malcolm and Wendell."

"If it would make you feel any better, I'd be happy to check on him and the critters every now and then. Where is he today?"

"In the office, probably pretending to work on his novel. I know he isn't writing, though. He's stewing, boiling, obsessing about Anthony. I mean, we were both shocked over his death, but I think I am more shocked by how it's affecting Jake. He's certain foul play is involved."

"What do you think?"

I wished I had a better answer for her. I shrugged. "All I know is that I'm worried about our relationship, our love, but I sense that Jake is too preoccupied to think about that. I'm not sure we can survive our differences on the topic of Anthony's death."

TEN

Jake

I'd wanted tonight to be wildly romantic; tomorrow night Lindsey would be too distracted for romance thinking about her trip to Austin, Texas—my hometown—for round two of her conference appearances.

At this very moment, though, a distraction of my own was brewing: the nagging need to write something—an opening paragraph, an outline, a few character profiles, *anything.* I needed to prove to both Lindsey and myself that I'd really begun to work on my book. My goal for today's daylight hours? Write, write, write—something! No stalling. No excuses. Just do it!

I knew Lindsey was upstairs laying out the clothes for her trip, humming happily all the while. This morning's playlist included, "Whistle While You Work" and "Somewhere Over the Rainbow."

I poured myself a water glass filled with wine to get my creative juices flowing, deciding to give that home remedy one more try. I sipped a little, then typed a little. A few words magically appeared on my screen: *A college student is missing; a baby is missing; a dog is missing—* *Could I base an entire detective story on a missing dog?;* *a newly wedded couple is missing.* Then nothing. A few minutes later there was only more nothing. Only two lines of text in my Detective Novel file so far, and they didn't have enough substance to be the mere premise of a story. Writer's block? Maybe. Or maybe, I wasn't a writer.

"Hey, Wendell. Let's go for a walk."

At least I got *those* words right. Wendell leaped in circles, then bounded for the door. Once again I admired Lindsey's foresight: the few breakable knick-knacks in her house had been strategically placed above three feet to avoid destruction by tail wagging or any other type of dog enthusiasm.

The mail would likely have arrived by the time we returned, which meant I could avoid getting back to work a little longer, and ... Damn! I'd done it again. My negative thoughts about writing must go! I could really use a transfusion of Lindsey's *I think I can* attitude.

Our walk over, Wendell curled up by my feet as I sat back down at the desk. I'd been right about the mail, and as soon as I was settled, I took a sip of my wine and started to open the envelopes I'd carried in with me. The first envelope contained a bill, and I set it aside. Then I picked up the next one. The address had been handwritten; it appeared personal. I tore it open and began to read.

Dear Jake:

Read this and read it carefully. The contents of this letter will have an effect on your life.

I blame YOU for my death. Here's why:

- *You are a spy. You spied on me under the guise of dog sitting and food delivering.*

- *You are a traitor. Your words and actions turned Lindsey against me.*
- *You are a two-timing, no good son-of-a-bitch. By setting up secret meetings with Shawna, you turned her against me, too.*

Beware! You will soon regret the day you were born.
Anthony

I dropped the paper, stunned. My hands shook, and my face burned despite the chill that surged through my veins.

Anthony? He was dead. We'd buried him over a month ago.

My shock began to fade, making way for a flood of questions. Had he written the letter prior to his passing? If so, how had it only just arrived? Who had mailed it? Had he known he was going to die? Should I add suicide to my list of possible causes of death?

It occurred to me that I should be writing these questions down, so I created a new text file: *The Mysterious Dr. Sommerfield.*

This letter smelled a lot like Shawna's craziness. Anthony could have pre-arranged something with her, and she could have mailed it for him. Or, maybe Anthony wasn't involved at all. Perhaps Shawna blamed me for Anthony's death no matter the cause, and she'd written the letter to get back at me.

My glass now empty; I felt emboldened, so I called Ms. Shawna Storm. I would get to the bottom of this.

"Hello, Shawna. Been writing letters lately?"

She hesitated before answering. "No. Who would I write a letter to? What are you talking about?" She sounded bored, disinterested. Was she trying to throw me off?

"Today I received a letter," I informed her. "From Anthony."

"What?"

"I think you wrote it. If you didn't, you were at least in cahoots with him, and you mailed it for him."

"You son of a bitch!"

"Ah, ha! Those exact words were in the letter."

"Oh, come on. There's probably a whole gang of people who would call you that."

"I beg to differ."

"So you're going all college-boy on me now? *I beg to differ?*"

Shawna was angry, I was frustrated. Our conversation escalated into a shouting match.

"You must know *something* about this letter," I wasn't about to let her get away with this.

"How dare you. I didn't write it or deliver it."

"OK. Maybe you didn't write it, the letter did have Anthony's signature on it. I guess that proves something."

Shawna laughed at my deduction. "Oh, yeah. That's proof of something, all right. Proof that you're an idiot! For one thing, he had several signature stamps at the office. For another, do you even know what his signature looks like? Of course you don't. There is no way for you be sure he signed it."

That shut me up for a few seconds, but I wasn't discouraged. After all, I was new at this business of solving mysteries. "So, Shawna, in your desperate attempt to make me look foolish, you just admitted that you could have written the letter and used one of Anthony's signature stamps or just signed it yourself."

She sighed heavily. "You know, Jake, in spite of the fact that I wish I had some friends, you need to back off. I don't need an obnoxious, snoopy, amateur detective in my life."

During our one brief phone conversation—to my dismay—Shawna slid bumpily down a laundry list of emotions: boredom, disinterest, anger, and sarcasm. When she hit the ground at the bottom of that slide, her emotions deteriorated to pitiful.

"I wish I'd never had surgery," she wailed. "I wish Anthony was here. I wish I'd had a decent dad." She kept on with her list of twisted wishes, and by the time she'd voiced her last one, she was whimpering like a little girl.

I hung up, completely at a loss, and was still staring at my cell phone when Lindsey appeared in the doorway. Looking up I noticed the odd expression on her face. At first neither of us spoke. Then she said, "Jake, have you been drinking?"

ELEVEN

Lindsey

T he day was gray, the clouds thin but widespread. Jake and I didn't talk much on the way to the airport, but we held hands. That small contact felt nice. I wasn't as tense about the conference or my keynote address this time because I knew what to expect and I was prepared. Everything was under control. Jake had my back at home, and Lad took on a similar role at the conferences.

Two books of fables were packed in my carry-on book bag today, and the flight to the Austin-Bergstrom International Airport would allow me enough time to skim through them. I knew some fables, like *The Boy Who Cried Wolf, The Ant and the Grasshopper,* and *The Wolf in Sheep's Clothing.* Who doesn't know those? But as I read through the book I was amazed by how many others existed.

The Tree and the Reed and *The Belly and the Members,* to name a couple. And oh my, all the morals involved! For example, "United we stand, divided we fall" is a great moral, and from that point on I would always picture *The Four Oxen and the Lion* should those words ever pop up. My personal favorite, "Honesty is the best policy," came from *Mercury and the Woodman*.

I glanced up from my books and out the window, spotting treetops, rooftops, and tiny cars on the streets below. We would soon touch down near Austin, Texas. Another chapter in my life was about to unfold.

I spotted Lad right away; he was hard to miss. He stood out like a monolith in a field of daisies. I'd hoped to find a lightened up version of my Advance Man today, since we knew each other better now, having experienced several up-close and personal moments, but that was not to be. He was his all-business, serious self.

I appreciated being taken care of, but to be honest, the whole "Lad aspect" of these conferences felt unnatural, overbearing. Having someone constantly at my side, catering to my every need was simply too much at times. Laura had said she thought it sounded cool. She never had to live with it.

I was the first to speak. "So when do I get to sit up front?"

"It's safer in the back."

I was tempted to ask why a teacher needed to be kept safe, but I didn't. Lad offered no conversation. Following his lead, neither did I. We rode to the hotel in silence. While I unpacked in my sleeping room, he kept busy in the sitting area of my suite, attending to notes, paperwork, and a phone call or two. I noticed two brand new dresses hanging in the closet, each complete with shoes and accessories. Strange. Why did they do that? Did it really matter how I looked, what I wore? *Do I get to keep the clothes?*

With my unpacking tasks complete, I sat calmly across from Lad at the round table, ready to begin our preconference meeting. Before we started, he set a hot mocha on the table in front of me and handed me a bag filled with colorful sticky notes in a variety of sizes.

Surprised, I glanced at him, wondering if I'd detected a slight twinkle in the man's eyes. Then I corrected myself. Of course not. He wasn't the twinkling type. But how had he known I would like the notes and love the mocha?

"I know everything," he said, and apparently he did. He could read my mind, too.

Did I like that? He was definitely helpful, I'd give him that. But so stoic, so serious. A "just the facts" man. My thoughts drifted to Jake, who was also a "just the facts" man these days. The facts. What were the facts? I had to admit that Jake had a point with regard to Anthony, his death, his funeral … the facts were missing. They might even be hidden.

"There's been a change in the schedule." Lad's words interrupted my thoughts. "Your keynote address will occur on Saturday, not Friday."

"Oh? Is something wrong?"

He shook his head. "Just Ms. Meriwether's whims. Plus, some people she wants to impress can't get here until Saturday."

"Okay. That shouldn't be a problem, right?"

"Right. Any questions?"

"No, but here's the CD I want to use with my keynote presentation. You said you wanted a copy."

"Correct. I'll drop it off with our tech gal. She'll want to add some sparkle." He lifted his eyebrows, looking uncharacteristically concerned. "Don't take offense. She does this for everyone—even for Ms. Meriwether. That's what we pay her for." He stood with a nod. "I'll be back in an hour with dinner."

And he was gone.

During the flight to Austin I'd vowed that no matter how busy I got or how distracting the conference events became, I would call Jake every day. Now that I was alone, I picked up my cell phone, skimmed through my contacts until I found *Jake, My Love* and tapped the screen. It had only been a few hours, and our conversation brief, but it felt great to hear his voice.

The next morning I visited the Ladies Room before going in to the hall. Ah, the privacy and sanctity of being within those walls. The room was Lad-less. But it wasn't empty.

"Hello, Lindsey," came a friendly voice. "You're going to love what I did with your keynote presentation visuals."

"Oh, hi," I said, turning toward the attractive young brunette. "You must be—"

"Sarah Bellings." I would have shaken her hand, but she had hers in the sink. "Don't worry," she assured me. "Everything you created is still there. I just added some digital effects and some subtle advertising for your future products and the company itself. Ms. Meriwether got wind that a bunch of big-wig buyers would be in the audience on Saturday so ..." she said, shrugging with a grin, "hey, we take advantage of opportunities. Do you have any questions for me?"

Did I? I thought quickly. Yes, indeed I did, though I was a little surprised by my own bluntness. "Uh, do you know Lad very well?"

She replied with hesitation, "No. He's pretty private."

That was the understatement of the year. "Definitely a man of few words," I agreed. "But what about his name? I'd never heard that name before now, and he certainly doesn't look like a 'lad.' That sounds like a name for an innocent young boy."

She chuckled. "Believe me. That he is not."

What did she know? Overcome with curiosity and a desire to investigate, I asked another question.

"Does he have a last name?

"Oh, yeah. He's got quite a name, actually. I'm surprised he hasn't told you about it. His name is the one and only personal thing he likes to talk about."

"Okay. So … ?"

"First name Lowell, middle name Andrew, last name Donovan. Quite a mouthful, huh? Suits him though. Ask him about the origins of his name someday," she said, then she looked away and slid her dripping hands under a loud, powerful dryer. Apparently, our conversation was over.

TWELVE

Jake

The funeral had jump-started the mystery. Anthony's odd and threatening letter had raised the stakes. Today, a new problem pushed my panic button. When I'd returned from the airport, I discovered our back gate was open and Wendell was gone. GONE! Losing Wendell was just about the worst thing that could happen right now—or anytime, for that matter.

I scoured the neighborhood, calling his name and knocking on doors, showing a photo of him to strangers. After three long hours I called Laura, hoping she'd be home from school, and enlisted her help. We called animal shelters, veterinarians, and emergency animal hospitals. Nothing. No leads. No one had seen him. And Wendell was the kind of dog a person would remember seeing.

It was as if he'd vanished into thin air. We left the gate open for now, just in case he wandered back, but any positive thoughts I'd had at the beginning of the search now took a back seat to an insurgence of dark, creepy sensations.

Lindsey and I had not left the gate open when we'd headed for the airport, and Wendell hadn't just opened it and walked away. Sure, he possessed the talent to open the gate, but he just wouldn't have. He would not leave the house or the yard even if the doors or gate stood wide open. No. Someone had taken him. Someone had stolen the dog. The letter did refer to my 'spying' while dog-sitting. Could this be part of Anthony's plan or Shawna's revenge?

I didn't know what to think or what to do. The loss of Wendell would devastate Lindsey, and she would blame me—maybe even hate me for it.

Desperate for answers, I asked Laura to drive around some more while I canvassed the surrounding neighborhoods. While walking I found myself glancing over my shoulder like a cautious fawn in a forest. Was I being followed? Watched? Would I be the next one to disappear? Or was I being unreasonably suspicious?

As the sky grew dark, I sent Laura home. If Wendell didn't show up by morning we'd make and tack up some missing dog flyers while we continued our search. I had decided not to burden Lindsey with this information yet, but my silence, my withholding of information turned our bedtime phone chat into a Lindsey monologue, scattered with some small talk from me. At least I knew *she* was all right.

Unable to sleep, and convinced more than ever that foul play had occurred, I opened the Mysterious Dr. Sommerfield file and typed in some notes about possible suspects and motives, even though the only real evidence of foul play I had at this point was the letter to me. Wendell's disappearance might not be related, but either way, it involved some kind of foul play, too.

Suspect #1 is Shawna Storm, the girlfriend. Her motive—she wanted Anthony, but he dumped her the second he discovered the truth about her sexual lies/betrayals, and he called her horrific names (however true). My take? She was mentally unstable to begin with.

Suspect #2 is Hank Sommerfield, Anthony's father. His motive—really don't know, but there is some strange animosity since the he didn't show up for the wedding, and Lindsey knew nothing of his existence. I don't think they had anything to do with the letter, but maybe the strange funeral. I just don't know.

Suspect #3 is ... Lindsey, the ex-wife, my girlfriend, and the love of my life. Deep down I know this is impossible. She is incapable of hurting the proverbial flea. Anthony had divorced her to be with Shawna. Linds was hurt badly by his actions—which included taking Wendell from her last fall. She definitely had motive, but she is incapable of lying, let alone violence, so—?

My gut screamed that Shawna was the one. She had to be involved in some way. I lay on the couch, thinking about my notes, and I said a little prayer for Wendell before falling asleep. I wanted to be close to the door just in case he showed up and gave it a scratch with his paw. But no such sound ever came.

Laura and I continued our search the following day— Laura even took the day off from school. She's so helpful. She also reminded me not to neglect Malcolm during this stressful time. We were methodical in our search, checking every house and every backyard.

The sun had set, dusk was upon us when we'd made the decision to visit Shawna. We drove right up to her front door, parked the car, and rang the bell. She was not happy to see us—no surprise there—and she demanded a search warrant, which, of course, we didn't have. Loud, heavy metal music blasted from the hallway leading to the master bedroom, and we called out to Wendell anyway. I thought if he had been in the house, he might bark, or at least do something to let us know he was there. We came up empty.

Later, I awoke from a restless sleep to unusual, loud squawking and flapping coming from downstairs. Malcolm? He'd never created a racket like that before. Never. I pulled on my boxers and rushed toward the noise.

"Hey, little guy. What's going on?" I asked. The sun wasn't up yet, so I flipped on the light in the kitchen to see him better. Strangely, my presence didn't calm him; the squawking and flapping continued. I ran to the back door and stared out.

Wendell! My God! He stood a few feet from the back door, a rope tied to his collar. I could see he'd chewed through the rope to set himself free.

"Wendell! Where've you been, big buddy? We missed you!"

He bounded inside, seemingly healthy and thrilled to be home. After feeding him and making sure he had everything he needed, I called Laura to give her the good news. I also sent Lindsey a text message, choosing to text rather than call because I didn't want to wake her so early. Now that Wendell was back, alive and well, I could tell her the story of our search—at least a short, textable version. I still wasn't ready to share the bizarre letter from Anthony with her, though. Didn't want her to worry about that. Not yet.

Her text reply did not arrive until late evening, and she was obviously not happy with me. *How could U be so careless? How could U leave the gate open? Poor dog. U R 2 distracted with your conspiracy theories. I am worried about U.*

She worried about me? Well, I was worried about us. It seemed we were drifting further and further apart. I needed to see her, *be* with her. Hell, I could do that! Within an hour I'd purchased a ticket online. My flight would leave early the next morning. I figured it would be a nice surprise for Lindsey, and we could visit my parents, too, if she had some time off. I hadn't seen them in quite a while, and I wanted them to meet her. I called Laura to request her help, and she said she would be happy to stay over and take care of the pets in my absence.

Feeling fine, I headed up the stairs three at a time to pack. Lindsey, my love, ready or not, here I come!

THIRTEEN

Lindsey

I am not paranoid, I tried to convince myself. I really wasn't. But, as I stood off to the side, scanning the entering crowd, a thin veil of perspiration dampened my forehead. An eerie feeling swept over me, and with that feeling came a heightened awareness. Someone was watching me. I felt it. I knew it. But who? The participants didn't yet know who I was or what I looked like, and staff members had no reason to stare. After all, they'd seen plenty of me already.

I scanned the crowd again, wondering if Lad was the looker standing somewhere in the back. But no. It couldn't have been him because he was always near the portable platform stage, always close by. My eyes saw nothing suspicious. Could it be that pre-presentations jitters had come back to haunt me? Perhaps.

The meeting hall was very similar to the one in Boulder. The only noticeable differences were the pleasant teal color of the wall coverings and the larger number of chairs—over four hundred people were expected. As the room filled up with happy, talkative elementary educators, the noise level increased exponentially. No dropping pins would be heard at this conference. I wondered idly if Elisabeth Meriwether's mere presence could quiet this chattering crowd as quickly as it had in the past.

I spotted Lad on the opposite side of the platform, and he gave me a hint of a smile with a nod. It was almost show time, and I realized with a burst of adrenaline that I was more than ready. I *wanted* this. I wanted to be the next educational rock star, if there was such a thing! If there wasn't, I'd invent it.

This morning, as I began, my knees were slightly wobbly, my mouth a tad dry, but I could tell my words, gestures, and eye contact had greatly improved since my first performance. The audience applauded often and even laughed now and then. Feeling confident, I strayed from my prepared material and told a personal story about a recent dream I'd had. A dream about a conference just like this one.

"I was standing at the podium," I told them, "and educators were sitting in the audience, just like we are today. I began to share my experiences at school working with kindergarten children and helping them become writers."

As I spoke, I felt the dramatist within me growing, and my unplanned storytelling added a new dimension of entertainment to my presentation. Encouraged by the rapt expressions on their faces, I continued. "As we all know, delightful conversations and misconceptions are part of every school day. For example, the time a little boy in my class named Marvin confused 'crops' with 'crocs,' and when little Willy thought the cinders from Cinderella's fireplace were 'people that did bad things.'"

A sympathetic chuckle passed through my audience and I smiled warmly at them, meeting as many eyes as I could.

"Well, you get the idea," I said. "But in my dream, not one person cracked a smile. No one moved a muscle. Before long my nice little dream took a twisted and unreal turn. Was anyone out there? *Anyone*? It felt like I was seeing a *crowd-shot* from a movie, where the director had filled in the background with fake people. I didn't know what to do, so I moved closer to the audience."

My voice softened to a slow, dramatic whisper, and I was thrilled to realize that yes, I could have heard a pin drop! I'd never mesmerized an audience of grown-ups before. This was fun! I continued with my dream story.

"I touched a woman in the front row, and she tipped over, creating a domino effect. After that, the whole row of people behind her fell flat, and I realized no one was real. I was speaking to an audience of cardboard people. I screamed and awoke, so relieved that it was just a dream."

Today's audience laughed and applauded. "I'm so glad that you're all real," I said, leaning into the microphone to speak over the noise. "I have a lot of exciting things to share today."

My unscripted comments were received with far more enthusiasm than anything I'd spent hours preparing ahead of time. Interesting. I hoped to remember most of what I'd said. Perhaps Lad could help me with that. At the end of my presentation, I received a standing ovation. What a thrilling, dynamic day! I was floating on air.

After shaking hands with the teachers who approached the stage, I was surprised to feel two strong, warm hands resting on my shoulders. I turned and saw Lad—wearing a huge, unfamiliar smile on his handsome face. I'd never seen that before! I could tell he was pleased. This was becoming a day of many 'firsts.'

"You were fantastic," he said, drawing me away from the crowd. "We thought you'd be good, but the speed with which you are developing yourself as a presenter, well, it's unusual."

I couldn't stop grinning. "You get some of the credit, Lad. You have been helpful beyond belief." I didn't even think before I gave him a huge hug. While feeling happy and safe I mentioned the strange feeling of being watched that had come over me earlier. He said he'd check it out, and I felt confident he would.

Timing is everything, and at that particular moment, my timing proved to be problematic. As I pulled apart from my quick, innocent embrace with Lad, I spotted Jake standing right next to us. What would he think?

"Jake! Oh my God! What a surprise!" My questions poured out. "Is everything all right? How long have you been here?"

My feelings were mixed. I was shocked, but I was also tremendously relieved. I never expected to see him here—especially after the unfriendly text message I'd sent him the night before regarding Wendell's disappearance.

He beamed. "I saw the whole thing. From the moment you were introduced until now. Wow, Lindsey. You were great! I had no idea you had that kind of public speaking talent."

I blushed still hoping my impromptu hug with Lad hadn't bothered him. "Neither did I," I admitted. So he'd been there all along. Maybe Jake's presence in the audience had given me that feeling of being watched. I'd solved my own little mystery, I thought with satisfaction.

"Are you done for the day?" he asked.

I glanced at Lad. He gave me a nod, then walked away.

"I could be," I said, thrilled to be standing on the stage with my arms around Jake's waist. I grinned up at him. "I have to be ready for tomorrow, but that's going to be a fun, easy day. Just one more workshop and a couple of meetings. The only part of the conference that still causes me stress is my keynote address, and I don't have another one of those until November."

"Well, then. How does a picnic by a lake sound? Maybe a little fishing, too. Have you ever been fishing, Linds?"

"No." Then I thought about it. "Well, maybe. I think I went with my dad a few weeks before he and mom … died. Pretty sure I just watched, though. I recall sitting on a long pier and watching the tiny fish in a bucket that he used to catch bigger fish." I shook my head slightly, clearing my thoughts. "This lake that you want to go to— it's a small lake, right?"

"Yes, small and as smooth as glass. Have you got something else to wear?"

As we went to my room so I could change, it occurred to me that Elisabeth had not yet asked for the last three 'homework' assignments she'd given me. That was a good thing because I hadn't completed them yet. I couldn't understand why those two personal questions were so difficult for me to answer. But now that Jake mentioned a picnic, if I stretched my imagination a bit, that might pass for the 'do something for myself that I've always wanted to do.' Sure, I thought, mentally rolling my eyes. A picnic that included fishing. Oh, yeah. I've wanted to do that for a long, long time. But I stopped my sarcastic thoughts before they went any farther. Sarcasm was so unbecoming, and not my style, but then, neither was fishing.

FOURTEEN

Jake

I didn't like him; I was never going to like him. And, I didn't trust this guy she called Lad. In my book, even his name was worthy of suspicion, but I'd suck it up for Lindsey's sake. I understood he was a necessary part of her life until these conferences were over.

I was determined to make sure our time together in Austin was great, even memorable. I had it all figured out: a picnic and fishing this afternoon, a late, romantic dinner at the best-darned seafood restaurant in town, then a relaxing evening in her hotel suite. While she was changing, I noticed the Jacuzzi and added a soak in the tub complete with my hands giving her a neck and shoulder rub to my plans.

Tomorrow, as soon as Lindsey's work obligations were complete, we'd take a drive to my parents' place on the edge of town. I couldn't wait to see the surprised look on their faces. We'd never been what I'd call a close-knit family. Not that there was any real animosity—there wasn't. Let's just say we'd never be accused of being too warm and fuzzy. And then, when our wonderful time together here had come to an end, Lindsey and I would return to Tucson on the same plane. I'd unveil that part of my plan a little later. I'd thought of everything.

I chose the city park lake, which wasn't great for a real fishing experience, but *catching* fish was not high on the day's list. Today was all for Lindsey, complete with fun, relaxation, and comfort. Last summer I'd detected a negative reaction from her during a horrific storm in the Zuni Mountains. It was if the sight of water gushing down the dirt road and the tiny waves created by the strong wind on the impromptu river had frightened her. I was pretty sure the watery sight triggered memories of the death of her parents, who had died in a boating accident on the rough waters of Lake Michigan many years before. I would see to it that nothing like that ever happened again. Not while I was around.

She curled her legs under her on the blanket I'd brought from the hotel, and she looked happy. Really happy. Like I hadn't seen since ... our episode in Wendell's tunnel.

"Thank you for arranging all this," she said, waving a hand at the last minute pretzels, nuts, and packages of cheese and crackers I'd bought and set out around her. "Especially these." She giggled, picking up a little plastic bottle of wine and waving it at me. "It's all so wonderful."

I didn't mind the teasing. I was just happy to hear that giggle. "Okay, okay. It was the best I could come up with in the bait store. But don't you worry. You won't think tonight's dinner and post-dinner doings are so laughable."

"Oh? You have plans?"

"I do," I said adding a confident wink.

She laughed again. "You're so funny, Jake. I can hardly wait for this evening's *doings*."

We sat in a comfortable silence enjoying the fresh air and the sunshine. We could push thoughts of Anthony's death and Shawna's life far away for a while. The next twenty-four hours had all the ingredients necessary for cookin' up a new beginning, a fresh start.

She spoke first. "I'm really sorry for writing that rude text to you. I don't know why I did it. I guess the thought of losing Wendell—"

I interrupted her apology with a kiss. "I know, Linds. It's okay. We were both upset that day."

We were back on track. We ate, we kissed some more, and I threw a line in the water, pretending to fish. I shared how proud and amazed I was at her incredible transformation from kindergarten teacher to national presenter, and I meant every word. I'd been blown away, listening to her. She spoke with such authority and confidence, using terminology that would dazzle any PhD or EdD, yet she'd maintained her fun-loving, sweet personality throughout.

"There is a lot more freedom of speech around adults," she explained. "I just had to find another voice, another way of speaking. Miss Lindsey, the kindergarten teacher, using proper words and phrases for five- and six-year-olds, wouldn't fly around several hundred teachers. Especially teachers who were delighted to be in the company of other adults and away from their classrooms for a few days."

"That makes sense," I said, "and you're amazing at it. I just hope you don't become so famous, so independent, that you won't want—or need—a guy like me."

Her eyes softened, and she shook her head very slowly. "Oh, Jake. I love you. I love you so very much. I want us to be together forever."

Just then I got a bite. Shocked, I looked back at the water, and my rod bobbed as the city fish nibbled at the farm-raised worm. I allowed it plenty of opportunity to swallow the hook, then I gave it a small jerk. I had him! I hadn't planned on catching a fish today, but since it was right there on the end of my line, I certainly didn't plan on losing it, or on missing the opportunity to display a rare, manly moment. Lindsey rose to her feet and watched with excitement as that fish put me to work. Either it was a huge fish, I thought, or it had tangled the line around something in the water because try as I might, I couldn't simply reel it in. In my enthusiasm, I gave the rod a much swifter, firmer jerk—maybe a little too firm—and before I knew it the fish was flying through the air … and, oh no! It smacked Lindsey right in the face. She let out a scream. Well, who wouldn't?

"You're okay," I assured her, using a paper napkin to wipe her cheek. "We'll wash off the fishiness and you'll be fine in a minute. Really."

I could tell she was not so sure about that. "Get the wet-wipes from my bag! Hurry! Oh, yuck. Eeew!" she choked, flapping her hands wildly on either side of her. Then she spit, and I stared in disbelief. I'd never witnessed that before. My lady was not happy.

The moment passed, and she recovered from the unpleasant fish encounter. The good news? The flying fish hadn't left a mark. I was sure that someday she'd laugh about this, but from the look on her face, that probably wasn't going to be today. I tossed the flopping fish back into the water and began to rethink our dinner plans. A nice, quiet room service meal of anything but fish might be best.

After the hysteria all but gone, we stayed by the lake a little longer, holding hands and enjoying a loving conversation. When she asked about the details of my trip out to see her, I explained that Laura was taking care of the pets. I also told her I had been able to do some writing. She looked thrilled to hear that.

"I'm so glad, Jake. You were getting far too obsessed with the whole foul play aspect surrounding Anthony's death. I'm relieved that you've moved on from that."

"Uh ..." I scratched my head, unsure of how to continue. "Hmm. To be honest, it would be more accurate to say that I've moved on *with* that. You see, the more I discover, the more I'm certain foul play involved."

Lindsey gathered up our picnic items and hurried toward the car, glancing back once to shoot me a furious glare.

"Jake," she said. "This has got to stop! I want no part of your insane obsession."

I was shocked by her reaction. For a second it felt like I'd been the one smacked in the face with a fish. The ride back to the hotel seethed with silent tension. She wouldn't even look at me.

Lindsey went immediately to the Jacuzzi tub and soaked without me. A few minutes later, Lad came in, using his own key to her room. He said "Hi," then walked right past me and in to see Lindsey, who was *in the hot tub*, naked.

What the hell? Who did he think he was? And yet Lindsey, my sweet, conservative woman, didn't appear to be the slightest bit shocked by his actions. I heard them talking to each other as if this were an everyday occurrence rather than an inappropriate, odd phenomenon.

What should I do about it? That was the pressing question of the moment.

I was already in hot water with her—though, literally speaking, Lad was much closer to actually being in hot water with her than I was. Damn! Pacing back and forth from the window to the TV screen, my resentment toward this man reached an all-time high. It even took me back to thinking about the mysterious letter from Anthony.

Was Lindsey a 'two-timer'? Was this one of the letter's paybacks? A set-up to hurt me? To change my life forever? But that would mean Lad was involved, and neither Anthony nor Shawna could have set that in motion. My brain was overloaded with questions. How did detectives solve mysteries and have a life, too?

Lad left, and I should have kept quiet. I knew that. But I didn't. I was about to explode in more ways than one. I waited until she came out, looking all snug and rosy-cheeked from the bath, then I let it out.

"You know, Lindsey, I'd hoped we might have a good time together here in Austin, but …" I shook my head and took a deep breath for courage. "You seem so into your work, and the staff guards you like you're some kind of priceless diamond. You're happy to talk all about it, but when I bring up something important in my life, you call it an insane obsession. I have to say it: you're not acting as if you want a life with me."

She bristled. "That is a two-way street, Jake. When I'm in Tucson and I have time and a strong desire to be with you, to *share* with you, our relationship is practically non-existent because you are off in your own twisted Wonderful World of Mystery. That makes me sad, it makes me worry, and, yes, it makes me a little bit crazy!"

This was coming out of nowhere. She'd been the one to encourage me to write in the first place. What was she so upset about? "What am I supposed to do?"

"I wish you could let it go," she snapped. "Let it all go. Return to school or work at one of the desert nurseries. Remember? You'd said you wanted to do that."

That was the last straw. Having little left to lose, I went ahead and told her all about the threatening letter I'd received from Anthony, blaming me for his death. If that didn't convince her that something was amiss, I didn't know what else I could do. But incredibly, she wanted no part of my story. She didn't want to listen, then refused to accept what I'd said. When I added that my next move would be a call to the police, she lost it.

She jumped to her feet. "You've gone completely nuts!" she yelled. "You're confusing the facts with your fiction. Now you're just making stuff up."

I got slowly to my feet, staring at her with disbelief. How could she say all these things, treat me like this? Furious at her lack of trust, her lack of support, and figuring out that my presence was doing us more harm than good, I left. As I strode toward the hotel's main entrance, I noticed Lad lurking in the lobby and just shook my head.

I drove the rental car toward the airport and was able to hop on a departing flight back to Tucson that same night, all the while feeling misunderstood, unappreciated, and … justifiably jealous.

FIFTEEN

Lindsey

He didn't knock; he never knocked. Lad just walked right in and found me in a miserable state of mind. My tear-stained, mascara-smudged face must have given me away because he immediately sat by my side, put one arm around me, and coaxed my head to his shoulder. He didn't say a single word, but that was typical.

I tried, but failed to stifle my sobs. Hyperventilation wasn't far off. No words had been spoken, but Lad began to rub my neck with his strong, warm hands, easing the tension I held there. What he lacked with regard to conversation, he more than made up for with his soothing hands and his delicious scent. I began to feel slightly better—especially as his hands moved upward, moving gently through my hair and massaging my head. I'd had no idea a head massage could feel so incredibly wonderful. Mmmm. Was I seeing a different, softer side to Lad?

"Now that's *not* typical," I accidentally mumbled out loud.

"I'm sorry, what?"

I blushed. "Oh, I don't know. I'm just talking to myself. It's been a crazy day. Feels like I've been riding on a roller coaster for hours. Tired. I'm just … tired."

"Do you want to talk about it?" he asked.

Not wanting to revisit the argument I'd just had with Jake, but needing a distraction, I asked Lad to stay a while longer and tell me about his name. Turns out Sarah was right on. Lad's steel gray eyes lit up the moment I made my request.

"I would be more than happy to do that," he said, "but you, your emotional state, your physical well-being, and your readiness for tomorrow's conference participation are of the utmost importance to me. So I propose we have this conversation in the Jacuzzi while you soak your troubles and tensions away. Let's go."

"All right. Just give me a minute." *I would soak tonight with my suit on.* "Okay," I called, as I sank down into the steamy water. "Come on in."

I was shocked when he entered the room, stripped down to his boxers—I assumed that his black business suit was neatly resting on the back of a chair—and then sank into the hot bubbling water with me. I was about to say something, except I was instantly, though oddly, distracted by his appearance. Seeing Lad in the flesh for the first time was like seeing a ghost—the ghost of Anthony. I blinked. Were my eyes deceiving me? Both men were tall, dark, and handsome though Lad seemed taller. I hadn't noticed the other similarities until tonight. The wide shoulders, the narrow waist, or the defined muscle tone. Their faces, however, looked nothing alike.

He sank completely underwater, head and all, then smoothed his thick, dark hair away from his face as he surfaced. "Lad is short for Lowell Andrew Donovan," he told me. "My parents gave a lot of thought to my naming. Donovan was my father's last name, and it has quite a history. It means 'dark warrior.' Anyway, that part was a given."

He sat in the tub, talking as if this were a perfectly normal thing for him to do. I, on the other hand, was a little nervous having him so close, and with so much of his skin showing. Eventually, his story—and his obvious enjoyment in telling it—began to distract me from the twinges of discomfort.

"Andrew was my maternal grandfather's given name, and Mother wanted that to be part of my name. She told me it meant 'strong.' The 'L' stands for Lowell, which apparently means 'Young Wolf.' They chose that name together after they'd gotten to know me a bit, saying it suited my personality." He grinned. "So here I am." He put up one finger. "The young wolf—" then two more. "—and the strong, dark warrior. LAD."

"Oh, my. That's quite a story."

He nodded. "Are you feeling more relaxed now?"

Before I could say yes, the room's phone rang. "Let it ring. You need your rest, and Jake needs time to cool off."

It didn't matter that I was sitting in steamy hot water. As soon as he'd said that, I stiffened and a chill zipped up my spine.

DOGS AND CHILDREN AND POEMS, OH MY!

SIXTEEN

Laura

"Another Saturday night, and I ain't got no boyfriend ..." I sang while searching through Lindsey and Jake's collection of DVDs. Carrying a tune was not included in my list of talents, but what did it matter? Like my little song said, I was on my own, and fortunately, Wendell and Malcolm were kind critics. They kept their thoughts about my lack of musical talent to themselves. "Oh, how I need a cute guy to talk to ..."

Sadly, the song's lyrics were true. Since my divorce eight years ago, I'd successfully maintained a wall, keeping any possible new relationships at bay. Life just felt safer that way.

Until I'd met Jake, that is.

How well I remembered that first night a year ago. He was bartending at the Coyote Café, and I was waiting for Lindsey, my best friend, to arrive. We talked, and he told me he was a student at the University of Arizona studying psychology. We had so much in common, so we had loads to talk about, which we did. For months. But the timing was all wrong. He was caught up in the complex task of finishing his doctoral thesis and, though neither Lindsey nor I were aware of this, he had a thing for Lindsey.

So ...

Another Saturday night ... and here I sat with a dog and a bird so Jake could be with Lindsey. The clock chimed the arrival of midnight, and still I couldn't sleep. I poured myself a glass of white wine from the fridge, invited Wendell to jump up on the couch to keep me company, and slipped "Two for the Road" into the DVD player, though my true self felt more like watching "Fight Club."

I was absently watching the movie while doodling on a scrap of paper when a car pulled into the driveway. Wendell and I both jumped up while Malcolm chirped loudly at the sound of a key unlocking the front door. I battled a momentary flash of concern, then stared helplessly at the door.

"Jake? What a surprise!" The words tumbled out of my mouth before my brain registered that something must be wrong. I clicked off the movie. "You're home! Welcome back."

He dropped his duffel bag on the floor by the door. "Yeah, I'm back," he said, not even acknowledging Wendell or Malcolm.

Something was definitely wrong. Something bad had happened. "Do you want to talk about it?"

"No!"

"Okay," I sang, happy to stay clear of the bad mood. "How about some wine?" He didn't answer, so I poured him a glass. He drank it so fast I poured him another.

The pacing started, then the words came. "First, I walk into her speech and find her in the arms of her bodyguard. Later the two of them had a conversation while Linds was naked in the Jacuzzi, and—"

"Wait! Back up. She has a *bodyguard*? Is she in some kind of danger?"

He blew out a breath through his nose, sounding disgusted. "No, I don't think so. I just don't know what else to call him. Oh, did I mention that Linds and I went fishing? Yeah. That was great. I hit her in the face with a fish, and we argued."

Huh. Now *I* needed another drink. "Jake, slow down and sit down," I said attempting to be helpful. "None of that makes any sense. Especially if you were trying to have a nice, romantic time with Lindsey."

I knew from my last conversation with her that she and Jake were having some issues, most of which were being brought on by the whole Anthony thing. Their problems seemed to have escalated.

Or maybe it was really about Mr. Bodyguard … in the hot tub.

That's when Jake told me about the letter he'd received from Anthony. He told me Lindsey hadn't wanted to hear about it, and she had absolutely refused to listen to any other information that helped his foul play theories move forward. Personally, I found Anthony's letter to be confusing. An odd piece of … what? Evidence?

It was uncomfortable seeing Jake in so much pain. I knew he and Lindsey had a good thing going on, but I also knew she was blowing it. Everything he'd just said confirmed it. She was doing the same thing with me. Sure, we'd had a good night, laughing about old times, talking about her problems—always her problems. She hardly ever asked about mine, though I'll admit I'm not one to really open up.

Lately it seemed to be getting much worse. She barely had time for us. She was so wrapped up in this new position—in her presentations and tours and impressive teacher packages—that she'd begun to leave the two of us behind.

Jake was a good man with a heart of gold. She'd encouraged him to write, to do what he wanted to do, but now she was throwing it all back at him with nothing but scorn. How could she hurt him like this when all he wanted was to make her happy? I poured him another glass of wine and went to the kitchen to grab some chips … all the while wishing he were mine.

"I'm so sorry, Jake." I handed him his glass. "I know you're only trying to do what's right. Lindsey's so busy these days, and well, I guess some people just don't appreciate a good thing when they have it. So what's next?"

Without speaking, he took the wine and the chips into the office, sat at his desk, and turned on his laptop. I followed, aching for him. What he needed was a little tender, loving care, and I was just the person to deliver that. Standing behind him, I rubbed the tense muscles of his shoulders, digging in hard with my fingers. He didn't object, but picked up the landline and made a call. I assumed the call was to Lindsey, but I didn't know for sure. What I *did* know was that no one answered. Jake slammed the phone down and began to pound the keys on his computer instead.

While I massaged his shoulders and neck, enjoying the heat of his smooth skin, my eyes watched the words appear on his screen.

No one at the funeral knew the cause of death.

No one at the funeral knew exactly when he died.

Lindsey, Mrs. Madera, Shawna (or so she says, I have no proof), and I all received cryptic notifications of the funeral.

Anthony's letter arrived AFTER the funeral, blaming me for his death. How is THAT possible?

He tapped on the sides of the keyboard, obviously pondering what he'd written, then he started up again assaulting the letters of the alphabet. My fingers dug into the knotted muscles, but he barely seemed to notice.

Shawna has got to be involved. That is the only logical conclusion. But how?

And now there's Lad—WTH?

Jake was terribly distracted. Was he frantically writing to take his mind off Lindsey and the argument? Or … was Lindsey right? Was he obsessively determined to solve this mystery of his own making? Regardless, he was oblivious to my efforts. I tiptoed out and crashed on the couch. Morning would be here soon enough. I could try again then.

SEVENTEEN

Jake

My eyes opened slowly and my senses were soon baffled by a puzzling contradiction. I felt excruciating pain in my back and neck while breathing in the delicious aroma of coffee brewing and pancakes cooking. Apparently, I'd slept with my head on my arms and my body hunched over the desk. That explained the pain, which cheered me a little. I did love it when a situation's cause and effect was not only detectible, but also made sense. Next on the list: I'd have to determine the basis of the delicious breakfast smells. Maybe Lindsey had changed her mind, followed me back to Tucson on a red-eye flight. That would explain why she hadn't answered her phone late last night.

But it was Laura who greeted me when I rounded the corner of the kitchen. "Good morning," she said, giving me a warm and bubbly smile. Why was she still here? So much for making sense. Now that I was home, the pets were back in my care.

"How is Lindsey today?" she asked. "Is she still mad at you?"

I answered without thinking. "I haven't had a chance to talk with her yet."

"You mean she hasn't called you?" She clicked her tongue, scolding. "She should be apologizing to you for not having your back. Couples need to support each other even through disagreements. Otherwise the relationship won't work."

I shrugged. Not much I could do about that.

"I figured you could use a good breakfast," she said, putting a plate of pancakes and eggs in front of me. She squeezed my shoulder. "Just so you know, I'm here for you, okay?"

"Yeah. Thanks."

"I'm heading home, but feel free to call if you need me."

After she left, I wolfed down the last few bites of pancake, refilled my coffee cup, and—with renewed energy and great determination—went back to work.

Lindsey seemed to think my attention was more on Anthony's mystery than on her, which wasn't true. In fact, despite her arguments, I was determined to solve this mystery *for* Lindsey. For her peace of mind as well as my own. In my opinion, this needed to be done. If it wasn't, she'd never be able to stop thinking about Anthony and Shawna—but she *might* stop thinking about me. I couldn't let that happen. And since everything had escalated last night in her hotel room, time was of the essence.

I jotted down my own Research To Do List, starting with an Internet search for Anthony's death, or at least an obituary. If that proved to be unsuccessful, I'd call hospitals for death info and/or dates. I would determine the funeral home involved and pay them a visit. With that accomplished, I'd have a few concrete answers by the time

Lindsey returned from Austin. And, hopefully, she'd stop thinking I was a raving maniac.

It was a beautiful October morning, so I decided to begin my workday in a shady spot in the backyard. I carried Malcolm's cage out and hung it from a special hook attached to the desert willow tree. He chirped contentedly while Wendell snoozed at my feet. Coffee steamed to the left of me, and my laptop awaited input.

First piece of business: I conducted a Google search for "Anthony Sommerfield." A few entries about his chiropractic practice and his internship popped up, but nothing else. I tried "Death of Dr. Sommerfield," and "Anthony Sommerfield Obituary," and "Sommerfield Funeral," but all I got was nothing and more nothing. I entered those same keywords into the local newspaper's website search link, not really expecting anything to show up, but hoping. Again, nothing.

Moving down my list, I looked up all the hospitals in Tucson and jotted down their phone numbers. Time to make some calls. I still had a good, positive feeling about today in spite of its fruitless beginning. I dialed the first number and a receptionist answered.

"Good morning," I said in my friendliest voice. "I'm trying to determine the exact date of a dear friend's death. His name is … *was* Anthony Sommerfield, and he—"

The woman on the other end of the line interrupted my request. "I'm sorry, sir. I can't give you that information. You'd have to be identified as a close family member and, preferably, stop by in person. So if you—"

"Of course. I understand." Frustrated, I almost hung up, but then I had an idea. I could almost feel the cartoon light bulb hovering over my head. "Can you tell me, please, if any patients seen in the Emergency Room or any who had been admitted between August 28 and September 3 died in your hospital?"

She hesitated briefly. "Since you put it that way, hold on a minute." I could hear her fingers tapping rapidly on a keyboard, then she reported, "There were no deaths in this hospital during those seven days. Does that help?"

"Very much. Thank you."

I crossed that hospital off my list, feeling encouraged. At least I now knew what to say to get the basic answer to one of my questions. Eight hospitals and six urgent care centers later, I was none the wiser. A few fatal illnesses had occurred in town, but those had all been elderly patients.

I refused to be defeated so early in the day. Funeral homes were next on the list. I found far more of those than I'd expected, but on the positive side, I discovered I didn't have to be clever or sneaky to obtain the desired information. My first question was straightforward, simple.

"Were the funeral arrangements for Anthony Sommerfield made at your establishment?" Easy enough.

On my sixth call, I received the hoped for "Yes." Barely able to contain my excitement, I asked if I could get more information about it and learned the director would be in the office in about thirty minutes. Good. So would I.

I took Malcolm and Wendell inside the house and put away my laptop, then got ready to go. I didn't take much with me, just a small pad of paper and a pen. I knew I'd need those things. I didn't know how those TV cops and detectives remembered all their facts since they hardly ever wrote anything down.

My hand was on the doorknob when I felt a strong, magnetic pull from Wendell's pleading eyes. He wanted to go for a ride. I shrugged. "Okay. Come on."

The funeral home was not what I'd expected. It was more like a hole in the wall. Uneasy with the look of the place, I decided Wendell was coming in with me. If they didn't like pets inside, they could tell me that after I'd already overstepped their bounds. We walked in and I discovered the inside was as rundown as the outside. The place was a dark, dreary room, sparsely furnished with a desk, a phone, and lots of old filing cabinets. No computer in sight. How could they conduct business in this decade without a computer?

The guy behind the desk appeared busy with paperwork. He looked startled, to say the least, when Wendell and I stood before him.

"How can I help you?" he asked in a monotone, not taking his eyes from Wendell.

I explained that I needed to ask some questions about the funeral arrangements that had been made for Anthony Sommerfield. He scratched at his ear and wrinkled his nose. "Sure. Have a seat."

We both sat. I know dogs don't have "people thoughts," but I could swear that Wendell looked uncomfortable. He glanced up, his big brown eyes practically begging, *Can we go now? This place gives me the creeps.*

"When did the cremation take place?" was my first question.

"I don't know."

He didn't know? "You don't do cremations?"

The man cleared his throat and the side of his mouth quirked up in an odd smile as if he'd just heard a bad attempt at a joke. "Yes, we do, but Mr. Sommerfield's urn was left on the doorstep, like an abandoned baby. Thought I'd seen everything when I picked that up. It arrived sealed and ready for burial."

"Uh …" Stranger and stranger. My foot tapped the wooden floor, and Wendell whined. "How did you know what to do with it?"

The man leaned back causing his chair to creak. "Oh, that was like taking toffee from a toddler." Funny, he didn't look like a guy who would say something like that. "It came with a check that more than covered the cost of what the instructions asked us to do. It was the easiest money we've ever made here. They asked for nothing out of the ordinary from our end."

"There's another 'end'?"

"The cemetery plays a different role. They always do. You might want to talk to them."

Finally, a helpful piece of advice. "Okay. I'll go there next. So what you're saying is that no official identifying documents arrived with the urn?"

He sat a little taller, thinking about the question, and eventually let out a resigned breath. "Okay. I know where you are going with that question, but …"

In fact, I had *no* idea where I was going with that question, so I was relieved when he continued.

"… you're right, laws were broken. But I had no choice. There was no way for us to know where the remains had been cremated, so it wasn't possible to do any follow up."

I got the feeling this so-called funeral director was no stranger to breaking the law. This was the shadiest looking operation I'd ever seen.

All three of us stood up, and Wendell's tail wagged with relief. I shook hands with the man behind the desk—we'd never gotten around to exchanging names—and thanked him for his help. We were almost out into the sunshine when I turned back and asked, "Who wrote the check?"

"Oh, I don't know that, either. It was a cashier's check."

One step forward, two steps back. Damn! I had new information, but nothing about it could be called a solid clue or a solution to any aspect of the mystery. But the whole thing still stunk of wrongdoing. We headed to the cemetery, since the one thing I knew for sure was the location of Anthony's plot.

I was stopped just before reaching our destination. "Sir? Sorry, but no dogs allowed."

"Oh?" I pointed toward Anthony's resting place. "Hey, man. This was his dog," I lied, sort of, trying to replicate Wendell's convincing, sad expression with my own eyes.

He thought about that for a moment. "Oh. Okay, sir. Go ahead."

"You look familiar," I told him, flashing my friendliest smile. "Were you here for the burial about a month ago?"

"Sure. I'm at all the burials in this section. And that one?" He chuckled lightly. "Well, let's just say it was a little different."

"Really? What do you mean?"

"The hole. We dug it as if all the urns and urn vaults were ready for burial, but as it turned out, there was only the one." He shrugged. "Must have been a misunderstanding."

"*All* the urns?"

"You don't know much about funerals and cemeteries, do ya?"

"No, I sure don't. The only time I was in a cemetery was one Halloween when I was just a kid. And I was scared out of my mind!"

He just nodded and continued. "Yep. Room for five in there, not just one." His words threw me for a loop. "Hey, I'd love to stay and chat, but I have to go change into my Sunday best for the next service. Don't stay too long, ya know? I mean, with the dog and all."

My eyes followed the worker as he hurried off. I turned back just in time to witness Wendell lifting his leg over Anthony's small bronze grave marker.

"Wendell, no! Stop that!" My voice trailed off.

Too late. I reluctantly admit that I almost enjoyed Wendell's indiscretion; nevertheless, I used the remaining water in my bottle to rinse off the marker, hoping any bad karma he might have set in motion would be washed away. As we drove to the airport to meet Lindsey's plane, I made Wendell swear he wouldn't tell her about that last event. We even shook on it.

EIGHTEEN

Lindsey

Ah, nothing to do and nowhere to go. I liked the sound of that. Sleeping in was just what I needed, so I did what any hard-working woman would do: I rolled over and went back to sleep. Unfortunately, the sleep wasn't restful, my dreams were unpleasant. Jake and I were sitting on a stage, and an audience filled with uniformed police waited for us to begin. He and I seemed to sit for hours, saying and doing nothing, until the officers began chanting, *Speech! Speech! Speech!*

Jake stood—I thought to defend me—but then he said, "Sorry, everyone. She just returned from being in the spotlight, from being worshipped and adored. She can't talk to you now. It takes her days to come down to earth and be like us ordinary fellas."

My dream-self turned and stared at him. "I just need to be mad for a while," I screamed, and the police officers all covered their ears with their hands.

I probably would have yelled some more, but I was awakened by a loud knock at our real life front door. I let

Jake answer it. After all, he was closer, and I wasn't dressed. But now that I was wide awake, I grudgingly got up, threw on some sweats, brushed my teeth and hair, and wandered halfway down the stairs—just in time to see an odd exchange between Jake and a policeman. I even heard their last few words.

"But we need to do that," Jake was insisting, sounding almost desperate.

"For the last time, Mr. Lee, there is no body to exhume. Just cremains. You know, ashes."

Jake shook his head. "There has to be some information in that urn that will help solve this crime."

"Mr. Lee, as I told you before, the process of cremation practically eliminates the ability to find clues. Especially the cause of death."

I watched from the stairs with horror. Apparently, Jake had taken Anthony's death on quite a road trip while I'd been away. He'd gone from merely stating *something's not right*, to declaring to the police that it's *a crime*. I didn't know whether to laugh, cry, or run away.

The policeman continued. "I'm really sorry, sir. The guy is dead and buried. In my book that is not a crime. Besides, you've given me no hard evidence to work with."

"What do you call this?" Jake asked, waving Anthony's letter in the officer's face. I couldn't believe such a whiny, screeching sound could come from Jake's mouth. It was actually quite embarrassing. "I call it a smoking gun!" he declared. "We've got a smoking gun right here."

The policeman crossed his arms. "No, sir. What you've got is a plastic squirt gun, and that's not nearly enough." He spotted me over Jake's shoulder, nodded a brief acknowledgment, then left.

Jake was in rare form. He spun toward me, looking furious. "What? Why are you looking at me like that?"

Just like the policeman, I crossed my arms, not just annoyed, but disappointed. What was happening to him? "Oh, Jake," I said. "You're taking this whole thing way too far. Why are you doing that? No one's asked you to. Not his parents, not his ex-girlfriend, and certainly not me. So why?"

He stared at me, his mouth open. "My God, Lindsey. I would think you of all people would want to know what really happened to Anthony."

Shaking his head with disgust, he paced back and forth across the living room. Malcolm didn't make a peep. Wendell watched carefully from the kitchen. Everyone's nerves were on edge.

"And did you hear what he said?" he ranted, waving his hands in the air. "He called them 'cremains.' Sounds like some kind of pastry!"

He was losing it. *We* were losing it.

"Good grief!" I cried, then I headed back upstairs to get dressed. What else could I do?

To distract myself from Jake's latest insanity, I decided to get my brain busy by working on something altogether different. The information Laura had left for me to read, about the Dogs at School Reading Program, turned out to be very interesting ... though a little complicated. Wendell would have to pass several tests in order to be certified for this program.

"Wendell," I said, and he cocked his head to one side. "It says you must be able to quickly drop any food or toy on cue, and ignore any distractions like a tennis ball bouncing right by your face. Hmm." Just the word 'ball' had him standing up, his tail wagging wildly. I changed my mind. "Maybe you don't need to be a *certified* reading dog. Let's just do it for fun. I'll bet Judy will let you listen to her first grade students read, whether you're certified or not."

105

I was excited, driving the familiar route to school. It felt like forever since I'd last been there.

"Miss Lindsey! Miss Lindsey!" Some of the students shrieked with joy when we walked in. Others were too intrigued with the giant dog in their classroom to notice me. I was relieved to see that Wendell wasn't the slightest bit anxious, even though he was surrounded by a roomful of rambunctious kids. This was a whole new experience for him.

"Hi, Mrs. Lopez," I said. "Thank you for letting us visit your class this afternoon."

"You are both welcome any time," she assured me. "Let's go up front so I can properly introduce you." Then she whispered, "Do you mind if the students ask a few questions about your dog?"

"Not at all. That would be wonderful. Do your students raise their hands to be called on?"

"Does tortilla begin with a T?"

I chuckled. "I'll take that as a yes."

The children sat on floor mats, Wendell and I waited, then Mrs. Lopez asked if anyone had a question. A dozen hands shot up.

"Miss Lindsey, does your dog bite?"

"No, he doesn't. Although ... he does take bites of his dog food. Does that count?"

The kids laughed, and one of my students from last year asked if Wendell still had his giant bed. I said that he did, and that he liked it very much. Flashback memories surfaced, reminding me of the day the bed had arrived at school, and I remembered how little Bobby had fallen sound asleep on the soft cushion. So many horrific facts were revealed shortly after that.

"Does he have any brothers and sisters?"

"How old is he?"

"Did you teach him how to read?"

I smiled at that one. "That's a great question. He doesn't read, but he knows a lot of words."

After a few more questions, Mrs. Lopez suggested that the children begin reading to Wendell. All the students wanted a turn, so we sat on the floor in the classroom's Library Corner, and the teacher sent three students at a time, each one held a small, eight-page reading book. Wendell was sufficiently attentive and appropriately exuberant when a student read a book containing words like *cat* or *squirrel*. He displayed his puzzled look when one of the stories had a character named Malcolm in it. Every time he heard that word, he looked at me as if I should come forth with an explanation—or at least the bird.

Emma, another child I'd had in my class last year, was the last child to read. She carried with her a tattered, handmade book. A book of poetry.

"Can I read you two poems, please?" she asked sweetly. I nodded and smiled, knowing she'd written them herself. Emma's talents and emotional maturity were far beyond those of a typical seven year old.

My teacher has a giant dog
Who has a giant bed.
It was tan and soft and cozy.
That's what Miss Lindsey said.

"There's more!" she announced, seeing my pleased expression. With a smile and a nod, I encouraged her to continue.

The little boy got sleepy
So he laid down his head
My dog will share the bed with him
That's what Miss Lindsey said.

"Oh, Emma! That was a wonderful poem!" I said, meaning it. "And I'm so happy you remembered about that unusual day back in kindergarten. When did you write that poem?"

"I wrote them all over the summer. I got the ideas from my kindergarten art journal."

"Oh, look," I said, pointing at Emma's book. "You used the picture you drew that day."

"Mom helped me glue it into my poetry book. She helped me with the word 'laid,' too. We had to look it up. She does a lot more things with me now that dad is gone. Can I read one more poem?"

"I would love that."

Emma turned to the last page in her book of original poems and began to read again.

> *My dad's chopper screeched and clanked*
> *Before it hit the ground.*
> *I thought the men inside would cry*
> *But they didn't make a sound.*
> *The trumpet's song was oh, so sad*
> *As the flag came into view.*
> *Mom said my dad was very brave*
> *And we'd be brave now too.*

Emma's second poem brought tears to my eyes. I took a deep breath and tried to avoid the blink that would send those tears rolling down my cheeks. Had I read her poem in the privacy of my home I would have sobbed openly. Emma didn't cry today, but I could tell the pain was still there; she was still being brave. Wendell must have sensed the little girl's sadness because he gently patted her with his giant paw and gave her ear a dog kiss. She hugged him tightly, and he accepted her gesture without any fussing. Such a tender moment. Far more than reading occurred in this classroom today.

I hugged this brave little girl, knowing she was far wiser, kinder, and more intuitive than most adults, and more tears filled my eyes. With the tears flowed an idea, a modification to my Children's Art Book project. I decided, right then and there, that each volume would be dedicated to a special, deserving child, beginning with Emma and her courageous thoughts and words.

We stayed behind for a few minutes so Judy and I could catch up a little. She insisted that Wendell and I come back as often as possible, and we didn't argue with that. Walking through the courtyard on our way to the office to sign out, Wendell stopped to sniff—but then … Oh dear. My big dog hunched his body into a position that left no doubt in my mind what was about to occur. Darn! I hadn't brought a bag. How could I have been so forgetful?

"Would one of these help?" asked Mr. Tom, the custodian. He waved a plastic bag, then scooped up the rather large pile himself.

"Hey! Thank you! I was going to do that," I said weakly.

"Not a problem. Seen Shawna lately?"

That was unexpected. "No," I said slowly. "I didn't know you knew Shawna."

"Oh, yeah. We go way back. We were neighbors in Phoenix." He gave me a quick smile. "See you later!"

I stared at his back as he walked away.

"Lindsey! Hi!" called Mrs. Wilson, the principal. She'd stepped out of her private office and caught us just before we'd reached the school's front door. "How lovely to see you."

"Nice to see you, too," I said.

"Rest assured your long-term sub is a good teacher," she told me. "She's not you, of course, but she'll do. Oh, and here," she said, flapping a sheet of paper near my face. Sometimes that woman was anything but tactful. "I should have given this to you sooner. Better late than never, huh?"

Glancing at the page, I could see it contained a string of three short emails originating from Bobby's foster mother, Jennifer Fields, going to Child Protective Services, and finally to Judge Martz. How timely, since I'd just been remembering little Bobby, all curled up on Wendell's new bed. I'd read the emails after I got to the car.

"I see you've got the famous dog with you today," she said, raising one eyebrow.

"What?" I giggled. "He's good, but he's not famous."

"Oh, I think he is. He looks exactly like the dog in the morning paper." I watched as she thumbed through the newspaper pages and found a photo of a mastiff—peeing on a grave marker. I recognized Wendell right away. Good grief!

I put on a fake smile to mask my horror. "The dog does look a little bit like Wendell. It is definitely a mastiff, but Wendell's bigger." I had no desire to read the caption under the photo. After an awkward, goodbye hug, I quickly departed with the famous dog.

After reading and rereading the email, then sleeping on it, I decided to give Bobby's foster mom a call. What harm could come from simply talking with her? I had spent almost an entire school year with him, and if any of my experience, ideas, or strategies might help her care for this troubled little boy, I figured I should share them.

"Hello. Is this Jennifer?"

Breathless, as if she'd been running on the treadmill, she replied, "Speaking."

"This is Lindsey, Bobby's kinder teacher from last year. I got a message that you wanted to talk with me."

"Oh, yes! Thank you for calling." I could hear growling and screeching in the background and realized Bobby was in one of his moods. "It's actually not a good time right now. Could we meet tomorrow at the U of A Mall? By the wildcat sculpture?"

"Uh, sure. What time?"

"A respite worker arrives at 2 p.m. so I could be there by 2:15."

"All right. But, um, can I ask a question?"

"Sure."

"Why is Bobby at home on a school day?"

"That's a real long story," she stated, then ended the call.

Curiosity activated, visions of the abuse he'd endured the previous year pounded like a hammer inside my head, tugging at my heart. Reassuring myself—at least for the moment—that his life was better now, that he was safe and being cared for, I made my own stay-at-home plans for the day.

Since traveling was now part of my life, my way of thinking about routine domestic tasks had changed. I think being away from home and living in hotels was the reason I'd discovered happiness in dusting, washing clothes, and even emptying wastebaskets. I looked around the house and realized the remainder of my day would be jam-packed with that kind of joy.

Jake helped with the big and obvious jobs, like sweeping or wiping up actual spills, taking out the trash, and tending to our pets. He was a clean freak in the kitchen, keeping it spotless and bright, but everywhere else was a different story. Our home office was a disaster. He'd taken over that room with books and articles about writing—in particular crime writing, 'real' crime, and accounts of actual investigations. He'd also taken over my stash of poster-sized sticky notes, and he'd stuck them to any empty wall space, planning to use them like a chalkboard or whiteboard for his thoughts. I came across several coffee cups that looked more like science experiments than containers holding liquid for human consumption. That was okay. From talking with other women, I gathered that even with this evidence in hand, Jake was more domestically helpful than a lot of men.

I did what cleaning and straightening I could downstairs then decided it was time to indulge in a snack. Placing my plate of sliced apples, cheese, and one tiny piece of dark chocolate on the coffee table, I sat back serenely on the sofa with Wendell near my feet. He was much happier when I wasn't rushing around attached to things like spray cans filled with furniture polish and roaring vacuum cleaners.

When the apples and cheese were long gone, I reached for the piece of chocolate and accidentally bumped the plate, which fell onto the floor. I dove for it, and so did Wendell. I couldn't let him eat chocolate. I knew what it could do to his digestive system. Our heads banged together, and I let out a small cry, but Wendell didn't seem to feel anything. His huge head was like a rock, and he was entirely focused on the chocolate as it rolled under the sofa. Fortunately, the size of his head kept him from retrieving the treat, and I found it with little difficulty. I grabbed several magazines and scraps of paper that were also under the sofa, then made a mental note to vacuum up all the dust bunnies and trolls that were living there.

I flipped through the magazines before placing them in a pile destined for the trash, and was in the process of placing the loose papers on the top when something caught my eye. I frowned, examining the colorful gel pen doodlings I knew I hadn't drawn. I noticed a lot of hearts on the page, and the words *Jake & Laura* or *Laura & Jake* had been written inside them. Could Jake have—no. No way. He was not a gel pen guy or the doodling type. Staring harder, I saw the words *Mr. and Mrs. Lee* written over and over, and I felt slightly dizzy with disbelief. Laura had written this. She had been here watching the animals, and I also knew her handwriting. Had she been daydreaming ... about Jake and her? How dare she do that? Two words written on the back of one of the sheets proved to be more than I could stomach. *Laura Lee*.

Waiting until I'd calmed down did not occur to me just then. I didn't bother to use the well-known strategy I'd taught and required my students to use—*when something upsets you or makes you angry, count to ten slowly before saying or doing anything*. I didn't do any of that. I drove straight over to Laura's apartment, speeding most of the way. My fingers tapped furiously on the steering wheel as my jealous anger and rising indignation overtook my sensibility.

"Hi, Lindsey," she said when she opened the door. "What a surprise!"

I gave her my most furious expression. "What a surprise, indeed!"

"What do you mean? What's the matter, Linds?"

I thrust the scrap piece of paper in her face and saw immediately the shocked look in her eyes. Oh, yeah. She knew what I'd uncovered. "You tell me," I demanded. "What the hell is going on, Laura?"

"What do you want me to say, Lindsey?"

"Say it isn't so! Explain. Explain the meaning of your words, your thoughts, your plans for *my* live-in boyfriend."

I saw the steel come into her eyes, and she folded her arms across her chest. "I don't have to explain anything. I can think and feel and do whatever I want. I can even draw little hearts, if I want to. It's a free country, and you're not the boss of me."

If she thought that popular elementary school phrase would deflect my anger, she was wrong. "How dare you?" I hissed. "How could you even *think* about coming between Jake and me?" My throat was swelling with fury. "I thought you and I were best friends."

"Yeah? Well, how dare you come barging into my house with all these accusations over a page of doodling? You need to leave. Now."

Laura, apparently just as angry as I was by this point, bullied me out the door, and when I hesitated, she gave me a little shove. That did it! That was the proverbial last straw that broke this camel's back. I crumpled up the incriminating page and threw it at her just before she slammed the door.

NINETEEN

Jake

This morning a significant breakthrough would brighten my day. Someone would make a mistake, slip up. If not, I'll go vegetate in the blue tunnel and be satisfied that my lot in life is that of a dog walker.

"Come on, Wendell. Let's go for a walk."

We walked for an hour, turning down streets that were new to Wendell. I'd been up and down them multiple times when he'd been missing, but he had a lot of new territory to sniff and mark.

Recently, I'd resorted to carrying a small voice recorder, just in case I got an idea for my book—or more likely, the crime waiting to be solved. Like a reminder, the gadget waited eagerly in my back pocket for input, and I suddenly became aware of its presence. I hadn't seen the hint of a clue, nevertheless, something prompted me to pull the recorder out, press the red record button, and start whispering into it as we walked.

"The dog and I are midway down Maple Street, and the hair on the back of my neck is suddenly standing straight up, as if a major lightning strike was about to occur. The thing is, there is not a cloud in the sky. Why do I feel this way? Is someone following me? Is someone watching or spying on me? Why would they do that? Lindsey would say I was being paranoid, but I have a reason to feel paranoid: Anthony's threats. Are they really going to happen? Will I regret the day I was born just like he warned in the letter?"

My phone's standard ringtone began to play, and I jumped so high I could have landed on a desert ironwood tree branch. "Hello?"

"Hi, Jake. It's Mrs. Madera. I hope I'm not bothering you."

Shaking off the temporary malfunction of my heart, I let her know I was glad she'd called.

"I, uh, I thought of something you might find interesting. Want to meet for coffee tomorrow?"

Anticipation surged. "All right, but today would actually be better. Would today work for you?"

"Uh, sure. I didn't want to be pushy or rush you or anything. It's probably not that important but—"

"Meet me at the Coyote Café in thirty minutes. I'll whip us up the best coffee you've ever tasted." I ended the call, and Wendell and I trotted all the way home.

Lindsey sat at the kitchen table, busy sorting some student artwork when we arrived all breathless and sweaty. She looked up at me, but her smile and sparkling eyes were nowhere to be seen.

"Is everything all right?" Her voice lifeless, a monotone.

I couldn't tell her about Mrs. Madera. She'd flip out if she knew I was still pursuing my detective path. "Yeah, we'd walked further than we'd realized, and the time got away from us so we hurried home. How is your work coming along? You seem to be spending more time getting ready for the San Diego Conference than you did for the others."

"You're right about that. I'm putting together a mock-up for a book Elisabeth might publish early next year. It'll feature some of my own students' art journal work as well as the work of others." She'd answered my question, then refocused on her work.

"Sounds good." I leaned over and kissed her on the cheek. Perhaps I was just seeing a look of concentration, nothing more. "I'm going to be at the Coyote Café for about an hour—something I've got to work out. I've got my cell, so call me if you need me."

I dashed out the door, and since I had a few minutes to spare, I swung by Shawna's place. No real reason, but I always carried the hope of learning something new. My gut wouldn't let go of the feeling that she was somehow involved with the death, the letters, or something I'd not yet discovered.

Her Hummer wasn't in the driveway; I parked the Jeep and rang the bell anyway. There was no answer, but since I was still ahead of schedule, I walked around the house's exterior, looking for ... what? I didn't know. I tried to peer into a few windows, but the place was shut up tight, as usual. Shawna had something against sunlight, so she always kept any possible traces of sunshine from entering her house.

My mind drifted back to the day when I'd come by to pick up Wendell the year before and ended up snooping around. It had been partly for my research, but also to learn more about this odd woman who had taken possession of Anthony, Lindsey's husband at the time. The place had been so dark, and I'd needed to use the flashlight from my Jeep's glove box just to keep from stumbling. Thinking back, I'm pretty sure that's when my sleuthing tendencies took hold. I'd snuck around, cautiously scanning the interior, hugging the walls as if I expected zombies to jump out. I'd held that flashlight like it was a weapon.

I remembered approaching a room, a room with a closed door. Just before entering, I'd whispered to the dog, "Ready, Wendell?' then dramatically flung the door open. I was shocked and stunned by the loud screaming, screeching sounds coming from that dark room. Wendell bolted; I was close behind.

I could laugh about that day now—I didn't at the time—because I'd learned that Shawna had pre-set her TV to record some horror movie and it just happened to click on as we entered.

I didn't need a flashlight today, and I wasn't about to go inside anyway. But I couldn't help feeling curious about what I might be able to see from the outside. I walked past a tree, still looking up at the house, then let out a short string of cuss words when my foot sank into a fairly new, large pile of dog poop. Damn! I could tolerate cleaning up after Wendell at home, but scraping an unknown dog's soft, smelly poop off my shoes? Well, that's a whole different and gross ball game.

Wait. Why would there be several days' worth of semi-fresh dog poop in Shawna's yard?

I glanced at my watch, realizing more time had passed than I'd planned on. I was late. After carefully wiping my shoes in some fallen leaves, I scrambled back in the Jeep and headed out, pondering new questions the whole way.

Mrs. Madera was waiting for me just inside the entrance of the café. She appeared to be happy to see me, but I could see an underlying aura of nervousness. I tried warming her with a smile.

"Are you sure you want just plain coffee?" I asked agreeably. "I can make anything. I still work here, you know."

"That's very thoughtful of you, Jake, but coffee with a little cream and a dash of cinnamon would be real nice."

Not wanting to rush her, I managed to come up with some small talk about the pleasant Tucson fall weather as we sipped our hot drinks. I didn't want her to feel anxious, so I didn't bother telling her that I'd turned on my recorder. Anxious to get the conversation going, I broke the ice by asking, "Do you remember at the funeral telling me that you took care of Anthony? That he was like your own child, or something like that?"

She nodded sadly. "Yes, and that was the truth. I don't think he ever showed anyone but me his needy, vulnerable side. He hid it well. And I'm pretty sure that even I saw only a glimpse of that part of his personality." Her face darkened with grief. This woman had obviously cared about Anthony. She appeared to know him better than Lindsey or Shawna or anyone else did.

"That Shawna person was the beginning of the end for him," she stated, staring into her coffee. "If only he'd stayed with Lindsey, he'd be alive today."

I couldn't agree with all of that because I was incredibly grateful that he hadn't stuck with Lindsey, for obvious reasons.

Maybe it was a little too eager of me, but I jumped in with, "So you think she's responsible for his death? I'm sure there was foul play."

She leaned in, her eyes narrowed. "Oh, Jake. You really think that? Foul play had not occurred to me. Not now, not ever. I blame Anthony's death on his own bad choices and his damaging reaction to the shock of his sexy, hot woman actually being a man. That's what did him in. You knew about that, right? Her being a he?"

"Well, yes." I knew all about Shawna. "Eventually, I found out. Tell me more about his deadly reaction to discovering the truth about her."

Mrs. Madera gave me an annoyed look and shook her head. "I believe my word was *damaging*, Jake, not *deadly*." She rummaged through her large purse and pulled out a paper calendar. "Okay. Here's what I wanted to share with you, but keep in mind, I don't have any exact dates, just approximations. And some of what I'll say is … my own opinion, not necessarily fact."

"Got it." Better than nothing.

"Well, right after Anthony left Shawna, he decided he wanted to move back with Lindsey. I don't know the details about that, but soon he ended up homeless and alone. He always seemed anxious, afraid, and even humiliated. He didn't know how to deal with any of it."

"What did he do?"

"Well, he slept at the office for a while. I don't know where he lived or slept after that. He never said. Since he wasn't able to cope with anything less than feeling on top of the world, he began to self-destruct. I'd seen this before, but only in short-lived, minor ways. This situation turned him into a ticking time bomb."

"Wow. I figured he was pissed at Shawna, but I never suspected he'd have such a melt-down."

"I did. That's why I covered for him."

"What does that mean? Covered how?"

She took a deep breath. "Like I said, Anthony can't stand to feel anything but great. And after all that, he was experiencing the worst scenario, the lowest point in his life. He began to spiral out of control with the aid of drugs and alcohol, and, of course, his stupid efforts to feel good made him feel awful. He cut back his office hours to only two days a week, and when he did come in, he was in real bad shape. One afternoon, after the last patient of the day had gone, he actually cried. He was like a baby in my arms. Through the sobs he called himself a loser," she said, frowning, "and yet he blamed everyone else for his misery."

"Do you think this might be a case of suicide?" That scenario made more sense to me after what I'd just heard.

"Absolutely not!" she snapped.

"I don't understand. How can you say that after what you'd witnessed and everything you've just told me?"

She frowned again, clearly annoyed at the interruption. "I'm not finished, Jake. After a while, Anthony began to cycle out of his deep depression. About two weeks before he died he found new energy. His ambition came back, and it appeared he was turning it around as if he'd suddenly found a new reason to live. If you recall, I did mention that he'd even gone off on a three-day weekend. Some kind of holiday. He was almost the Dr. Sommerfield we all knew and …"

She didn't say the word, but she obviously loved him in some way. A motherly way?

My thoughts went to that three-day vacation. If Anthony was truly turning it around, even taking a little time off, that provided even more reason to suspect foul play. Where had he gone during those three days?

"Thanks for calling me about all this, Mrs. Madera. I really appreciate your sharing all that information. If only I could talk with Anthony's parents."

"You haven't talked to Hank or Katie?"

"Well, sure, a few words at the funeral. They didn't have much to say, and I didn't have much to ask because, at the time, I didn't know they were his parents. Anyway, I don't know how to reach them. After you'd mentioned their names I tried to find some contact information but none was publicly available. They must like their privacy."

"I found their phone number back at the office when I was packing up some of my things."

"You did? Really?" Finally, that needed breakthrough! Hank and Katie *had* to know something. "Let's go get it?"

I made the call from the now inactive chiropractic office with Mrs. Madera by my side. It surprised me that she still had access, but she only shrugged and assured me the rent was paid until the end of the month. I dialed the number and pressed the 'speaker' button so she could hear, too. After announcing who I was to Anthony's mother she handed off the phone to Hank, Anthony's father. His mood hadn't changed from that of the man I'd seen at the gravesite. He still didn't have a trace of sadness in his voice. To my relief, he seemed willing to talk about his deceased son, though.

"Do you and Katie know anything about how he died?" I asked. "No one in Tucson seems to have any information about that."

"Why do you care? What's it to you?" he asked gruffly.

"Lindsey, a friend of mine and Anthony's former wife, is very upset by his death as well as all the mystery surrounding it. Knowing what happened would give her a little peace of mind so she could get on with her life." That was my on the spot answer, and I liked to think it was fairly close to the truth, even though Lindsey kept insisting that I back off.

Hank softened his tone and began telling his story. "We don't know anything about his death, but we sure know about his life. Katie and I couldn't have kids, so we went through the long process of adoption here in California. We adopted six-month-old Anthony, and he was a difficult infant. He cried often and loudly. But we knew some babies were like that. We did our best.

"But around the age of two, we saw signs of trouble that were beyond our understanding. It was almost as if our cute little toddler had a split personality, if there is such a thing. Every year he got worse. Some days he was smart, helpful, even charming. Other days, I could swear I was in the presence of pure evil. By the time he went to elementary school he'd actually tried to physically harm both Katie and me. More than once!"

He let out a deep sigh, sounding tired, and Mrs. Madera and I exchanged glances. Hank continued without prompting from us. "At that point we were still making excuses for him. We believed we could overcome any genetic flaws he might have inherited from his birth parents, and by the time we realized we had a huge problem, it was too late. We were years beyond the trial period, and he was not returnable."

I listened with shock and disbelief. "What did you do? How did you cope with his odd behaviors?"

"I'm a chiropractor myself, and I naïvely thought that with daily adjustments and a super healthy diet and lifestyle, he'd come around. But nothing helped—at least not while he still lived with us. I gotta say, life with that boy was hell."

Hank kept talking, telling me his story, but he did so with little detectible emotion beyond his initial anger. I assumed that was his coping mechanism. But Katie displayed enough emotion for both of them. Hearing her sobs over the phone line was heartbreaking.

"What about psychiatric help?" I asked. "Wasn't there medication or therapy or someone that could fix these … these problems?"

"Oh, we tried that, but, like I said, Anthony could turn on the charm when it suited him. He couldn't maintain his good side for very long, but it was long enough to convince several doctors that we were the ones with the problems, not him. We were even investigated by Child Protective Services several times."

I watched as this conversation took its toll on Mrs. Madera, too. Her shoulders slumped, and tears rolled down her cheeks. Had she known any of this? Suspected anything of this magnitude? Then, I wondered if she'd ever experienced any of his evil behaviors? I'd ask her later. For now, I reached for her hand, and she didn't object.

"Sometime during his middle school years, he began hiding in our bedroom and spying on us during our … intimate moments. We're not sure how long this went on. He was clever. As soon as we discovered this, I put a strong lock on the door, but that solution triggered one of his longest and most evil periods. He even started a fire under our bed one night. Can you imagine?"

His stories were unbelievable. "Didn't the police or psychiatrists have anything to say about all of this?"

"Oh, sure. They said we were 'enabling' his bad behavior. We needed to use 'tough love.'" He barked out a laugh. "I would love to know … how the hell does anyone 'enable' *crazy*? Eventually, we just gave up on getting help."

Mrs. Madera and I didn't need to hear any more. She was probably the only person on the planet who felt sorry for Anthony, but I could also see confusion on her face as she wept for his parents.

But Hank had a few more things to say. "As an adult he seemed to gain far more control of his personality disorder—that's what I called it, anyway. As you know, he followed in my footsteps and became a chiropractor. A very successful one at that. Or so we heard. We hadn't been face to face since the beginning of his sophomore year in college."

He took another deep breath, and this one he let out slowly. He sounded very old in that moment. "So, yeah, to be honest, we were relieved to learn that he was gone. We just needed to see him put into the ground. You have no idea what it's like to constantly be looking over your shoulder, expecting harm at every turn."

I told them how sorry I was, for both their loss and their troubles, but I still had to ask the tough question. "Where were you and Katie between August 28 and September 3?"

"I know what you're thinking, and I don't blame you for thinking it. Katie and I were on a 14-day Alaskan Cruise during that time frame. In fact, we had to cut our vacation a few days short to return for the funeral. Go ahead and check."

They had motive. No doubt about that. But they had an alibi, too. I was mid-sentence saying thank you and goodbye when Hank interrupted me.

"There is one more thing, though it probably doesn't really factor in. We did hear, unofficially, at the time of his adoption, that Anthony had a twin. We never knew for sure. We were never able to find any facts about that."

Mrs. Madera and I sat in stunned silence for quite a while after I'd hung up.

On my way home, it dawned on me to wonder who had paid the rent on that office. Did I need to search for a twin? Could his twin, if there was such a person, be involved with any of this?

TWENTY

Shawna

I'd waited at home for Julie's phone call. Where else would I be? I didn't have any friends. I didn't even have a job. The phone's ringer alerted me … right on schedule.

"Hi, Julie," I said, leaning back against my headboard. "What's on your 'Cure the crazy guy' agenda for this week?"

"Oh, I don't know. I thought I'd leave that up to you. What do you want to talk about today?"

Julie always did that shrink thing. She turned everything back on me. Okay, then. Two could play at that game, and she'd asked for it.

"I need friends," I informed her, "a social life, and a job. I *really* need a job. I'll be completely out of money soon. If you think I've got problems now, you won't want to see what financial ruin does to my delicate psyche."

She didn't react to my challenge. "What kind of job did you have in mind?"

"The only thing I know how to do is dance while 90% naked—actually, make that 94%. And I was *very* good at that. Maybe the best in town," I said, my voice smooth and sultry. She didn't react, so I went back to talking business. "You tell me. What could I do?"

I wasn't actually trying to be difficult with Julie for the fun of it—though I've done that a time or two. The truth was, I really hadn't a clue as to what I should do with my life. I had even less of a clue as to what kind of employer might hire me.

"I can help you do some brainstorming," she offered calmly, "but only you can make the decision. Tell me, when you were a child, what did you want to be when you grew up?"

I chuckled wryly, but I told her the truth. "Well, I spent most waking moments wanting to be a girl, a woman, and I worked very hard at that."

"What else?"

"I remember a few fleeting moments when I wanted to be a fireman or a cowboy. In a general way, I thought being an actor would be cool." I had no idea how old I was when those little fantasies had flashed through my brain. All I knew was that they'd quickly fizzled out. There were no firemen or cowboys wearing frilly dresses. A few actors, maybe.

"Good," she said, surprising me. "That's a start. Now you have a homework assignment. Make a list of any type of work you can think of. It doesn't matter how silly or impossible it might sound to you. Write it down. I'm going to call you back in forty-eight hours, and we will go over your list. Write down everything that comes to mind. Do not edit yourself. Got it?"

At least it sounded like something that would keep me busy for a while. I hesitated. "Yeah, I got it. But there is something else I need right now."

"All right. What's that?"

"Taking it slow—the reversal of my transformation—is not working for me. I think it would be easier, less painful, to go cold turkey. And I want you to tell me how to do that."

I knew she wouldn't like that idea, but frankly, I didn't care. This was my body, my life.

She took her time, thinking over my request while I hummed the *Jeopardy* final question theme into the phone. I knew I could be a real pain in the ass. That came so naturally to me. In fact, a vision of an advertisement flashed before my eyes. It read—Wanted: A Pain in the Ass, five years experience preferred. I'd be a great candidate for that job.

"I have a question," she said. "You seem far more certain about your life's path now than you were a few weeks ago. How come? When we started working together, we decided this was to be a cautious experiment to determine your most viable, helpful, and desired life options. What's going on?"

"I can't explain it," I lied. I knew exactly what was going on, but I didn't want anyone else to know what I had planned.

"But look how long it took for you to kill off Sean and go for the 100% Shawna. I'm sorry, but I can't recommend rushing like this."

I gave her a long, dramatic sigh, letting her know I didn't really care what she did or did not recommend. "Okay, you've given me your professional opinion. Thank you very much. Now let's move forward."

Julie let out her own frustrated sigh. Whether she decided to help me or not, I'd already decided I was pressing the fast-forward button, beginning today. Why? Not telling.

"I'm working for you," she said, "so if that is what you want, let's give it a try with some role playing. What are you wearing right now?"

"A simple knit dress. Nothing fancy. Why?"

"Well, that won't accelerate your process, will it? From this day forward, pack up the girly stuff and wear pants. You do have some, right?"

"I do. The men's clothes that I wore while working in the salons up in Phoenix are in the locked closet in the small bedroom."

"Well, go change. I'll wait."

"What, now?'

"Yes, now. Go."

Julie was using her *I mean business* voice, and since she was complying with my wishes, I went to change. I even hurried.

"Now what are you wearing?" she asked when I got back to the phone.

"Khaki slacks that are way too baggy and a black polo shirt that is way too tight. I look like a dork."

"Okay. Well, that's a start. Describe how are you sitting."

"Uh, I'm at the dining room table on a chair."

"Details. I need *details*. Where are your feet? Your legs? Your arms?"

"My legs are crossed—"

"How?"

"Geez! At the knee."

"Nope. If you must cross your legs, place the ankle of one leg on the knee of the other. Otherwise, feet flat on the floor."

I slammed my feet on the floor, not entirely happy about this. It seemed I now had more assignments than I'd had in high school. "Done."

"And, I want you to go shopping. We can't have you feeling like a dork. Get some nice, snug jeans and wear them. Stop tucking your male parts out of sight. Let it all hang out, so to speak."

"I'll try," I'd told her the truth. "But that will require a purchase of more than jeans. All I have here at the house are my custom made bikinis. My ass will be as flat as a pancake again when I give those up. Such a bummer."

I laughed at my own joke, but Julie got quiet. I decided I would be the one to stay silent the longest this time, and I won. She couldn't resist, had to dig deeper. She was a curious woman, which I guessed was a good thing for someone in her profession.

"Tell me more about that," she said.

"Which that?" I asked, wishing I could see her frustrated face.

"The bikini."

"Oh, all right. My ass is naturally flat. Always has been. That wasn't a great physical trait for an exotic dancer, so I had special bikinis made that had hidden padding. It was really clever padding made to perfection, and it also assisted in hiding my ... well, you know."

I think she'd heard enough about *that* because she quickly continued with her list of instructions for me. "Okay. Buy some loose fitting shirts for now, while you still have your double D breasts. You might also want to pick up a stretchy ace bandage to help minimize those obsolete assets. How are you doing with tapering off the female hormones?"

"I haven't gotten around to that yet."

"Well, I strongly suggest that you do." She sounded a little frustrated at that, which I understood. If I really wanted to reverse all this, I did have to cut back on the hormones. I knew that. Just been putting it off. "And you know there is breast reduction surgery in your future if you really go through with your reversal."

"I don't want to think about that right now, but I'll get some clothes and cut back on the hormones."

"One last thing. Think about several male actors you like and admire, maybe even think are hot. Watch and study their moves. You will have to fake it till you make it."

"I can do that. I'll do it today."

Changing the subject a little, I told Julie her baby brother was still hounding me, accusing me of being the one who had harmed Anthony. I hated the way Jake talked to me lately. He used to be so helpful when he thought I was a sexy, hot woman. I guess those days were gone for both of us.

"So, Julie," I tried gently. "Hypothetically, if I had hurt Anthony in any way, or if I were involved in what Jake is calling 'crimes,' would it be better in the eyes of the law for me to be the messed up guy who wanted to be a woman, or the transgender human trying to recover his manhood?"

She sighed. "Go get a haircut," she replied. "I need some time to think about that one."

TWENTY-ONE

Lindsey

I detected exhaustion and worry in Jennifer's eyes though she carried herself with determination and confidence. We shook hands and sat on bench near the wildcat sculpture as college students hurried by, and I asked how I could help with little Bobby.

"I can't get through to him," she said, obviously frustrated. "He's so *angry*. I want to help him, but he resents everything I do."

I nodded, sympathetic to her plight. "Jennifer, that's how he's been every since I've known him, so don't think for a minute that you're responsible for any of his problems or his actions. You do know about some of the abuse issues, right?"

"Yes. The CPS caseworker told me. She also let me know about his foster care history."

"His history?" That was news to me. "He's been in foster care before?"

"It's a brief history. He'd been in three other homes before coming to me. The other families gave up after three or four weeks of life with Bobby, and I can't blame them. He's tough. He has no self-control and is often defiant, destructive, and aggressive. He lies, he hits, and he's a bed wetter. My hectic job as a grocery store checker is more relaxing than being at home."

"I am so sorry," I said. I couldn't even imagine living that way. "How can I help?"

"Well, the injured camel arrived."

I blinked. "Uh, what?"

"You know about the straw that broke the camel's back?"

"Oh, sure. I know that camel," I said. *I really did.*

Jennifer explained that Bobby had been suspended three times since school had begun. The principal had said he would have been suspended every single day if they'd followed the Students' Rights and Responsibilities district document. The teacher and the school finally reached their own 'last straw' when Bobby's actions injured another student. He had been expelled, and Jennifer was informed that if she couldn't fine a private school to take him, home-schooling was her only other option.

She held out her empty hands. "I can't afford private school even if they would take him. I receive $21 a day as his foster mom. That barely pays for his food and clothes—I definitely don't do this for the money. There is no way a babysitter could handle him all day long while I'm at work, which means I'd have to quit my job. Stay home with him 24/7 and home-school him. That is simply not an option." She dropped her chin to her chest. "So I'm in a panic. I don't want to give up on Bobby; he needs stability in his life. But now I feel like the grim reaper has joined forces with the camel, and they are both sitting on my doorstep, impatiently waiting."

"How long has he been staying at home due to the expulsion?"

"Two impossible days. The fact is, even if I could find a sitter who could handle him while I was at work, I can't be his teacher. He won't even let me read him a story. I asked him what would make him happy, and for the first time he actually answered my question." A smile trembled on her lips. "He said he wanted to see Miss Lindsey. So here I am, hopefully arranging that."

"I could certainly visit with him," I said.

Then, with deep, pleading eyes, she asked me to be his home-school teacher, adding that since I was a certified teacher, I could probably be paid—something, by someone.

"I'm sorry, Jennifer. I can't do that. I'm on sabbatical from my teaching job and I'm also under contract with another company. And that job takes me out of town."

Her eyes morphed from pleading to fearful begging. "But CPS and the judge both think it's a great idea."

"Maybe if I'd taken the year off," I told her, then shook my head. "But I am working. I can't be his home-school teacher. That's not possible."

"Please!" Her eyes welled with tears. "I can't do this alone."

"What about your husband? Can't he help you?"

"I don't have a husband. I know kids are usually placed in homes with two parents, but in Bobby's case, they were desperate."

My heart hurt for Jennifer and Bobby. I agreed to a one-hour meeting with the boy after I returned from the San Diego Conference—hoping they'd both survive until then.

TWENTY-TWO

Jake

Tonight would be memorable. Determined to be both the creator and the reason for one of Lindsey's best nights ever, I planned to grill a splendid dinner of tilapia, zucchini, and red potatoes. All that and a side of candles, wine, and roses. In a couple of days she'd be winging her way to San Diego for the third of her conference presentations, and it was imperative to me that we feel good about our relationship, our future together, before we were separated again.

We pulled up to the house at the same time and I jumped out of my Jeep, motioning like a traffic cop for her to drive in ahead of me. After she'd parked, I watched her swing those beautiful legs from the car and step out. Face to face, we smiled, though our physical contact was limited to a swift, cool kiss because we were both loaded down with bags.

"Looks like we're on the same shopping wave length tonight." I held up my bags, but I kept my plan a secret. "Thought we could use a few groceries."

Mimicking my bag lifting, she said with exaggerated coyness, "And a few odds and ends for the house."

Once we were inside, she said she was really tired and was going to lie down for a few minutes before starting dinner. That gave me time to light the grill, prepare the food for cooking, chill the Chardonnay, then set the table. I think I can put the silverware in the correct place. Forks on the left?

"What's all this, Jake? Expecting company?" Her voice was light, and I glanced over with surprise. I'd thought she was going to lie down, but apparently she'd had her own surprise planned. All she wore was a short, silky Victoria's Secret cover-up—which covered very little.

"Have a seat, my lovely, scantily clad lady," I said, though I had difficulty taking my eyes off her. "Dinner will be served in about ten minutes."

Her look of surprise was worth a million bucks. I poured each of us a glass of wine and turned on some soft, jazzy music. She glowed, she smiled, and she smelled really good.

"A toast," I said gently. "Here's to you, to me, and to us. May we be in love forever."

The toast was sealed with a tantalizing kiss, and I detected a tear of joy clinging to each corner of her beautiful hazel eyes, so I initiated an encore.

"Mmmm," she purred as we drew apart. "Who says you can't live on love? Right now, I think we could. Who needs food?"

Food! My eyes popped open instantly, and I dashed outside to rescue our rapidly charring dinner from the grill. No damage, thank goodness. In fact, not only was it edible, it was cooked to perfection. I got lucky. Lindsey said she loved it, that everything was delicious. I had to take her word for it because my focus was on Lindsey not on the food in front of me. She was all I needed.

"Are you ready for dessert?" she asked, with a mischievous twinkle in her eye. "It's upstairs."

I had a pretty good idea of what she'd planned on serving, and I was good with that. Real good. She took my hand and led me up the staircase, and halfway up I turned toward Wendell and shook my head. He laid back down, his head on his paws, prepared to wait at the bottom of the stairs. He wasn't often banned from the bedroom, but he was catching on quickly.

The bedding was turned down, and she'd sprinkled a few rose petals over the sheets. A large bottle of sparkling water sat in a bucket, chilling on ice, and a plate of chocolate covered strawberries waited on the night table.

"My God, Lindsey. What's all this?"

"Jake, we are truly becoming one," she said. "And our great minds are thinking alike more and more."

"Our great bodies are, too." That just slipped out—I am a guy, after all—but she didn't seem to mind. She smiled.

"Tonight proves that. We both wanted to create something special for each other, and it looks like we did. Mr. Lee, you had your chance to run the show downstairs, now it's my turn. So come with me."

I'd expected a little food, a little love, but it seemed there was more than that to her plan. She led me into the master bathroom, ran hot water into the over-sized bathtub, and reached for a bottle of ...

"Very Sexy," she informed me.

"Yes, indeed," I agreed.

She giggled. "No, I mean the bubbling bath oil is called Very Sexy. I got it when I was in Boulder."

"Oh."

It was a good choice, a good name. But it certainly wasn't just the bath oil that was very sexy. Her next move took me by surprise. She carefully unbuttoned and removed my shirt, setting it aside as if it were something priceless. Then she nudged me to the edge of the tub and removed my well-worn flip-flops. I was certain my cargo shorts would be coming off within seconds, but what came next was even better.

As I sat on the edge of the slowly filling tub, I had the privilege of watching her undress. This was not just any 'undressing,' either. This was not how Lindsey removed her clothing at the end of the day when preparing to go to bed. This was … choreographed. And oh, boy. She had my undivided attention. It was like watching Natalie Wood performing sweetly erotic moves in the old movie *Gypsy,* except the gorgeous, tantalizing woman was my very own Lindsey.

I couldn't wait much longer. When she teasingly tossed away the last item of her clothing—a sheer pair of silky pink panties—my cargo shorts joined them in a pile of fabric on the floor. We embraced, skin on skin, before stepping into the hot, Very Sexy, bubbly water.

Heaven. Heaven in a tub. She sat behind me and rubbed my neck and shoulders, melting away the aches I'd acquired from spending so much time sitting with poor posture at my desk. We switched places so I could return the sensual feeling, then she reclined against me. I held her in my arms, breathed in her scent, feeling whole. We both needed this closeness. We needed it now and forever.

"The water is losing its heat," I eventually informed her.

She nodded. "And we have things to do."

"Uh, huh." I handed her a towel, eyeing her speculatively. "Do you have any specific order in mind for these 'things'?"

"Yes, I do. The strawberries will need to wait a little longer."

Back in the bedroom, she lit the candles, opened the sparkling water, and we rehydrated ourselves. I kissed her with my eyes before I could touch her; she was so sweet, young, and beautiful. I wished I could place this moment, this feeling, this lovely vision, in a time capsule to be preserved forever. Moving closer, I traced her delicate lower lip with my fingertips, then ran my fingers over every inch of her body, producing tiny moans which quickly intensified. We lay in bed, and before I knew what was happening, she'd slid out from beneath me and was on top, her hands exploring. This was a first for me. I'm pretty sure it was a first for her, too.

I enjoyed the easy access to her firm, round bottom and did some exploring of my own. I loved the sensation of her breasts pressing against my chest and the nibble of her soft lips as they kissed my ears. Just when I thought nothing in the world could feel any better, tousled locks of her perfumed hair tumbled down, tickling my face, then my chest, and traveling … slowly… lower.

This was a night of many firsts for both of us.

Afterward, she curled up into the curve of my body. "I loved your surprise dinner," she said softly. "That was so thoughtful of you, and it was delicious. Thank you."

I kissed her nose. "I loved your after dinner dessert surprise. Or should I say *surprises.* Thank you!"

"My pleasure."

"Oh, no. *My* pleasure."

We both laughed until we heard Wendell bark. The sound was sharp, almost urgent.

"I think he's trying to tell us something," I said. "Let's take him for a short walk before we all call it a night."

"Great idea. While we walk, we can talk. I want to tell you about Bobby."

Wendell was not at the bottom of the stairs where I'd assumed he'd be. Instead, he stood at the living room window. His big head had pushed aside the curtain, and he growled softly with concern. This was not typical behavior for Wendell. I'd seen him do this only one other time.

Someone—or something—he did not like was out there. My mind immediately went to the threatening words in Anthony's letter, and I turned the deadbolt locks on both doors. The walk would have to wait.

TWENTY-THREE

Lindsey

S ince I'm a desert rat—make that a *kangaroo* rat, they're a little bit cuter—and seek shelter from the blazing hot sun for much of the year, I had a heightened appreciation for San Diego and the cooler weather brought about by its proximity to the ocean. The mere sight of the sparkling, glassy blue water from the airplane's small window put a smile on my face. From a distance, I loved water, as long as it remained calm.

After a brief Town Car ride from the airport to the hotel with Lad, I was able to add the scent of the salty sea to today's mental list of physical delights.

As usual, no small talk took place between us. Lad was still all business, though I wasn't quite sure how rubbing my neck and shoulders and soaking in the Jacuzzi with me fit into the business category. Perhaps he did that for all the keynote speakers.

He seemed a little on edge today, though, and I'd never seen him display that trait before. He hovered at my side more than usual. *Why is he doing that?* The only new information he'd felt I needed to know about pertained to an extra autographing session following my keynote address on Friday. Not a problem for me. Meeting participants up close during book signings was my favorite, most enjoyable part of every conference.

On the morning of my keynote presentation, I'd gone down to the ballroom early to take a look around—without my escort. I felt a little bit naughty, a new experience for me, one that brought on a grin. But the moment I saw the enormity of the room, my knees went weak, my whole body trembled. This was the worst case of nerves I'd ever had and I now wished Lad was at my side.

Then a clinking sound like metal on metal drew my attention. Weak knees and all, I turned and looked in every direction for the source of the sound. I noticed some chairs jiggling against each other, the hanging light fixtures swaying. Oh, my God! Earthquake? Was this an earthquake? I was in California, after all.

The mere concept of the earth moving beneath my feet sent panic racing through me. Should I return to my room? Did I want to be on the 14th floor during an earthquake? I didn't know. I'd never experienced this particular phenomenon of nature before, but I'd seen some movies. *No. I don't dare let my thoughts go there.* I continued to tremble and sweat beaded up on my forehead. Fortunately, when the shaking subsided, and I saw no evidence that anyone but me was shaken up by the event, my twinges of fearful panic dissolved.

An hour later, the ballroom was packed with over a thousand participants. I stared at the crowd. Though I'd wanted to be an educational rock star, I wasn't quite ready for an audience of this magnitude. The screen that would project images behind me was so huge it looked like it belonged in a movie theater rather than an educational conference. The sound of the participants chattering with each other—likely about the earthquake—was deafening.

The unwelcomed traits of nervousness had returned, and I could not blame the earthquake this time. The shaky hands, quivering voice, dry mouth, wobbly knees, dizziness, and even a touch of hyperventilation, all needed to vanish before my big moment arrived.

I turned to Lad and tried to say *Oh, my God*, but the words barely formed.

Lad grinned and handed me a pill I recognized, along with a glass of water. The dry mouth medication. I'd gladly down one of those today.

I scowled at him. "Why didn't you remind me about the possibility of earthquakes?"

"Didn't want you to worry."

"Well, now I'm worried *and* nervous."

Lad stood calmly by my side. "You will be great," he said. "They will love you." He held out another small pill. "This medication will take care everything else. It is sublingual. Just slip it under your tongue."

A new kind of apprehension swept over me. I rarely took medication of any kind. What if this one didn't agree with me? What if it made me feel sick or weird? Weird definitely wouldn't work at the conference. What if … what if … Damn. It was too late to ponder the effects of the pill. I had to trust that he'd only give me something he knew to be safe. The opening music played, and Elisabeth Meriwether strolled onto the stage to say a few words of introduction. My hesitation vanished, and I dropped that little pink pill right under my tongue. Show time!

Even in my high platform heels, I walked with ease to center stage as the audience welcomed me with applause. I turned to them, beaming, and feeling good. *Really* good. The words came easily to me, and I rarely referred to my notes. I was able to focus on the teachers, their needs, wants, and interests. Only one thing bothered me today: there was, quite literally, too much distance between the teachers and me. *Nothing shackled me to the podium; the microphone was cordless.* Stepping down from the stage, away I went, walking out into the audience.

For a few fleeting seconds I wondered if the flow of the presentation would be upset since many in the audience would not be able to see me now. I knew everyone could hear me just fine, but I worried I might be standing out of sight. Then, glancing over my shoulder I saw myself on the big screen, larger than life, and realized a cameraman must have been close by, taping my every move. I hadn't looked at myself since Lad had brought the make-up artist to my room before the presentation. She'd done her magic so quickly it hadn't occurred to me that I might look different. I stared at the gorgeous woman on the screen, wondering if my perception was accurate or if that was one of the pill's effects.

After shaking hands and thanking about a dozen teachers for coming, I looked over and saw Lad give me a not-so-subtle, fairly urgent nod toward the stage. I responded by holding up my pointer finger as if to say, "Just a minute," then I led the huge group of energetic teachers in a chant they could use when they were leading their own students through a guided art lesson.

"I watch and I listen / as you draw / then I draw the same—*clap, clap.* I wait—*clap, clap*—and repeat—*clap, clap.*"

As we chanted the words for the third time, a few teachers formed an impromptu conga line while others added their own percussive touches with finger snaps, pencil taps, and cowbell slaps. I had to laugh—who carries a cowbell in their purse? Following their lead, I danced rhythmically back to the stage.

Near the end of my keynote address, that funny feeling of being watched snuck up on me again. Why now? Why here, when everything was going so marvelously well? Could it be Jake again? I didn't think so, but something was definitely different today. Even Lad seemed ultra alert, scanning the crowd with discriminating intensity. Needing to rationalize his actions and my atypical concerns, I attributing both to the size of today's audience. Yes. That made sense.

With the presentation over, I could relax. Or, maybe not. Lad approached, and I braced myself for an unemotional scolding, which never came. Without taking his eyes off the departing crowd he stated, "You were great! No. You were *better* than great."

I grinned. "Thank you! And thanks for that magic pill. You were right. It really took the edge off."

"Placebo," he informed me.

"What?"

He shrugged, enjoying the joke. "Placebo. The pill was a B12 vitamin. The magic was all you."

The autographing session took place on the tiered terrace overlooking the bay, and I was astounded to see the line curved around the corner and out of sight. Lad told me it was filled with female educators and a smattering of men. Some things never change. Unfortunately, no balance of men and women ever exists in elementary education.

I signed each participant's not-yet-completed version of what would someday be a published book, and was amazed by the level of excitement and appreciation coming from most of the teachers.

"I can't wait to implement some of your ideas, Ms. Lark."

"My mother was at your Colorado conference, and she gave me her copy of your teachers' art journaling handout," said a very young teacher. "Now I can give her this one."

"We're right in the middle of a *Frog and Toad* literature study," one woman said, "so I'm going to try that Frog Story lesson first. But my little guys aren't writing much just yet. What do you recommend I do for the writing part?"

I suggested that she instruct her students to write words that rhyme with frog and/or toad, and then I jotted down a short list of suggested words along with my signature. She walked away happy, clutching the packet of papers to her chest.

The positive comments kept coming. I only heard one woman worry that she would not be able to conduct the drawing part of the lessons, but she said she was willing to try.

I smiled up at a tall man approaching the table, wondering if he was a classroom teacher, specialist, or principal. "Hi there," I said.

"Make it out to Sean, if you don't mind," he said, placing his copy of the booklet on the table.

"I'd be happy to do that for you." I glanced up, and was about to confirm the spelling of his name, when I got a good look at his face. "Shawna?" I gasped. "Is that *you*? Oh, my God!" I stared in utter surprise. I had never seen her dressed completely like a man before. The effect was mind-blowing. "What are you doing here?"

"There are many things I need to say to you, beginning with an apology."

From the edge of the terrace, Lad inched closer. He gave a negative shake of his head and drew a little slash across the neck, meaning "cut it short." I was certainly good with that, but Shawna wanted to keep talking.

"Shawna, we can't talk here," I said nervously. "There are people waiting in line behind you."

She shook her head. "I am Sean now. Please don't call me Shawna. She doesn't exist anymore." Her eyes drifted past us. "See that pale blue bench down there by the boardwalk? I'd like it if you would meet me there around 6:00 p.m."

Say no; just say no. I sighed. "All right. I will be there."

Hours later, I waited for her on that bench, questioning my own sanity. The last person I should be here with was crazy Shawna. But she had seemed so sincere. Maybe I could help her somehow.

The dark blue water barely rippled. I hadn't known a body of water this large could ever appear so glassy and still. It wasn't quiet, though. Seagulls screeched and pelicans plunged comically in search of dinner while I waited, taking in all the evening's ocean view had to offer. The last trace of sunlight shimmered up through wispy clouds and rested on the horizon.

This had been a good day. Strange, but good. I really hoped I was not about to send my entire stash of positive, blissful thoughts on a downward, negative spiral by agreeing to talk with Shawna—or *Sean*. In spite of the fact that he—uh, *she* had stolen my husband, I felt unaccountably sorry for him. I'd heard about his earlier life, and I couldn't imagine anyone surviving so much physical and mental abuse at such a young age and for so long. If my accepting Sean's apology would help him regain some kind of life and move on from the horror, then I believed I should let him do that.

At 6:15 I began to wonder if maybe he'd changed his mind, gotten cold feet. That would be okay. My feet were cold, too. Literally. In fact, every inch of me suddenly felt chilled as a result of the slight temperature drop and the damp seaside air, so I slipped into my lightweight jacket.

"Lindsey?"

I looked up and smiled. "Hi, Sean." He'd changed his clothes since I'd seen him in the autograph line, and I had to admit he looked good. He wore tight jeans, a cream-colored, button-down shirt under a tan linen sports jacket, and navy topsider shoes. He shopped well. Unfortunately, he didn't wear his purchases well. Everything about his stance, his motions looked awkward, forced, and fake.

"Thanks for meeting me." He pulled a sheet of paper out of his jacket pocket and smiled at me with apology. "My notes," he explained. "I don't want to forget anything."

"Good idea," I replied, hoping to ease his obvious discomfort though it did nothing to dispel my own. "I have sticky notes all over to help me remember what to do or say."

Despite my best efforts, I couldn't shake the visions of Shawna from my memory: Shawna on a poster outside the strip club in Tucson, Shawna dressed only in a red sequined bikini bottom and a strategically draped sheer red scarf ... and Shawna with my husband. Unexpected hatred surged up from my chest and lodged uncomfortably in my throat.

He cleared his throat and began. "I am sorry for taking Anthony away from you. If I'd known you then, I might not have done that. It's just that, well, he reminded me of my father a little, and he was so hot and sexy and—"

"I don't need the gory details, Sean," I said through clenched teeth. "You're sorry, and I accept your apology." Sure, I felt sorry for him, but what did he expect? That suddenly we'd become best friends?

"Could we walk a little? There's more I need to tell you." Before I could say no, he stood, so I stood. We started walking down the cement path toward Seaport Village. "I wanted you to be so mad at Anthony," he continued, "and act so crazy toward him that he'd want to stay far away from you. That's why I made him take your dog. And for that I am really, truly sorry."

"Okay." Everything about this conversation increased my discomfort. "Is that all? Are we done?"

"Almost."

We passed dozens of happy tourists among quaint shops, musical groups, and face painters. Delicious smells from the many food establishments tickled my nose and tempted my tummy. But my former enemy wasn't done speaking.

"You and everyone else must call me Sean from now on. Always. I will no longer respond to Shawna. Shawna does not exist." He smiled broadly, pleased with his statement. It was obvious to me that he'd wanted to make that perfectly clear. "There is one more thing I want to say, and it involves Jake. Let's go over there and have a drink," he said, pointing at a restaurant with outdoor dining.

It stood on a pier-like structure at the far end of this popular tourist attraction. That was farther than I'd wanted to go. I shook my head and glanced at my watch. "I really need to get back. I've got two more days of conference work to do, and we have a staff briefing this evening."

"Just one drink. You'll be headed back to your hotel in twenty minutes or less. I promise. Okay? Please?"

My gut said no, but my mouth said, "All right. But just one, then I've got to go."

I did want to hear what he had to say about Jake, but as it turned out, all he wanted was to thank Jake and me for setting up the initial call to Julie, Jake's psychiatrist sister. He said that connection and the weekly phone counseling sessions that followed had really helped him along in his search for his true self.

"Lindsey," he said, staring intently at me. "I understand why Anthony loved you and married you. You are a good woman. Someday I will be a good man. I'm a man now, and I'm working on the *good*."

Admittedly, his words sounded appropriate for these odd circumstances. "I'm happy to hear that. I think you are definitely moving in the right direction." I hesitated before making my next statement, but I made it anyway. "Anthony's death must have been difficult for you, too."

He shook his head, took a sip of his martini, but said nothing. I took his silence as an opportunity to leave, but when I reached for my purse he put his hand on mine.

"Sean," I said quickly, suddenly afraid. "I am sorry for all the abuse you suffered as a child. I hope you are able to find your very own happily ever after."

He leaned in closer and whispered, "Guess what? I already have, and it's you. I love *you*! You, my princess, are the one for me."

In a sudden move, he squeezed my jaw and pressed his lips against mine while I shook my head wildly, trying to escape. Shocked, horrified, frightened, and disgusted— all those words applied—I ripped away from him and ran across the wooden deck toward the sidewalk. Almost blinded with emotion, I ran, heart pounding, right into the strong and safe arms of Lad. I'd never been so glad to see him.

"Sorry Lindsey," he said, speaking gently into my ear. "I knew that one was trouble, I just didn't know how much. I should have seen that coming and intervened before she got that far."

I glanced up quickly. "*She*? You said, 'she.' Why?"

"Slip of the tongue, I guess. It's no big deal," he said.

I was unconvinced by his lie. What was going on? Did Lad know Shawna?

He walked me to my hotel room and used his own key to open the door. I stood back as he searched the suite to make sure no intruders were lurking.

Satisfied, he returned to me. "Are you going to be all right?"

I nodded, still shaken. "I just want to take a shower and go to bed."

"Sounds good. You've got the panel discussion, the luncheon, and your basic workshop tomorrow. I'll see to it that you are not bothered."

"Thank you, Lad. Good night."

He nodded and closed the door. I double locked it behind him.

I stepped into the shower and the warm drops of water both soothed and cleansed. I needed to feel clean. Craved it. How could just one creepy, unwanted kiss create such a sensation of disgust, even *violation*, within me? I figured another ten minutes of decontamination in the shower, a good tooth brushing, a phone call to Jake, and I'd be as good as new.

As I headed toward the dresser to retrieve the long, silky nightgown I'd purchased for this trip, I heard a noise outside my door, just like the notorious *bump in the night*. The security peephole on this door was lower than most, so I only needed to stand on tiptoe to see out. The source of the sound became obvious immediately. Lad was camped outside my door, seated on a chair he must have dragged over from the sitting area by the elevators. No one would get by Lad tonight. I'd sleep well.

A delicious piece of dark chocolate had appeared on my pillow just as it had the previous nights, but tonight an envelope waited with the chocolate. Smiling, feeling all was right with the world once again, I crawled into bed, turned on the TV, and unwrapped the candy.

I slid my thumb under the flap to open the envelope, removed the note, then gasped, nearly choking on the chocolate.

This could not be happening.

Dear Lindsey:

Read this and read it carefully. The contents of this letter will have an effect on your life.

I blame YOU for my death. Here's why:

- *You are guilty of neglect. You were unsupportive of my need for Shawna.*
- *You are guilty of fornication. You made a fool of me with the string of men at our house.*
- *You are guilty of abandonment. You were not there for me when I needed you.*
- *You are guilty of making the Money Pig threat. Now it is your turn to be threatened.*

Beware! Soon, someone new will be buried in the Money Pig's family vault.

Anthony

I gasped for air, not knowing what to do. *Think. Think.*

How had the letter gotten in here? Only hotel staff and Lad had keys to my room, and Lad could not have delivered this letter, since he'd been with me most of the time—though not all the time. No, I refused to believe Lad was involved in any way. If it wasn't Lad, a hotel staff member must have delivered the letter, but who had given it to that person and told them to put it on my pillow?

Thinking only added to my anxiety. I had to *do* something, take action. Yes, I was fearful, but now I was also angry. This was real. Someone was trying to hurt me … and Jake.

Jake. I had to talk with him. In spite of the late hour, I made the call. *Come on, Jake. Pick up. Answer the phone.* No answer came, and I had no choice but to leave a message. "I got one. I got a letter. I'm scared, Jake. And

Shawna—I mean Sean—was here. Call me. Please, call me."

I waited a half hour but got no call back. I had to talk to someone who might understand. Did I dare call Laura? We weren't on the best of terms at the moment, but it was either Laura or Lad or no one. Who did I trust? Unfortunately, there was no answer at Laura's place, either. I remembered Laura's doodles and felt suddenly sick for an entirely different reason: was she with Jake? Was that why neither one of them answered their phones?

I redirected my focus back to the letter, which stated I was guilty of abandonment. Was Jake abandoning *me*?

Sometimes, like right now, the distance between us seemed insurmountable. Some of that distance was actual physical distance. Other times we'd have mental or emotional disconnects, like the ones I'd been feeling with Laura lately. I didn't want to experience the feeling of abandonment ever again. When my parents had died, I'd felt it deeply. And though they'd had no control over leaving me forever, it hurt just as much as if they'd planned it. As I'd been shuffled around from one foster family to another, I'd felt unwanted, but not abandoned. A foster home wasn't a forever home. I'd known that. I didn't like any of them anyway.

Then there was Anthony. That was abandonment, only much, much worse. Now he had the nerve to say *I* abandoned *him?* Ugh! Wait. He was *dead.* Those couldn't be his words … or *could* they? The letter had been typed, even the signature; anyone could have typed it.

If I didn't talk with some one right away, I'd soon be climbing the walls. I unlocked the door, and Lad was waiting when I opened it.

"Please come in."

We sat on the sofa, and he waited silently for me to begin. That was difficult; I didn't know where to start. He was a wonderful man, always there for me, but I knew next to nothing about him, or whether I should trust him. Would I ever be able to trust anyone completely? God, I hoped so.

I handed Lad the letter and watched his face while he read it. As usual, his stoic expression never changed. "When did you get this?"

That first question was easily answered.

"Do you think Anthony wrote it?" he asked.

"I don't know, but Jake got one, too. He thinks Shawna, Anthony's girlfriend, wrote it. And … well, Shawna is now *Sean*. Or Sean was Shawna—"

"Yeah. I get that."

"You do?"

"Yes. I'm observant. And probing."

TWENTY-FOUR

Jake

Sleep had not held a prominent position on my list of things to do lately. Really, I should have put it at the top because I was so tired I couldn't think straight. It had been nice of Laura to insist that I take a break and go out for pizza with her. She'd been so helpful whenever Lindsey was out of town. I'd have to think of some way to repay her kindness.

Knowing that I'd more than likely spend another hour at my desk, I brought Malcolm into the room to join Wendell and me. We were quite a trio. I shared a few bites of leftover pizza with the dog, but I didn't think the bird ate pizza. And I did not want to take the chance of making him sick.

I missed Lindsey. Plain and simple. Though she was never gone for more than six days at a time, it felt longer. I imagined her in San Diego, working and sleeping not far from the ocean, and worried about her more than ever this time. I did what I could and prayed for good weather and calm water, so she wouldn't have to experience any aspects of her childhood anxieties.

I'd stared at the computer screen long enough. With Lindsey on my mind, no writing would get done tonight.

"I give up," I said to the pets. "Let's go to bed."

When I plugged my cell into the charger, I noticed a missed call and a voicemail from Lindsey. That brought a smile to my face. But, then I listened, not believing what I'd heard, and returned the call immediately. The lateness of the evening didn't matter. Lindsey did. She sounded incredibly relieved to hear my voice. I thought she might start crying, but hoped she wouldn't. I needed her to talk and think clearly.

"Lindsey, baby, what's going on? You got a letter? What kind of letter?"

"Just like the one you got, Jake. Only it's even more threatening."

I had her read the letter to me, and my mind filled with questions. "I think I understand all the threats except for the Money Pig reference. What's that about, Lindsey?"

"That's an old Hans Christian Andersen tale about a piggy bank," she told me. "It's a little on the weird and morbid side. Not a child's tale, for sure. The nutshell version: all the toys come to life, put on a strange play, and the Money Pig watches. To show his appreciation he declares that one of the players would get to be buried in his family vault when their time came. But before he made out his will, he fell off a high shelf, shattered into many pieces, and all the money he held within his belly danced away. His pieces were swept up and put into the trash."

"Uh, OK. I still don't get it. What does that have to do with you?"

"The day he left me—or maybe it was the day he came to take Wendell from me, I really don't remember—

I shouted that I hoped he turned out just like the Money Pig. It was a stupid thing to say. I didn't expect him to know what I meant, but maybe he looked it up."

"Or maybe he told Shawna, back when they were still a couple. And since she was also a fairy tale aficionado, she might have explained it to him."

"I suppose that is a possibility."

Lindsey didn't sound sure about that idea, though. And the more I thought about it, the more it did not make sense. But lately, what did?

"Jake, what if that means I'm going to be buried, or that I will break, lose all my money, and be put in the trash?"

The fear in her voice pulled at my heartstrings, stretching them to the point of tearing. "Let's not worry about 'what ifs' right now, okay, Linds? I want to hear about Sean's visit."

Lindsey shared, in great detail, the events of the evening. I could tell she needed to talk it through, and I was horrified at the tale she told. He'd *kissed* her? This was such an unexpected turnaround. I was speechless.

Sean *could* have been the author of her letter. With a nice tip he'd have been able to entice one of the room service or housekeeping staff to place it on her pillow, and he was certainly close enough to make that happen. But even that scenario had its problems. The fact that the letter had appeared the same evening that Sean had made an inappropriate pass at Lindsey was far too obvious. It would lead any decent detective straight to his door. Or had his advances just been poorly planned or even spontaneous?

"Jake, hold on a minute. An email just popped up on my phone's screen. I'd better check it. It could be about tomorrow's schedule."

"Okay. I'll wait. If we get disconnected, call me right back."

Neither one of us was as smart as our Smartphones. The possibility of losing the call while navigating to her email was real. I heard a click. Yep. She was gone. But my phone rang two minutes later.

"Well, that was strange," she said coldly.

"What do you mean?"

"I'll read you the email, and you tell me. It says, 'Payback time. The string of men at your house has been replaced by a string of women. One even stayed the night. How does that feel? My revenge has only just begun.'" She paused. "What women are at the house, Jake?"

I huffed. "The bigger question here is who sent that email?"

"Answer me, Jake. What women were at the house?"

I had to think about that. "I don't know. I had food delivered a few times, and one of those times the driver was a woman. I *think* our UPS driver is a woman. Come on. This is crazy, Lindsey. The author of my letter, your letter, and now this email is obviously trying to turn us against each other. Don't you see that?"

She was unrelenting. "Which woman spent the night?"

"That was just Laura, but I can explain."

"I'll bet you can," she snapped. "And when you do, you can also tell me where you were tonight and who you were with."

"Uh, Laura called, checking on how I was doing with my pet-sitting. She suggested I meet her for pizza. What's wrong with that?"

Her voice was as hard as steel. "While we are on the subject of Laura, did she happen to mention the fight she and I had not so long ago? Because if she did, and you still went out with her, it's over between us, Jake. Over."

"What?!"

"I suppose you know nothing about her cute little drawings of hearts with your name inside of them."

"Hearts?" What was going on? "What hearts? Lindsey, you're upset about the wrong things here. You're mad at the wrong person. I'm here to help you, love you, make sure your life is joyful and safe. You've got let me do that. You need to trust me!"

"I don't trust anyone or anything right now."

I blew out a breath. "And I don't blame you for feeling that way. The plot is definitely thickening, becoming more complex and twisted and … potentially dangerous."

Her silence—*our* silence—dangled in cyberspace until I could bear it no longer. "What does Laura pet-sitting and sharing a pizza with me have to do with the crime?"

"If there was a crime at all!"

"Come on, Linds. You know, at the very least, that some creepy, weird stuff is going on. Don't you? After all, you got a threatening letter, too."

She caught her breath, and even though I was starting to get annoyed by all this, I wished I could have gathered her in my arms in that moment.

"Oh, Jake," she said. "I'm sorry. I'm not really mad at *you,* but I am even more upset with Laura now than I was a few minutes ago. She's really crossed the line—again. Maybe the letters never had anything to do with Anthony *or* Sean. Maybe *she's* the one writing the threatening letters, trying to break us up so she can have you."

What? A sudden vision of the Lost in Space robot waving his arms saying 'Warning, warning!' clogged up my thinking. *My brain is malfunctioning.*

"Oh, I just don't know. The entire series of events since Anthony's funeral is overwhelming and disturbing.

But Jake, I need to apologize about one thing. I thought you were exaggerating, but now I am definitely giving some serious thought to your foul play theories. What do you think about my theory?"

I was completely lost. "Your theory?"

"Yes. Haven't you been listening? My *Laura* theory. I know she wants you, Jake. She's wanted you for a long time. She made that perfectly clear last spring, and again a few weeks ago. And now, I find out that she'd spent the night at our house when I was gone. It doesn't look good. She really might want to break us up."

This was coming out of nowhere. But I gave some thought to what Lindsey was saying, then imagined Laura's friendly visits, neck rubs, and phone calls, and conceded that she might have a point. I'd been pretty clueless to her advances, though, if that is what they actually were.

"Okay, Lindsey. I do hear what you're saying, and I understand some of it. But I've never had the slightest interest in Laura. You must know that. And I don't think she was privy to the knowledge required to write the statements and threats in our letters. Does that make sense to you?"

"I suppose it does. But that brings us back to—"

"The email! Check it again. There has to be some key information in the address."

"Uh, I never wanted to see it again, so I deleted it several minutes ago."

"Check the Trash!"

"I, uh … sent it to my spam folder then deleted it forever."

"Oh." I couldn't conceal the disappointment in my voice. If only we'd been able to trace the email address. Yet another dead end.

"I'm sorry, Jake. Can we restart this conversation?"

Now that Lindsey was finally willing to consider the idea that a crime might have taken place, I shared some of my current thoughts with her. It felt great to open up about this, help her understand why I'd been so caught up in the mystery. I even let her know that Anthony's parents had been at the funeral, but I felt telling her about my phone conversation with them was too much for tonight. Maybe someday. Then again, maybe not.

We agreed that Anthony's death and funeral were unarguably suspicious. Either his parents or Shawna—I meant Sean—could've played a part in that. The letters? The new email? I hadn't a clue. Lindsey was right, though. It seemed the letter writer's purpose was to harm us or at least break us up. Romantic terrorism. But my gut still told me that Shawna—Ugh! Sean—was deeply involved. Especially after arriving in San Diego and making a pass at Lindsey just prior to the letter showing up in her hotel room. I could think of no other suspects ... suspects? Could there be more than one letter writer? With no definite answers, anything was possible.

My thinking traversed from the letters to Anthony's death. Mrs. Madera seemed to care more for him than anyone else did—she would never wish him harm. Could he have upset a patient or a competitor to such a degree that they'd retaliated with murder? That seemed far-fetched, and they wouldn't have been connected to Lindsey or me. Or had someone from his past returned to inflict some of his or her own revenge? I had no idea. As far as I was concerned, Shawna Storm was guilty of something. Guilty until proved innocent.

"Lindsey, do you want me to fly over to be with you? I will in a heartbeat. I'm not comfortable being away from you, and you shouldn't be alone right now."

"Oh, I'm not really alone," she assured me. "Lad is camped outside my door. No one is getting in, and he said he wouldn't leave my side for the duration of the conference."

"And you trust this guy? Completely? 100%?"

Lindsey hesitated a few seconds too long.

"I'll catch the next flight out."

Lindsey's last two days at the San Diego Conference were uneventful, but I was glad I was there. We were able to take a few walks on the beach at low tide, enjoy delicious seafood for dinner, and ride the carousel at Seaport Village. Lad kept his distance, but I knew he was never too far away. We were never completely out of his sight except for the time we spent in Lindsey's room, and even then I wondered.

We did not see Shawna/Sean for the duration of the conference.

But did he see us?

GIVING THANKS, RIGHT HOOKS, AND ROSES

TWENTY-FIVE

Lindsey

Home. It was good be home. The San Diego Conference had been exhausting; let me count the ways: The earthquake, the new nervousness, Shawna/Sean's shocking visit, the threatening letter, my Laura theory ... Jake and I were in desperate need of some quality time together.

The first few days back in Tucson were filled with sleeping in, relaxing in the backyard with my guys, and leisurely jotting down ideas to work on between now and the final conference in Seattle next month.

I should clarify and say that *most* of those first days back were spent relaxing. I had made a commitment to meet with Bobby, see him face-to-face for the first time since that day we'd discovered the physical abuse inflicted on his tiny body. No part of that meeting would be relaxing—that was a given.

When I walked into the mid-town library where we'd agreed to meet, his face already held a stubborn scowl. I inhaled and braced myself.

The large woman holding his hand frowned critically at me. "Are you Miss Lindsey?"

"Yes, I am. And who are you?"

"I am his transportation. I was contracted to deliver the boy here today. I'll be back in exactly one hour to pick him up."

Before I could finish thinking how strange that was, Bobby had wrapped his arms around my waist and burst into tears, crying, "Miss Lindsey! Miss Lindsey!"

We found a comfy sofa and we talked—well, *I* talked. Bobby constantly wriggled and thrashed, but at least he remained in the vicinity of the sofa. The hour slowly ticked by. He appeared to be well nourished, clean, and physically healthy, but he also demonstrated indications of Emotional Disability (ED) and Attention Deficit Hyperactivity Disorder (ADHD), which we'd suspected last year at school. Now, based on some of the details Jennifer had shared with me on the phone, I understood Conduct Disorder could be added to list.

"Let's read a book together," I suggested, then I held my breath, waiting for his response. He cocked his head— just like Wendell—and scooted next to me. Good. That was a start.

"I suppose you're gonna make me talk about the cover."

Another good reaction. He obviously remembered how we'd read books last year in kindergarten. "It would be nice to talk about the cover. This one looks pretty interesting, don't you think?"

"All I see is a stupid turtle and a crazy-eyed bunny. What's so interesting about that?"

"I don't know, but that's a good question. Let's find an answer."

We did a little book talk about the illustrations, and that went well until page eleven, on which the hare took a nap under a tree, and the tortoise plodded past him.

"Stupid, stupid bunny," Bobby muttered, then his little face formed a roguish smile. "I'm gonna make him sleep in a dog bed. He'll hate it."

His declaration raised a few eyebrows on nearby patrons. His tone of voice and choice of words made no sense to them. I, however, knew exactly where his mind had drifted. Last year we'd learned that Bobby's own father—or at least the man who lived in his house—had literally treated Bobby as if he were a dog. The little boy had been kept in the garage, his food in a dog dish on the floor, and he'd slept in an old, dirty dog bed.

We never made it to the end of the twenty-four pages of *The Tortoise and the Hare*, let alone to the moral. Maybe, I mused, the moral was really for me, not him. Perhaps I'd need to proceed slow and steady if this race to help Bobby was ever to be won.

Other than that one hour with the boy that tugged at my heartstrings, the rest of my time at home was blissfully spent. Jake catered to my every need—and I mean my *every* need, from making lunch to making love and everything in between. So when the cordless phone in the kitchen rang, I was not surprised when he jumped up off the backyard, cushioned lounge chair to answer it. When he came back outside holding the phone, he was chatting away. Secretly, I'd hoped it wasn't Laura he was being so friendly with. Her name hadn't come up since that last long distance phone conversation when I'd hysterically aired my concerns.

"Okay, Mrs. Wilson," he said, handing me the phone. "Here she is."

"Hi Lindsey. I won't take up too much of your time. Besides, there isn't much time. The thing is, I'm in a jam.

Our kindergarten class is scheduled to go on a field trip to the Arizona-Sonora Desert Museum tomorrow. The teacher's husband just called to say that she came home ill today and won't be able to go with her students on the trip. When I heard that, I immediately thought of you— the best kindergarten teacher for miles around."

"Thanks for that vote of confidence," I replied, all the time wondering, *what does she want?*

"Well, you deserve it, and I hope you will agree to my proposal, Lindsey. You see, the trip is already bought and paid for, the bus ordered, the parent volunteers and several teaching assistants are confirmed to go. But if we don't have a certified teacher, I'll have to cancel the whole thing. The children will be so disappointed."

I felt a little dizzy, thinking about that, and I couldn't figure out why. It's not like it was a difficult request, but I needed to sort out my emotions before making such an unexpected commitment.

"I do appreciate that you thought of me, Mrs. Wilson, but I just returned from a conference, and I usually need a few days to unwind after that. And ever since you gave me those emails, I've been trying to help Bobby in my spare time. I need to think about it. Can I call you back in an hour?"

When I explained Mrs. Wilson's side of the conversation, Jake stared at me with disbelief. "What's your hesitation, Linds? You could do that in your sleep."

True. I was hesitating. Why? Did I want to be the certified teacher responsible for twenty-some kindergarten students away from the school? I could easily find the time; lack of time could not be my excuse. But then there was Bobby. An hour with him was exhausting both physically and mentally. I'd need a nap after each session with him.

Logical. Practical. I needed to be both as I thought this through. "For one thing, I don't know any of these students," I blustered, feeling strangely defensive. Jake had no idea how challenging it was to make teaching five- and six-year-olds look easy. It never was. "It's only November, and they've been students for less than three months. Besides, I have no information about each student's needs, personality, or behavior. That is a recipe for disaster."

"But you're so great with those little guys."

"It takes time to train students, to develop a rapport with them, to establish an environment of respect. Without these key ingredients, there could be problems."

"But … but you kind of want to be a teacher for a day, don't you?"

Jake knew how I'd answer that question. I loved teaching children and I missed it. But he also knew how tired I was.

"Yes. Yes, I do. That's why I'm torn. Right now I want to devote all my energy to the upcoming conference, and to you. I also want to design a new way to use the basic Art Journaling concepts, but I want it to be different somehow. I won't feel I'm ready for the next conference until I've accomplished that. And right now, I don't even know what *that* is."

He shrugged. "I don't know. It seems to me this field trip might be the perfect opportunity. The students bring out the best in you. You get ideas from them. I've seen it happen."

I shook my head, still confused. "Maybe if I had an idea before the students boarded the bus, maybe then I would do it. But I need to let Mrs. Wilson know soon."

"The way I see it, this is one of those 'two birds with one stone' scenarios," he said. "Conduct one of your art journal lessons at the desert museum."

"Oh, I don't think that would work. There's no way I could teach them this process on a field trip."

"Exactly! Don't *teach* anything."

I glared at him. "Are you being difficult on purpose, Jake?"

"No." He wiggled his eyebrows at me. "I'm being brilliant."

I was smiling now. He had my attention, though I was pretty sure we were just bantering for the fun of it. "Then I need details. And this had better be good."

"Here goes." He held his hands, thumb tips together, fingers up, out in front of his eyes as if he were imagining something on a screen. "I can see it all now. You'll carry little sketchbooks and pencils in one of your big teacher bags. When you arrive at an exhibit the kids really like, tell them they each get to pick one, just *one* thing they see—it could be a plant, a rock, or an animal—and draw it. They must try to make it look real. You'll know what words to use to explain that to the kids."

My creative wheels started turning, thanks to Jake, and I began to fill in additional details. "When the children get back to the classroom they'd label or write a fact about the thing they'd drawn. Then, using colored pencils they could add realistic colors to their drawing." I looked at him in amazement. "Jake, you're a genius!" I frowned. "One slight, potential glitch. The teacher might not have those supplies in her classroom."

"It would be my pleasure to contribute the sketch books, pencils, and colored pencils. And I'll even volunteer to go with you all."

My eyes widened with surprise. "That is really sweet of you to offer, but I couldn't ask you to pay for all that. You're only working a couple of shifts a week at the Coyote Café."

"You're not asking, but I am insisting."

I beamed. "Now you're a *generous* genius. I'll do it! Hand me the phone."

I loved that he'd wanted to go on the field trip with me, and I approved without a moment's hesitation. He was right: it would be fun, and Jake could see me in action. Plus, an additional male volunteer would come in handy.

"Geez, Lindsey," Jake whispered. "Is all this necessary?"

Before heading to the classroom, I had accompanied him to the office where he'd reluctantly filled out the required visitor and volunteer information sheets, then produced his driver's license for identification.

"I'm afraid it is. We teach children about stranger danger, and you are a stranger here. Nobody knows you except for me and—"

As if some ironic cue was directed from above, Laura walked into the office right then to pick up her mail and messages. The three of us stared awkwardly at each other, and the office manager suddenly looked away, sensing the tension in the room. I felt obligated to break the silence.

"Hi, Laura. I'm the teacher of record for Mrs. Frank's field trip today. She's out sick. Jake is volunteering. Isn't that great?"

Laura reached into her mailbox, retrieved a few papers and envelopes, and without making eye contact with either Jake or me, she hurried toward the door to the school's courtyard. I think she said something like "Uh, huh," but I wasn't sure. I hated the moment. Either I was witnessing jealousy because I was the one with Jake, or she was still angry at the fact that I'd barged into her apartment and instigated a fight. I'd have to find a way to rectify all this awkwardness in the future, but there wasn't time today.

Mrs. Frank's classroom looked like a kindergarten desert. She'd even set up the papier-mâché saguaro that the students had helped make last year for our Desert Performance. It felt good to be back in my old classroom, and I grinned when the bell buzzed. Ready or not, here they come.

As I stood at the door to greet each child—I could tell they were not used to this—they each had a response to my presence.

"Who are you?"

"Where's Mrs. Frank?"

"I know you! You were my sister's teacher!"

"What are you doing here?

I sang my 'Come to the Rug' song even though these kids had never heard it before, and I made sure I personally directed a few students to the right spot with the hopes others would follow. They did! We were off to a good start.

Right on schedule, we were ready to board the bus. Everyone had been to the bathroom—a must-do because the drive would take about forty-five minutes—and was assigned a buddy with whom they would sit. My seat buddy was Jake, and he already looked like he'd been through the wringer. That made me giggle. He would need a nap the second he got home.

We sang "The Wheels on the Bus" about a hundred times which was better than the chorus of "99 Bottles of Beer on the Wall" one little boy had tried to get going. I had no idea this generation of kids even knew that song, but apparently they did. Then I used some of the bus ride time to introduce Jake and let the kids know that he'd brought along some special drawing books and pencils for them to use at the Arizona-Sonora Desert Museum.

At last we arrived, and we all stood in line at the entrance, waiting for a museum employee to let us in. The parents and teaching assistants all had written instructions, maps, and a short list bearing the names of the students in their group for the duration of the field trip. All was going well until I spotted one little girl quietly crying.

I was grateful for the nametags Mrs. Frank had ready and waiting for me. "What's the matter, Jessie?"

She sniffed loudly and wiped the back of her hand across her face, mopping up tears. "I left it on the bus, and my mom is going to be *so mad.*"

"What did you leave on the bus, sweetie?"

"My purse. I have to have it." She looked up at me, her eyes wide and red from crying. "I have to have it *now!*"

"It will be safe," I assured her. "The bus driver will either be in the bus or the bus will be locked."

"No! It's my *'sponsibility,'* she shrieked. "Mom *said* so."

Her level of distress did not make sense to me. "Jessie, what's in your purse?"

"I ... I can't tell you," she said, dropping her chin to her chest. "I can't tell anyone."

She cried even harder, almost hyperventilating, then she slumped to the ground. Not knowing what behaviors were 'typical' for this child, I wondered if this could be an emotional tantrum displayed to get her way, or if it was an actual physical problem. We needed to know. I picked her up, and she cried, "My legs! My legs feel funny."

"Will you feel better if I go back and get your purse?" It was worth a try.

"Yes," she squeaked.

I handed the small child a tissue for her nose, then I asked Jake to hold onto her and follow along. The other adults knew where to go and what to do. I hurried toward the bus, which was probably already way out in the Buses Only parking area. When I got there, the bus driver was not in the bus, and the bus was not locked, so both of my assumptions had been wrong.

Jessie's tiny pink purse was easy to spot; it was cute, and I could see why the little girl didn't want to lose it, but still, her reaction to leaving it on the bus had been way over the top. Respecting a child's privacy was my typical *modus operandi* but not when my gut nagged relentlessly that something was wrong. And my gut not only nagged, it was shouting at me right now.

I opened Jessie's purse, and my skin crawled with what I saw. The purse was empty—except for three tiny pills. They were definitely not over-the-counter meds or candy. One of them looked like Adderall, a medication used to treat ADHD or sleeping and eating disorders. I didn't know what the other two were. Hurrying back from the bus, I flagged Jake down, hoping that Jessie hadn't spotted me. I would eventually give the child her purse, but it would be empty. And I assumed the purse's contents had more to do with her reaction than the purse itself.

"Jake, do you have any idea what kind of these pills are?" I asked. "I think our little crier was about to follow her mother's orders and self-medicate."

"No," he said, frowning at the meds, "but I have an App on my phone that lets me describe a pill and it tells me what it is. I can give that a try. If that doesn't work, I've got a guy I can call at the university who will probably know."

"Okay. You do that while I call the school nurse. If the kid needs medication, I don't want to withhold it from her, but a child this young cannot be in charge of prescription meds. That could have tragic results. Plus, it's against the law."

Within ten minutes, Jake knew what the pills were. The first was Horizant, used for treating restless leg syndrome. The second was Lorazepam, often used for anxiety. Lastly, he confirmed my suspicion of Adderall.

I felt slightly ill, thinking about all that. "I don't know, but that sounds like recipe for trouble. I've never heard of small children taking a combination of meds like that." I wondered how this little girl made it through each school day. Other than being distraught and anxious at the thought of *not* following her mother's directions, she seemed okay. Then again, she had said her legs felt 'funny.'

When I'd called the nurse, I was able to learn that no medications were ever given at school, and the child's health folder made no mention of any health problems. But her personal records folder held vague reports of some behavioral issues as well as excessive absences. Since I wasn't Jessie's teacher, the nurse was not at liberty to discuss those with me. I understood, but it didn't help the situation.

"What do you think, Jake? What are we going to do?"

He looked thoughtful. "I think what we might have here is one sick parent. And Jessie could already be experiencing withdrawal symptoms from the Lorazepam. My friend was more than a little shocked that a doctor would prescribe that for a child so young."

I nodded, keeping my eyes on the children. "I think you're right about that. I'll call the nurse back and ask her to contact the mother. We'll see what she has to say about the medication found in her daughter's purse. The school can decide what to do from there, but I'd be willing to bet this will result in a 911 call *and* a CPS call. I'll ask the nurse to have someone call us back on our cell phones when they know what's going on. We need to know what to do for Jessie while she's here with us."

"You know, Linds, if the mom is feeding her kid those medications, she's not only sick herself—possibly

Munchausen by Proxy is a factor—but she could also be dangerous. If the nurse calls her, she is apt to destroy any evidence that might be used against her. Without evidence, the police or CPS might not be able to do anything to help Jessie *or* to keep her safe."

I was impressed. "Wow. You turned on your detective switch really fast. Okay, so what do we do?"

"Law enforcement has to get involved. I'll run back to the main entrance and see if anyone from the sheriff's department is on the grounds right now. If not, I'll call 911 and get someone out here. They can keep Jessie safe while other officers check out the parents and the home. I don't see any other choice here."

I agreed with everything he'd said, and I loved hearing how his mind had figured it out so quickly. "All right. I'll keep an eye on the little girl from a distance. If she sees me, she is going to want that her purse. Who knows what she'll do when I don't give it to her. At the very least, there'd be lots of crying."

Jake ran off to do his part of the plan, and I kept vigil over Jessie as the group she was with took an interest in the mountain goats. I'd have Jake give those kids their sketchbooks when he got back. I could not take the chance of Jessie seeing me just yet.

Within ten minutes I spotted Jake heading my way with a uniformed sheriff. I wondered whether the little girl would feel safe or threatened by this person. We'd soon find out. I was asked by the officer to approach the group and get the child. She came willingly but demanded to know if I'd found her purse. I said that I had and that a man was keeping it safe for us. That was good enough for the moment.

She walked right up to the officer and said, "You're tall."

"I guess I am." He had a warm smile, and Jessie didn't seem the slightest bit afraid. "Do you want to see the view from way up here?"

She nodded a yes, so he picked her up and pointed out the mountain lion that was sleeping on the cliff within a nearby, walled exhibit. They struck up a conversation, he thanked us for our help, and off they went.

"What happens now?" I wondered out loud.

Jake folded his arms. "That depends on what they find after running some general checks on the mom and anyone else that might live in the home. They'll probably find a way to conduct a legal search, too. There is nothing more we can do."

"Well, then. I guess it's out of our hands. Let's go give out sketchbooks, find out what desert dweller fascinates these little guys the most, and encourage them to draw. We've got less than two hours before they'll want lunch."

"Maybe we should split up," Jake volunteered. "That way we can each work with three groups rather than both of us trying to get around to all six."

"Okay. Just remember that all the kids need to meet at the Pavilion by 12:30, and don't let any pencils or sketchbooks fall into any of the exhibits, and—"

He grinned. "I got this, Ms. Lindsey. See you for lunch. And, oh yeah … have fun."

With each passing day, my Jake was becoming easier and easier to love. Today's bonus? He was great with kids! I had no idea he would jump right in and work with the students as if he'd been doing that for years. In fact, I think he somehow got the kids in his groups to draw more realistic details than I did. It turned out to be an amazing and successful day. I had fun and so did the children. During lunch, I managed to stifle my comments pertaining to talking with mouths full of food to myself. That missing manner could be overlooked today.

The bus was waiting for us when we exited the gate. The children were tired, and so were the adults. I knew the ride back to school would be much calmer and quieter than the morning ride had been, but my peaceful, easy feeling was cut short when I heard a commotion coming from the middle of the bus.

"There's a pig in my seat! A pig in my seat!" shouted the little boy named Sam.

All the kids ran over to see the pig, then they squealed and laughed, swiftly regaining their second winds. I prayed Sam wasn't referring to the only overweight girl in the class. That type of humiliation could be devastating.

"Piggy! Piggy! Piggy!" chanted the children.

"Please take your seats, everyone," I said. "The bus is ready to go."

They did as they were told without incident, and when I got to the spot where the 'pig' was sitting, relief swept over me. It was indeed just a piggy bank: a cute, traditional-looking, pink piggy bank.

"Is this yours, Sam?" He shook his head. "Are you sure this is your seat?" He nodded, eyes wide, then he handed me the pig slowly and carefully, as if it were treasure. "Who does this little piggy bank belong to?" I asked with a smile, watching all eyes on board. No one claimed it.

Before I could say anything more, Jake was at my side with a few questions of his own.

"Hey, kids. Let's solve a mystery. Did anyone see this pig at school? Did anyone see this pig on the bus earlier today? Does anyone have a piggy bank like this at home?" Jake received negative responses to all his questions. Still excited about having a tiny, kindergarten mystery to solve, he carried the pig to the front of the bus and asked in his best detective voice, "Ms. Bus Driver? Did you see any one put this pig on the bus?"

The driver shook her head, then admitted, "But I did take a couple of breaks and left the bus a few times."

From the look on Jake's face, I thought he was on to something.

Then Sam shouted, "Shake it! Shake the pig!"

I looked at Jake, and he looked at me. We both shrugged, and he shook the pig, which rattled. The students heard it and knew what that meant.

"There's money in the pig!" Sam yelled. "Money Pig! Money Pig!"

As the bus pulled out of the parking lot and the children joyfully continued their chant, Jake and I locked eyes, held hands, and felt threatened once again.

TWENTY-SIX

Jake

Letters. Threats. Kisses. Pigs? What's next? I could only imagine.

Shawna was the key to everything. I was certain of that. Ever since the trouble at the San Diego Conference and the appearance of the money pig on the field trip, I'd wanted to confront her again and force her—*him*—to confess to or at least take responsibility for a few of the pieces of this *Anthony* puzzle. I called every day. I drove by the house at least once a day. But there was no sign of her, and my frustration was fast approaching the boiling point.

Less than two weeks later, on Thanksgiving, I took a little detour before heading home with the rolls and butter I'd been sent to purchase. To my surprise, Shawna's Hummer was parked in her driveway. Finally, she was home. No time like the present. I pulled in, parked my Jeep, and knocked on the front door.

A man greeted me—a new boyfriend? I was within seconds of asking him if Shawna was home. It took another moment before I realized I was looking right at her. I had not seen Shawna since she'd embarked on a resolute effort to look like the man she had originally been. The effect was quite shocking.

She eyed me sullenly, then said, "Oh, look. The Thanksgiving turkey has arrived. You might as well come in."

Once I was inside, she poured us each a drink, then she told me to say what I had to say and get the hell out of there. She had plans: places to go and people to see. All of this was a vast improvement from the time I'd entered her home last May. Back then she'd pummeled me with her fists, leaving me bloody and bruised.

"There are a few things we need to get straight," I said. "First, Lindsey is off-limits. Stay away from her, got it?"

"Are you jealous, Jake? Do you think she might find me more attractive, more handsome than you? I'm flattered."

I wanted to slug her … him, but I needed to keep the conversation going for a while. I proceeded with measured control. "I will help Lindsey file for a restraining order if you don't stay away from her."

"You don't need to be in such a tizzy, Jake. Besides, it was your sister's idea."

"Un, huh. I don't believe you."

"She told me to get out there and practice doing manly things. Experiment, she said. Take some chances. So you see, I was just doing homework. Really, it didn't mean anything."

"Yeah? Well, real men don't force kisses on women. Oh, and since you're trying to act all manly, lose the word 'tizzy.' No guy would ever say that." I crossed my arms. "You're telling me you went all the way to California to do some *homework*? Seems a little excessive."

"I didn't think so," he said, lifting his chin. "Lindsey is nice, and she feels sorry for me. I thought she'd want to help me since she cares so much about abused children."

I didn't bother to say how twisted that was, but I certainly thought it. I segued to the subject of Anthony's death, but he still flatly denied knowing anything about it. He declared that I was living in fantasyland and making up my own funky fairy tale.

"Well, I disagree. I think you had both motive and opportunity."

He shrugged. "That's true. I was furious with him. He was such a selfish bastard toward the end. But he was madder at me than I was at him. Can you imagine that?"

"Yes. Yes, I can. You deceived him big time."

He smiled like a cat on cream. "But I gave him the time of his life, too. He didn't complain much … until the end."

I was getting nowhere. "Come on. I need the truth, and I need it now. At the very least, I think you are involved in delivering Anthony's threatening, revengeful letters. Admit it. You did that. I *know* you did. You are going to pay for that, one way or another."

He shrugged. "Think what you want. You can't prove it, and I will never confess to such nonsense."

I changed the subject a little. "And then there's Wendell. You stole him from us. Were you going to harm him, too?"

It was odd, seeing him put his hands on his hips and toss his head as if he still had long, strawberry blonde hair to toss back from his face. In reality, his hair was dark and short now, and everything he wore screamed *male*.

His eyes narrowed. "What?"

Still, I wasn't getting anywhere. I knew I should cut my losses and just go home. But I didn't.

"Am I to assume it's a mere coincidence that a very large dog used the area by the tree out back as its bathroom, multiple times? Huh, Shawna? Are you opening up a doggy daycare?"

His nostrils flared with anger. "You were here? Snooping around again?" He stepped closer. "You son of a bitch. Take your conniving, skinny ass right out of my house or I'll—"

I shoved him. I shouldn't have, but I did. Not hard enough for him to even lose his balance, but he shoved back and took a swing at me. He connected, and my lip split. I tasted blood and I had to defend myself. He'd been incredibly strong back in his sexy, female dancer days, but now that he was dressed in men's pants, they seemed to have enhanced his strength exponentially.

A real fight ensued, which was shocking to me. I'd never in my life participated in an actual fight, and I wasn't very good at it. Garbled words flew out of his mouth as he continued to come at me, screaming something about kicking a man when he was down. The statement didn't make sense to me, but I wasn't given the time to stop and think or search for meaning. The last thing I remembered before waking up on the ground next to my Jeep were the shouted words …

"Don't you *ever* call me Shawna. Never again! Got that? I am Sean! Sean Hepburn."

TWENTY-SEVEN

Sean

"I can't take it anymore. I just can't take it!"

I suppose I should have said, "Hello. Happy Thanksgiving. Have you got a minute, Julie?" but I didn't. I was angry with her, angry with Jake and Lindsey, and angry with anyone else who might be having a nice day.

"To whom am I speaking?" Julie asked calmly.

"Shut the fuck up. Have you been drinking? You know damn well who this is."

"Maybe. Maybe not. I will be more specific. Are you Shawna or are you Sean?"

"I. Am. Sean," I said through clenched teeth. "Sean with a sore chest. You ought to try binding yourself up as tight as I have to do right now."

"You don't *have* to do that, you know. All the choices are yours to make."

"And I've made them!" I roared. "Most of them, anyway. I am Sean. Shawna is never coming back."

"Do you think you should slow down your transition?"

If she'd been standing in front of me right then, I would have punched her, too. Then again, maybe not. My knuckles were still sore from the beating I'd just given Jake.

"No," I replied. "I think we should speed it up."

"I see. Well, we can talk about that. But I sense something else is bothering you today. Do you know what that might be?"

Shrinks! Always asking questions. Always putting the hard work on the patient that needed the help. Where was the justice? The fairness? What did I pay her for?

"Now that you mention it, yes," I said. "Your brother is bothering me. He's still on his detective kick, and I am his prime suspect. Me! Can you believe that?"

"What are you suspected of doing?"

"He thinks—no, he is *certain* that I am responsible for harming Anthony. He thinks I am either delivering the letters that Anthony wrote to him and Lindsey before he died or that I wrote those letters myself. Now you tell me. Why would I do any of that?"

"I don't know. Why *would* you do any of that?"

Damn. With that question, Julie moved to the top of my mental anger list. She kept badgering me with questions, as if she were a cop or something. This obsession, this quest for answers must be a family thing. First Jake, now Julie.

She waited, silently. That was her way of making me do the talking, and she was good at it. I was not. The silence became uncomfortable. "I did not harm Anthony," I insisted. "Oh, we had some moments, and he pissed me off a lot toward the end, but he never got more than he deserved."

"What did he deserve?"

I plead the fifth. Julie was not going to manipulate me and get me to say something I might regret.

"Have you physically harmed others in the past?"

"You are trying to trick me; I'm not falling for it. You already know I've thrown a few punches, but I'm *not* the letter writer or the postman. Why would I write threatening letters to Jake and Lindsey?"

"You tell me."

Julie caught me off guard, and I began to answer her last question. "Well, that's easy, actually. Jake is the reason Anthony left me. It was all Jake's fault. And Lindsey—Little Miss Perfect—who could compete with *that*?" I snorted. "And then she had the nerve to scream in horror just because I held her face and gave her a little kiss."

"You did *what*?" Julie cried. Wow! She'd really come unglued at that news, which I thought was pretty funny for a shrink. I laughed out loud. Then it occurred to me that Lindsey's reaction was all Julie's fault, and I told her so.

"She would have been fine with my advances," I told her. "She probably would have liked it if my hairy face hadn't scratched her. And, Julie, I blame *you* for that because I followed your orders and stopped taking my female hormones. Wham! I grew facial hair overnight."

"My *orders*? What did you do?" She sounded shocked. "Go cold turkey on the hormones?"

"Hey. I wanted to feel manly, okay? I told you I wasn't messing around. But I wasn't ready to be hairy!"

She cleared her throat, slowing the pace of our conversation. "How do you feel right now?"

"Odd. I feel odd. I've felt odd all my life, and I'm getting tired of that."

"All right," she said, taking control again. "Here's the plan. You will slow down your transition—at least as far as interacting directly with women—and we will talk every day, *every single day* for the next two weeks. Frankly, under the sum of all the circumstances, once a week is no longer enough."

I chuckled darkly. "You think?"

I heard her take a deep breath and let it out. "Sean, until we talk tomorrow, be truthful with yourself. I want what's best for you. You know that. But you're headed for trouble right now. In not-so-technical terms, you're close to going off the deep end without your floaties."

I wasn't laughing any more.

TWENTY-EIGHT

Lindsey

I had high hopes for this Thanksgiving Day. The weather was perfect: not too hot, not too cold. Today would be good in other ways, too. Communication with Jake had improved greatly, easing the tension that had been smothering our home and our hearts for quite some time. All it took, really, had been for me to show a slight interest in his concerns and theories surrounding the death, the funeral, and now the letters, and put aside my contentious denial. His mystery was far from solved, but at least we were finding ways to cope with the unknown, now that we could move forward *together*.

In my mind, however, one nagging issue stood unresolved: my best friend Laura and the time she'd spent at our house, fantasizing about being the woman in Jake's life. I'd thought I'd said all I needed to say on that afternoon I'd stormed over to her apartment and let off enough steam to propel an old-fashioned train up a steep hill, but the added information of her 'sleepover' left me with a few more questions. In an attempt to both solve this issue and diffuse the situation, I'd invited Laura to join Jake and me for Thanksgiving dinner. While Jake was doing some last minute shopping, all issues would be resolved.

Laura arrived with pies—pumpkin and cherry—a can of whipped cream, and an awkward sense of hesitation. After a few sketchy moments of staring at each other, we hugged, opening a path to rational conciliation. Or so I hoped. I offered her a glass of wine while we finished cooking the feast, and waited for Jake to return.

We sat in the backyard while the turkey roasted in the covered grill saturating the air with an aroma too delicious for words. Wendell thought so, too. He kept a close watch. Malcolm wanted nothing to do with the cooking of the bird.

Laura still seemed apprehensive, and I knew I couldn't put off the difficult conversation any longer. Jake would return soon. "Laura, you know you're my best friend, right?"

"Sure. Absolutely."

"Then you know I must be honest with you."

She nodded and swallowed, preparing. "Yes. And I will be honest with you."

"Good. Because, as I said before, I felt like you were making a move on Jake when I was out of town. Am I way off base?"

Tears welled in her eyes. Tears of what? Sadness? Loss? Guilt?

"Oh, Lindsey," she finally said. "Jake never did anything wrong. In fact, he was clueless—kind of odd for a guy who obsesses over figuring things out. In September you'd told me about the problems you two were having, and it seemed like you were going to dump him over all this 'Anthony' stuff. You knew I liked Jake. I liked him long before you did. Remember? You were dating Emmett and Martin back then.

"We had a discussion, and you told me to 'go for it' with Jake." Laura sighed and looked down. "But even then, he had no interest in me. That night in October, when he arrived home a couple days early after seeing you in Austin, he was beside himself, thinking you didn't love him anymore and that you thought he was a lunatic. I just wanted to comfort him. I guess I also wanted to comfort myself."

She looked up again, meeting my eyes. "He paid no attention to me. It was really late, so I left him alone in the office with his laptop, and I fell asleep on your couch. Yes, Jake did ask me to come over here originally, but the pets were the reason he asked for my help. Jake is completely innocent."

I'd thought as much, but it was a huge relief to hear it said out loud. My heart ached for Laura, though. Her expression was so sad.

"Me?" she said quietly. "Well, I'm guilty of liking Jake and wishing I had someone like him in my life. For a few days I let myself believe he was available, but nothing happened. Nothing. And I'm truly sorry. I'll leave if you want me to."

I didn't want her to leave. She'd been like family to me for several years, ever since she'd taken the exceptional education teaching position at school. I wanted our relationship as best friends to continue, so I pulled her into another hug, and we wiped away our tears.

"Let's go inside," I suggested. "You can help me make the salad, and I'll mash the potatoes. Jake should be back any minute." He was taking forever. "How long can it take to buy butter and rolls?"

The table was set with fall placemats depicting deciduous trees with red, yellow, and orange leaves, and a centerpiece of small Aspen branches, pinecones, tiny decorative birds, set among fall leaves. Dark tan, bayberry-scented candles added to the festive décor. Jake's favorite CD played in the background, and the smells coming from the kitchen were to die for. All we needed was Jake.

Just then, the door opened. Jake stumbled in, his face dripping with blood. His mouth and eyes were swollen and turning darker with each passing second.

"Oh, my God!" I screamed.

After four hours in the Emergency Room, twelve stitches and a bunch of butterfly bandages, Jake and I returned to the house where Laura had waited with Wendell and Malcolm. We attempted to resume our Thanksgiving festivities but with much modification. Jake's dinner now consisted of only mashed potatoes, and though Laura and I were physically able to eat everything, we didn't have an appetite for much of anything. So we just ate pie.

Jake was more talkative now that he'd been patched up and had the benefit of some pain medication and a little wine. He told us Sean had attacked him, gone ballistic after being accused of crimes against Anthony and against us.

"I remember the threat he made just before I blacked out. He said, 'It's so easy for you to kick a man when he's down. Well, it's your turn now, Jake.' And I thought about those words as I drove home. But you know what? I have no idea what he was talking about."

I stared at him, knowing I'd heard those words before. Where? A fable floated to the surface of my thinking. "The Dogs and the Fox," I declared.

Both Jake and Laura turned toward me, confused. "What?"

"*It's easy to kick a man when he's down* is the moral to that fable."

Laura lifted one sardonic eyebrow. "Uh, huh. I can see you weren't kidding about switching your interests from fairy tales to fables."

Smiling, yet feeling so sorry for Jake's pain, I said, "I would never kid about something like that. But seriously, Jake, it seems to me that tonight Sean proved, beyond a shadow of a doubt, that he's capable of violence. He is definitely guilty of assaulting you. Shouldn't we call the police?"

"Now look who's sounding like a detective," Jake said slowly, trying to form a smile of his own. He grimaced, and his hand went to his lips. "Ow! Maybe we should wait."

"Wait? For what? This is the second time, Jake. Last June, when you found me in the Zuni Mountains, you arrived with a rather battered face after Shawna had slugged you. That's when she blamed you, saying you were the reason Anthony had left her."

"Yeah, but—"

Our discussion was interrupted by a knock at the door. Who would stop by this late on Thanksgiving? We rarely received unexpected visitors here at the house. I worried that maybe it was a remorseful Sean with an apology or round three ...

Laura told us to relax and stay put. She'd answer the door.

Within seconds, she stood in the kitchen doorway, shrugging and staring at us with saucer-wide eyes. A tall, stocky policeman towered over her from behind.

"Jake Lee?" He spoke without emotion, but we could see the shock in his eyes when he got a look at Jake. "I just answered a call. A complaint from ..." He glanced down at his notes then looked up again, regarding Jake's face skeptically. "Sean Hepburn. He said you have been harassing him, threatening him on the phone and at his residence."

I could tell Jake was still thinking, his response likely slowed by his meds, so I jumped in. "Officer, as you can see, Jake is the one who should be filing a complaint. He was viciously attacked by this … this Sean Hepburn." I turned to Jake. "Hepburn? Since when?"

He shrugged. "I don't know. I heard the name for the first time today."

The officer glanced back and forth several times, looking from Jake to me to Wendell and even to Malcolm. He must have thought Laura was the only normal part of this picture because he didn't look in her direction.

"I just came by to let you know about the complaint and ask you to stay away from Mr. Hepburn, otherwise he's requested a restraining order on you." He scratched his head and frowned. "Hey, if you want to file a counter complaint, you can. I strongly suggest we do that just in case there is any further violence."

Jake said he wasn't interested in pressing charges, but he explained his side of the story, the counter complaint was written, and a photo of Jake's injuries was taken for the record. The officer ate two pieces of cherry pie before he left, and Laura departed shortly after that.

We were exhausted. I put away the food, but otherwise left the kitchen in a Thanksgiving mess before taking Jake's hand and leading him upstairs to our bedroom. He noticed right away that the room had been set up for romance, and I sensed his regret, though he didn't say anything. The bed was turned down, candles ready to be lit, and a bottle of Merlot waited to be opened. Plans change, though, and that was okay. We showered together, and I helped Jake wash his hair, tilting his head to keep his new sutures dry. We climbed into bed afterward and snuggled between the fresh, fragrant sheets. I went to turn off the lights, and Jake reached over to light the candles.

"Jake, the candles will keep."

"That may be true, but I won't." His battered face attempted a crooked smile.

I wondered how he could possibly feel like making love after what he'd been through. Just hearing about Jake's encounter with Sean, then seeing his injuries and the pain … the whole situation had dampened my desire.

"Are you sure about this, Jake?"

He was sure. Tonight our lovemaking would be sweet and gentle, if not a little challenging. We were both careful, not wanting to disturb any of his physical wounds, and I took the lead. I insisted on that after I realized even the slightest movement of his head caused him pain and dizziness. In fact, I not only took the lead, I got on top and ordered him not to move.

"Tonight you are going to relax and lie perfectly still," I told him. "I'm in charge. Understand?"

"Yes, ma'am."

Though I was becoming a fairly good follower, I'd never been completely in charge when it came to lovemaking. In Jake's condition, I doubted he'd notice my shortcomings or lack of sexual leadership experience. However, kissing had always been our forte, and I couldn't count on that tonight; his mouth was far too sore. I'd have to come up with something different. I began by nibbling on his ears with my lips, and when I saw that he enjoyed that, I gently teased with my teeth. When my tongue got involved, Jake sighed. So did I, quickly dispelling my earlier belief that I wasn't in the mood.

Since I'd had success with his ears, I thought I'd try a few other locations. I kissed his neck and drew circles around his nipples with my tongue. I'd always wondered if guys liked that—I certainly did. He answered my question with a louder sigh, and his breathing sped up. So he liked that, too. I kissed my way down to his navel, and my mouth enjoyed his salty flavor while his manly, musky scent mixed with a hint of clean and soapy tantalized my nose.

I became aware that Jake's body was no longer relaxed. Involuntary tremors of arousal began as my hands traveled lower, and so many thoughts flashed through my mind. Was I still in charge? Was this the best time to revisit that uncharted territory we'd come so close to entering a few weeks ago? Jake was injured, and suddenly I was feeling virginal, but there it was. His hardness electrified me, and for a brief moment, that was all that mattered. I took it in my hand and kissed it, hoping my trembling lips and inexperienced tongue would please him. After a few hypnotic moments I felt Jake's arms pulling me upward until we were face to face.

"Oh, Lindsey," he groaned. "My sweet, sexy, loveable Lindsey."

Though I remained on top, Jake took over. So much for sweet and gentle.

Once our breathing and heart rates had fallen back to a normal level, we snuggled for a while, whispering sincere words of love. We dedicated ourselves to supporting each other always, no matter what challenges life hurled at us.

"I wish you didn't have to go to Seattle for the December conference next week," he finally said.

"Well, there's nothing I can do about that. I'm committed. But I'll be okay. I'll be careful. Lad will be there, and I know he will be extra vigilant—if that's possible."

After a dissatisfied grumble, he blew out the candles, and I kissed the back of his neck.

"I love you, Lindsey."

"I love you too, Jake."

TWENTY-NINE

Sean

Having to talk with Julie every damn day was a pain in the ass. There was always plenty of *How do you feel about this?* and *How do you feel about that?*

The next time she called, I decided to ask her a question or two, like, *Have you been able to call off the hounds yet?* meaning Jake and Lindsey, but mostly Jake. And, *Have you found me a job yet? Cause I can't afford you much longer.* That one would make her think. While she was thinking, I'd ask her how she felt about *that.* There, I felt better already.

Today was the day I'd set aside to clean my closet and remove all my sexy, girly clothes, shoes, and make-up, and replace it all with man-stuff. I didn't have much of that yet, and my old, male wardrobe—still hidden away in the small closet—was pitiful. It came from my gay guy days, and that was a far cry from how I wanted to look now: like a hot guy, a real man. But I still liked to shop, so once I had some money, I'd go out and get what I needed to keep looking great. Different, but great. In the meantime, I had the two outfits I'd purchased to wear in San Diego. Then I wondered if *outfits* was a word like *tizzy*? A word, a handsome guy like me shouldn't use.

My closet project ended up being more challenging than I'd anticipated. I loved my female clothes and wasn't a hundred per cent ready to dispose of them. Especially my fur coat. I'd had some fun, sexy times wearing that. The shoes were another story. As much as I liked the way they accentuated my long, gorgeous legs, I'd always hated the way they felt. I wouldn't miss that.

I tired quickly of the closet cleaning business. Besides, I'd worked up a hefty appetite after all that effort. Potato chips and beer sounded good. I could eat that now that I was no longer obsessed with keeping my almost perfect girlish figure. Not only that, but today, the day after Thanksgiving, was traditionally a college football day. Beer, potato chips, and football. It didn't get much manlier than that.

I'd made a deal with the mail carrier several years back, saying he was to honk if he put anything other than junk mail into my box. That way I wouldn't need to make the long walk down the driveway for nothing. Now that I wore comfortable shoes, the length of the walk really didn't matter. Someday I'd tell him not to bother anymore. I rarely received mail worth reading anyway, but then I heard a horn honk. Slightly curious, I headed down the driveway.

Sitting in front of the TV in my T-shirt, jeans, and loafers, my unhealthy, fattening snacks spread around me, I flipped though the small stack of mail. A letter in a business size envelope caught my eye, and I opened that one first.

Dear Shawna:

Read this and read it carefully, as the contents of this letter will have an effect on your life.

I blame YOU for my death. Here's why:

- *You were gorgeous but that was fake. You deceived me from the first day we met.*
- *You are a manipulator. You made me do things I didn't want to do.*
- *You are an impersonator. Need I go into detail about your disgusting secret?*
- *You made me hate myself.*

Beware! You will soon regret the day you were born.

Anthony

My hands started to shake, and a new understanding emerged. So this was what Jake had been accusing me of. He thought I'd been mailing letters from Anthony, or even writing *and* mailing them. Well, I hadn't written this one.

Except ... its contents felt strangely familiar.

But I hadn't written this. I was sure it wasn't me.

Or was it? No! Some sicko must have written it, but who? I stared at the letter, ran my finger over the words. *I did not do this! I did not write this! Did not, did not ...*

Or did I? Could I have been so out of it that I *had*?

Oh, hell. I had no idea. If I had written it, that would make me one crazy lunatic. But why would I write a threatening letter to myself? And not remember doing it? Knowing Jake, he would assume I'd done it just to throw him off, and I had to admit that did kind of made sense. He'd think I was delusional or worse. Hell, he probably already thought that.

An odd sensation began to rise up within my body, like a rumble, a vibration. I didn't like it or the way it was taking possession of me. I stood to walk it off, shake it off, and I noticed my breathing had changed, and I was panting like a woman in labor. There was no pain—not exactly, but it was obvious something bad was happening. I knew my body well. I was always conscious of the way it looked, the way it felt. Everything about this was wrong, all wrong.

I was unable to prevent the sweat from beading up on the entire surface of my face. All the symptoms suddenly combined, morphing in slow-motion and culminating with an internal explosion. Then I heard an unrecognizable sound and yet perfectly familiar.

"I can do crazy," I screeched. "Oh, yeah! I can do crazy in my sleep!"

The explosion faded swiftly after that, leaving only a mere tingling sensation, and I collapsed on the couch, descending into a deep, hypnotic slumber.

THIRTY

Lindsey

Bobby. What could I do to reverse all the damage that had been inflicted upon this little boy? What could anyone do?

This morning, the plane was full, but I had an aisle seat so at least my right arm had a little wiggle room. I'd be able to write a lesson or two for Bobby, after that I'd jot an entry in my old, mostly empty journal. My goal for the boy was to make the one or two hours a week I'd spend with him enjoyable, and that in itself was a tall order. He didn't know how to enjoy anything. If nothing else, I hoped to teach him that.

Wanting to incorporate fables into some of these lessons, I thumbed through my books in search of the perfect one for him. It was difficult, since most of the stories and their morals were a bit grim, even violent. That would not do. He needed no encouragement in those areas. Then I found "The Crow and the Pitcher," in which no one died, lied, or got hurt. The premise? A crow was thirsty but couldn't reach the water down deep in the pitcher, so it dropped pebbles into the pitcher until the water rose just enough so the bird could take a drink. The moral: little by little does the trick. That could work!

Another idea struck me as I was working. I could conduct a few guided art lessons based on one or more of my sessions with him, and I'd also let him draw whatever he felt like drawing. In the past, his art had been gruesome, grotesque, even scary, and it probably still was. We'd see. But the way I envisioned the Children's Art Collection that Elisabeth hoped to publish, included a wide variety of children's art. Bobby's art would definitely expand the width of the collection. And, who knew? He might just be the next Picasso.

Journal time. I craved the opportunity for some stream of consciousness writing. Why hadn't I found the time? I loved to write, and this much-needed therapy was long overdue.

Early December: On the plane

I haven't written in this journal since last June in the Zuni Mountains, and it's about time I got on with it. Lord knows I need somewhere to vent, to escape, to write things I wouldn't dare say out loud!

November was a crazy month. The Conference in San Diego, Sean showing up and making a disgusting pass at me—that was really creepy. Then I received my very own threatening letter from Anthony. Jake thinks it came from Shawna—oops! I mean Sean—but we have no proof.

How is it that Jake and I maintain any sense of normalcy? I guess some days we don't.

Then there was my face-to-face meeting with Bobby, and taking on the teacher role for the field trip, only to discover a sweet little girl with some big ugly problems. I also made peace with Laura. At least I think I did. We seemed to work things out, but I worry that our truce is temporary. It's true she had a thing for Jake long before I did, and, unfortunately, 'things' like that don't just disappear because you want them to.

Then Jake arrived home for Thanksgiving dinner all beat up and bloody, the result of a fight with Sean, followed by a visit from the police. Poor Jake. He tries so hard. Our life over these past three months could easily be scripted into a movie or a book! Ha! No, probably not. No one would believe it. Then again, they say the truth is often stranger than fiction ...

The flight attendant just announced that we'd be landing in about fifteen minutes, and I don't want to end my journaling with such negative entries, so I will add in some good stuff: my love for Jake ... and Wendell and Malcolm. The fabulous opportunities provided by the conference tours and subsequent publications. The sweet way that Jake makes love to me, and the way he tries to protect me, though I hope he isn't trying to protect me from the truth. I need honesty.

THIRTY-ONE

Jake

A swishing, thumping sound captured my attention. I glanced over and saw Wendell standing beside me, staring with pleading eyes only a heartless devil could refuse. He asked for so little, really. But this was a first. He was not alone. He'd dragged in the nylon bag that housed the famous "tunnel" he and Lindsey played with now and then.

"Okay, Wendell. Let's go have some dog fun," I said, putting down my coffee.

Removing the blue agility tunnel from the bag was easy, and setting it up wasn't too bad, but I wasn't sure what my next move was supposed to be. Not a problem. Wendell had a plan. He went to one end, stuck his head in and his rear up, then barked. I attempted to emulate the dog's actions at the other end of the tunnel, seriously hoping that no one was watching.

My efforts, which I thought went above and beyond, did not impress Wendell. I, apparently, did not know how to play this game. He bounded helpfully down to my end of the tunnel and gave me some direction by pushing my butt into the tunnel with his huge mastiff head, then barking some more. Every time he barked, I went in a little farther. I had to laugh—who was in charge here? Silly question, but at least I was learning the game. When I reached the midway point, he bounded back to his end, looked in, barked, then tore back to my location and proceeded to pounce on me from outside of the tunnel. Oh, boy. This is fun—for him.

This was no easy feat to survive, if I was being honest. Crawling flat on the ground, using only my elbows like a soldier in combat, was hard enough. Add being pounced on by a one hundred and sixty pound dog, and I felt like a contestant on *Survivor*. I'd definitely be voted off this little island in record time. How did Lindsey manage this? My pretty lady must be tougher than she looks to play this game.

After the tunnel episode, sitting at my desk was easy. With my body now relaxed a little, my mind kicked into thinking mode. I still worried about Lindsey and wasn't completely sure I liked the idea of Lad spending even more time with her than he had in the past—how was that even possible? He was already at her side every waking moment. That left only ... I shook my head, needing to eliminate that thought from my brain. I really didn't want to go there. I wanted her to be safe but ... did I want her to be with Lad *twenty-four hours a day*? No! Definitely not.

An email from Lindsey popped up, surprising me. I hadn't expected to hear from her until the end of the day. In the past, the first full day at a conference kept her going non-stop, running her ragged with the general session and company meetings until bedtime. Hearing from her like this, made my day. We began to chat.

Sean's legal last name really is Hepburn. And get this: it means Ancient Burial Ground. - Linds.

How do you know that? - Jake

Research. You don't have a monopoly on Binging and Googling. - Linds

What in the world possessed you to do that? - Jake

Curiouser and Curiouser. (Read that with an English lilt in your voice.) - Linds

Please explain. - Jake

It's from Alice in Wonderland. - Linds

Always the teacher. Thanks. I love you. - Jake

Love you more. Got to go. – Linds

I had to chuckle. Her English lilt would be better than mine any day. Too bad I couldn't just call her. I was still smiling when the ring of the doorbell, the bark of the dog, and the tweet of the bird interrupted my thoughts. By the time I opened the door, the FedEx driver was already backing out of the driveway. I waved and picked up the sturdy envelope, wondering—*don't we have to sign for deliveries anymore?*

The last piece of real mail I'd received had been that threatening letter from Anthony—or Sean, or some unknown weirdo—so I hesitated before opening this envelope. Was the fear of mail an actual disease or phobia? Seems the world was getting paranoid—or rightfully cautious—about poison, lately. Looking at this unexpected, mysterious package, I realized I could easily jump on that bandwagon.

I took a deep breath for courage then tore it open, and a grin spread across my face. I'd half expected to find poison or additional threats, but instead, I found my second surprise of the day: an invitation from Lindsey. She must have planned this before she'd left for Seattle. What an amazing woman.

TO: My dearest Jake

FROM: Your dearest Lindsey

WHAT: A romantic night in a quaint, woodsy cabin

WHERE: An hour's drive east of Seattle (see driving directions)

WHEN: Sunday after my last meeting

WHY: You have to ask?

HOW: Your plane ticket and rental car reservation are enclosed

IMPORTANT: We must arrive at the cabin by 4:30 for a big surprise

I laughed out loud. I hadn't been this excited since … heck, I'd never been this excited. Not even as a kid on Christmas. I had to call Laura to see if she could stay with the pets this Sunday, Monday, and part of Tuesday, but first, I'd fire off one last email to Lindsey.

With your work for December almost complete, let's get ready for romance. I will pick you up at your hotel on Sunday at 3:15 sharp. I miss you so much. Read that with an English lilt! - Jake

THIRTY-TWO

Lindsey

A s promised, Lad was within shouting distance every minute of the day and stationed near my door every night. *When did the man sleep?* He didn't seem to mind, though. In fact, I think he enjoyed adding 'bodyguard' to his list of roles. It came very naturally to him. Picture one of the guys from the movie *Men in Black,* and that was Lad.

He'd also requested my company for a private dinner in my room, saying we had a lot to discuss. That would be a first: discussing 'a lot' with my mysterious man of few words. I was curious. What did I need to know? I'd overcome my nervousness—well, at least I could push past it—even when my audience was huge. I'd already been informed that there were no last minute schedule changes, as there sometimes were. What else could he need to discuss? *Curiouser and curiouser* indeed!

We dined on a salad of basil, spinach, and other mixed greens, tossed with a lemon Tahini dressing, fresh pasta with basil pesto, and a squash and apple pizza on a thin, whole wheat crust. We'd completed the delicious meal without much discussion, but I was used to Lad now, his lack of conversation didn't bother me. The silence was relaxing, almost calming.

But if he really had something to discuss, I wanted him to get on with it. The suspense, the uncertainty of the promised discussion created dramatic scenarios in my mind. I broached the subject rather bluntly. "Lad, what is it we need to talk about? What's going on?"

He frowned slightly. "Some might view this information as a good/bad situation. I'm not sure how you will react."

Where had I heard *that* before? Oh, yeah. That's what Martin—a friend in my life before Jake and I had hooked up—had said just prior to making a date with me for the purpose of breaking up. I told myself not to jump to any conclusions and just let Lad speak. After all, what choice did I have?

"Nothing about your keynote presentation needs to change."

I nodded. Didn't sound like anything bad yet. I braced myself for the inevitable '*but*' ...

"But there are a few significant changes you need to know about."

I was confused. "Please, get to the point."

"The point is ... you will soon be bombarded with microphones, photographers, TV cameras, and reporters."

"Oooh," I mused, intrigued. "That's a pretty sharp point, Anthony."

Lad's knee began to shake like a kid with ADHD. "Why ... why did you do that?"

"Do what?"

He blinked, looking utterly shocked. "You just called me Anthony."

All the color drained from my face. I'd had no idea I'd done that. Why on earth … "I did? Are you sure about that?"

"Positive."

"I'm so sorry! I have no idea where that came from." I'd have to think that over later. For now I had to get back on point. "Here's a question for you, Lad. Why all the media? Why now, and why here?"

An uncertain smile formed on his face. "You got your wish, Ms. Lark. You've become that educational rock star you wanted to be, and the word is out. The world wants to take a look at Lindsey, hear your voice, and get a sense of your personality—things like that."

I sat up taller, shocked. "But I—"

"Oh, and FYI, a clothing rack with dresses, shoes, and accessories will arrive any minute now."

Just like clockwork, there they were, and I modeled all the outfits for Lad, feeling silly and awkward the whole time. He made his recommendations, and fortunately, I agreed with his choices. Next, he produced a list of everything I would eat and drink tomorrow. It seemed ultra-healthy and definitely not from the hotel's standard menu. He said the food had been selected to give me energy and keep me calm at the same time. He also made it perfectly clear that he would be at my side 24/7 because the paparazzi and the press could be overwhelming, not to mention the extra large crowd of eager participants.

I stared at him, stunned by all this. "Let me get this straight. You are my bodyguard, my butler, my PR executive, my big brother, my fashion consultant, and my dietician? Are you my make-up artist, too?"

He looked scandalized. "Absolutely not! I have people for that. Oh, and they will be here, in your room, at 7:45 tomorrow morning."

I fought back giggles at the straight delivery of his answer because I could see Lad was totally serious. He did not find any humor in this discussion. Maybe I should be taking this turn of events more seriously. Perhaps my lack of nerves was due to the fact that I really had no idea what to expect … and Lad did.

In the morning, he was there to make sure everything went without a hitch, then he escorted me through the main lobby and toward the ballroom. I felt great, and having looked in the mirror after the make-up artist had left, I knew I *looked* great. Really, I had no idea I could ever have looked this good. *I'm feeling a touch spoiled right now.* Lad pressed closely against my side as he led me along a specific route, which he said had been chosen to give the cameras access to me before my presentation. A few reporters shouted out questions despite having been told to wait until the keynote address was over.

"Events like this must be intimidating for a kindergarten teacher," one yelled. "How are you holding up?"

We kept walking, but I turned my smile toward the reporter and suggested, "Come and spend a day in my kindergarten classroom with twenty-six kids and we'll see who's intimidated." Everyone close enough to hear me laughed, including the reporter.

Keeping his eyes forward, though I knew he was observing everyone, seeing everything, Lad remarked, "Nice."

Most of the shouts were unintelligible, but one, from a female reporter, came through loud and clear. "Ms. Lark. If teachers are so underpaid, how can you afford to dress like that?"

"Don't say a word," came Lad's voice. "Smile and wave and keep walking." He barely moved his lips—as if he were a ventriloquist. That, of course, would make me the dummy. I smiled, glad to realize I still had my sense of humor even in this surreal situation. I think that came with being a kindergarten teacher. Maybe it was true that people did learn everything they needed to know in kindergarten. And since I'd been there seven years, well … just saying.

I'd trimmed about ten minutes from the explanation of the typical Art Journaling procedure in order to include some of the students' work from their Observation Journaling: the drawing and writing about real, non-fictional things. I'd returned to Mrs. Frank's class several times back in Tucson, and I'd guided the children through the completion of their masterpieces, conducted a whole group writing activity that produced several desert songs and poems about the plants and animals they'd seen at the museum. I'd taken photos of everything.

The audience today, though polite and eager listeners, was fairly subdued. I think the presence of all the lights and cameras proved to be a distraction for them. This all changed when they grasped the concept of this complementary vision of journaling and viewed the photos of the students engaged in this activity.

A voice blurted out, "There's no way that's going to work."

"It will work," I assured her. "You *can* do this with your students, and I'll show you how in detail if you attend tomorrow's workshop." That seemed to satisfy the teacher. I could tell her comment had come from a feeling of inadequacy, a fear of failure or even of just trying something new. Most humans were resistant to change.

I was told that Sarah, the conference's technical specialist, had outdone herself with my CD this time, and had added a fully orchestrated musical accompaniment to the songs and a lively percussive background for the poems. The first song, 'The Prickly Pear Blues,' came up on the screen, and the sound began. Immediately and unprompted, the teachers stood, clapped, and attempted to sing along. It was awesome!

A prickly pear is a cactus,
A prickly pear has fruit.
So red and sweet and juicy
With a rooty-toot, rooty-toot, toot!
Throw away that éclair
Eat a prickly pear ...

When the song finally came to an end, shouts rang out, requesting to sing it again. Amazing! The adults were acting just like children, and they were having a great time. So we ran it again, and the media folks had a field day capturing all the sound, movement, color, and excitement.

Then it was time for the poem. I worried that it might not be as upbeat or entertaining as the song, and wished I had switched the order around. Oh, well. Too late now. Thanks to Sarah, the clinking of a cowbell set the tempo: *clink, clink, clink, clink,* followed by short ascending and descending zips on a slide whistle. I had no idea what made the other sounds, but it rocked, and before long the whole place was grooving to the simple words of a kindergarten poem.

One, two cactus grew
Three, four vultures soar
Five coyotes
Six corn cakes
Seven slinky rattlesnakes
Eight lizards
Nine canteens
Ten bowls of pinto beans ...

The audience was still standing and applauding when all the lights suddenly went out—the room was completely dark except for a faint, bluish glow cast from the large screen behind me. There I stood, the only person in the entire meeting hall that was slightly visible. A strange hush fell over the crowd, and a solitary voice spoke. It sounded like a man's voice, but it had been adjusted, distorted somehow, almost robotic, computerized. The effect was chilling, terrifying.

"Listen up and listen good," it instructed the crowd. "Don't be fooled by the woman's fake sweetness. What you see is not what you get."

My heart raced. That message was directed at me. I was that woman. Not a cough or the taking of a breath could be heard ... until a pair of footsteps pounded, running back stage. Lad was on it.

I was escorted toward a side door just as the lights flicked back on, and Elisabeth Meriwether took my place at the podium. I watched her assure everyone that the brief interruption was merely a stray, emotionally unstable fellow who'd wandered over from the docks or the area near Pike Place Market. She made light of the situation as well as she could. She moved on smoothly, and soon the audience was back on track and bustling out of the ballroom for lunch. It would be quite a while before I felt 'back on track.'

Camera operators and reporters followed me around all day, hoping, I think, for another odd episode to add to their stories. Thank God, the afternoon passed without any additional incidents. Lad stayed close, and I thought I spied a few extra men tagging along with us as we moved from one location in the convention center to another. Had he called in extra help? Plain clothed officers? My imagination ran wild, though I was grateful for their reassuring presence.

I had to admit I was on edge after today's unexplained, unexpected guest had appeared. Wait. Let me rephrase that. He hadn't *appeared*—no one actually *saw* him. He was just … there. A strange, distorted voice in the dark. I concluded that being in the spotlight, being a 'rock star,' albeit an elementary educational one, had its downside.

Finally sequestered in my hotel room with the door closed and locked, my jubilation diminished and my exhaustion intensified. That was all right. The day was done; I could rest now. Turn down service had already been there, and I glanced over at the bed. Lying on the pillow along with the expected chocolate treat were three roses: a red one, a white one, and a yellow one. I loved their velvety petals and their delicate scent, and smiled wondering which thoughtful person had arranged for this pleasant surprise. Jake? Ms. Meriwether? Lad?

My tired mind drifted to my comforting knowledge of fairy tales and, in particular, the tale of Snow White and Rose Red. The red rose could represent Rose Red; the white rose, Snow White, but the yellow rose? I didn't know about that one. No fairy tale connections came to mind for a yellow rose. In German culture, I knew a yellow rose signified infidelity or dying love—what a horrible thought. Then I wondered if this yellow rose might represent the yellow rose of Texas, which was a much more joyful idea. Either way, I chastised myself for reading so much into the flowers. Especially when I was too tired to even think.

I heard Lad running water in the tub and, knowing it was for me, I slipped into the luxurious bathrobe the hotel provided and walked in, ready to soak my tension away.

"I'll be back later," he said softly in passing.

"All right. Hey, Lad?"

He paused. "Yes?"

"Thank you for all your help today. Especially with the … the conference crasher."

"Just doing my job."

"By the way, did you ever see the guy?"

"Nobody saw him," he said carefully. "All we know is that he knew how to shut down the lights in the ballroom, alter his voice over the speakers, then disappear quickly."

"What do you think happened? Who would do that?"

He hesitated. "It could have been an angry teacher fired from his job, maybe a jealous guy who applied for the Innovative Teacher of the Year and didn't get it … the possibilities are endless. But don't you worry. That's what I'm here for."

One more question came to mind. "Is it always like this? Are you always kept this busy helping keynote speakers?"

Maintaining his serious, all business countenance, he shook his head, then walked out.

I slid out of the bathrobe and sank into the hot water thinking about how good Lad had been to me. I'd come to appreciate his cautious ways, his attentiveness, and his knowledge. The intruder who had interrupted my keynote address had obviously taken a toll on him, too. His eyes carried signs of fatigue and unrest. I realized he most likely felt responsible or that he'd failed in some way.

Closure. I'd always liked closure. I'd met my contractual obligations, I'd performed well according to Elisabeth Meriwether, and with the published version of my Art Journaling Teacher's Guide soon to be released, sales and royalties would continue indefinitely. I'd be able to work on the Children's Art Collections series at home at my own pace. Closure. It felt great.

Waiting for Jake and the special plan for 'romance' was all I had left to do here. Then I could pack up and head home. I climbed out of the bath, dried off, and grinned into the mirror.

"Definitely got my shine on today. Nothing could take away the joy I feel right now."

When I heard a knock at the door, I flung it open without thinking, expecting to see Jake.

"Lad!" I exclaimed. "What a surprise. You didn't use your key." I reached quickly for my robe, though it was merely for my own comfort. I don't think Lad ever noticed whether I was dressed or nearly naked, unless he was scrutinizing my on-stage wardrobe. His expression never changed, and his eyes never drifted to any off-limit areas.

"Your part in the conference is over," he stated. "I'm beginning to cut back, wind down. Once you're on the plane and headed home tomorrow, my work with you is complete."

A profound sadness touched my heart, surprising me. I hadn't realized I'd miss him so much. "Oh, of course. I understand."

He stepped into the room and over to the sitting area. We sat. Looking as serious as always, he handed me a manila envelope. "In this envelope is a lucrative two-year contract, encouraging you to continue with the company as one of its main keynote speakers and educational consultants. You need to read it, think about it, and be prepared to discuss it tomorrow morning with Elisabeth and her staff."

He stood, then headed for the door. Just before stepping into the corridor, he turned and asked if I would like to go out for dinner or order room service tonight. I thanked him but explained that I had already made plans. Was that a hint of disappointment I saw on his face?

Still wearing only the robe, I stepped into the hallway, watching him leave. With amazing timing, Lad entered the elevator just as Jake stepped out, and they nodded at one another. Even though I stood a few feet away, I detected a scowl on Jake's face. I assumed Lad's expression would be unreadable.

"Jake!" I cried, holding out my arms.

Just like that, his frown disappeared, and he swept me up in an embrace. Inside the room, after a few minutes of passionate kissing and hugging, he surprised me by taking his hands off my body and stepping away.

"Come on, Linds," he said with a grin. "We gotta go! Let's get this evening of romance started."

I regarded him quizzically, since I'd thought that was what we'd just been doing, but apparently he had other plans. I quickly pulled on a pair of jeans and a sweater, matching his choice of attire. "All set."

"Don't you want to bring anything with you?" Now it was he who wore the puzzled look.

"Like what?"

"I don't know. A toothbrush? A jacket? Something to sleep in?" He swiped the air with his hand. "Never mind! Disregard that last item. You won't need it."

I laughed. "Jake. You're so funny. Sounds like our romantic evening will last all night."

"Yes, ma'am," he said tentatively, scratching his head. He looked a little lost, though.

"Sounds perfect." I grabbed a few needed items, including the manila envelope, and was ready to go. "I do need to read this contract tonight. Otherwise, you will have my undivided attention. That's a promise."

Lad stood like a sentinel in the lobby. He gave a stoic nod as we walked outside arm in arm and waited for Jake's rental car to be brought up from the parking garage. I glanced back over my shoulder as we pulled away and noticed Lad writing in his little black notepad. His presence gave me comfort, but it made Jake frown. I smiled anticipating our romantic evening and knowing I would soon erase that frown from my lover's face.

TOO HOT TO HANDLE

THIRTY-THREE

Jake

Keeping secrets was not her usual modus operandi, though today she managed to do just that quite effectively. I was curious and wanted more information about our special night, but I'd be patient and go along with her game, her teasing. For now, she held the driving directions and kept us on track, telling me when and where to turn.

As soon as we'd traveled beyond the busy, city traffic, I lifted her hand to my lips to kiss her pretty fingertips. We didn't talk much, but we did sing along with the radio. I thought by now she might have clued me in on the details of our romantic evening at the cozy cabin, but she didn't, so I assumed she intended to maintain the mystery. We were happy, and that's all that really mattered.

In my estimation, we would arrive at the cabin in about fifteen minutes. The radio went suddenly silent, and though we tried other stations, nothing worked. We were in a mountainous area, but I didn't think it made sense for us to be out of *every* station's range. Perhaps the radio itself was malfunctioning. It wasn't a problem for long, though. After all, I had a kindergarten teacher in the car with me. As if on cue, she said, "Oh, well," and began singing a vaguely familiar song from my own childhood, complete with hand movements!

> *Little cabin in the woods,*
> *Little man at the window stood,*
> *Saw a rabbit hopping by,*
> *Knocking at the door.*
> *Help me! Help me! …*

I wondered if she'd still be singing kindergarten songs when she was eighty. And would I still think it was cute?

Lindsey announced that our next turn would be in about a half mile, onto a dirt road. We were almost there. We hadn't passed anyone else, I realized. No cars, trucks, houses, cabins—*nothing* for miles. We were out in the sticks, no doubt about that. I was glad we still had well over a half tank of gas in the car.

"Look!" she said, pointing. "There's the collapsing old barn over on the left. That means our cabin should be on the right in .3 of a mile."

I spotted it, and I also noticed the road we were on ended at the cabin. A dead end. I turned the car off, and we turned toward each other, saying in one voice, "Little cabin in the woods!"

Thankfully, no 'little man at the window stood.' Hand in hand, we climbed the three wooden steps to the front door and I turned to Lindsey, expecting her to produce a key. She didn't, so I tried the doorknob. It was locked. We both shrugged simultaneously, and went around to the side door. Fortunately, it was not locked. I glanced at my watch and noticed it was just 4:22 p.m. Eight minutes ahead of the requested arrival time stated in her explicit instructions. Eight minutes until her 'big surprise.'

The place was rustic, to say the least, but also cozy and woodsy as promised. The river rock fireplace was set and ready to be lit. Extra wood had been piled off to the side, and a box of matches was conveniently located on the small mantel. An oval, wooden table located directly across the room from the fireplace was set with place mats, utensils, salt and pepper, and candles. Nothing fancy like Lindsey would have done back in Tucson, but perfect for this old cabin.

I heard Lindsey rustling around in the kitchen, probably searching for just the right pot or pan or dish, so I went ahead and began the process of lighting the fire. That wasn't as easy as I'd hoped it would be; the wood was either a little damp or green. The next time I looked up from my challenge, I could see her in the kitchen pouring wine into a couple of juice glasses, filling bowls with soup or maybe stew, and slicing a crunchy baguette. Everything smelled delicious.

I knew she was a pro when it came to planning, but she'd really outdone herself this time. She must have had some help—a partner in crime—since she'd been working at the conference almost every minute of every day, but it couldn't have been Lad. He was always with her. But someone …

Lindsey glanced up from her bread slicing, and our eyes met and lingered … until the match's heat reached my fingertips, breaking the spell. "Ow!" I grimaced and shook my hand in the air before applying the only pain killing medication available—my own saliva.

By the time she carried the food items to the table, the small fire was crackling, and we enjoyed a tasty dinner in our cozy little cabin. My curiosity almost got the better of me though—I wanted to know what the surprise was, and why her plan had specified 4:30. Maybe the dinner was the surprise. I wondered. No, dinner alone would not be thought of as a BIG surprise. So, since she hadn't said anything, I assumed it would be made evident any minute now. I watched her face for clues, but I saw none. She'd be really good at poker, if she ever took up gambling. A minute later, I noticed a sudden change of expression on her pretty face. She was suddenly tense.

"What is it, Linds? What's the matter?"

"Oh, it's nothing."

"Come on, Linds. I was one long paper away from getting my PhD in psychology. It's not 'nothing.' It is *never* nothing."

"I was blindsided by a memory. It came out of nowhere."

"Lindsey, it obviously bothers you, whatever it is. Please share it with me. Maybe I can help."

"Well, I just remembered the last time I stayed in a small cabin. We were in Durango, Colorado."

"We?"

"Yes, me and … Anthony. We were on our way to Estes Park to get married."

"Oh." Strange. If being in a small cabin was such a painful memory, why would she want to duplicate it today? "Do you want to leave?"

She glanced up with apology. "No! No, Jake. This is wonderful. I just felt a momentary wave of sadness. I'll be all right, especially since you're here with me."

I reached across the table and took her hand, stroked her knuckles with my thumb. "Lindsey, I will never leave you. We can get through anything that comes our way. We're a team, okay? A strong, loving team."

I went into the tiny kitchen to get two glasses of water and happened to glance in the fridge. I spotted a delicious-looking chocolate layer cake, but I decided not to bring it out yet. Our next course would be served in the bedroom. The cake would have to wait.

THIRTY-FOUR

Lindsey

The double bed was covered with a smoky-gray quilt about as thin as a postcard and decorated with faint traces of russet-colored deer. It appeared to be extremely old and worn. I leaned in, examining it, and wondered if the gray color was due to dust and dirt as well as age. Jake didn't seem to notice the state of the linen when he rolled back the quilt, but I did, and it wasn't good. Not that it was a 'used' kind of dirty, it was more like the bed hadn't seen much action or the inside of a washing machine in a very long time. Not unless you called dust falling from the old wooden walls, or dirt, pollen, and who knew what else blowing in through the cracks between the boards, action.

Just prior to our bodies making contact with the lackluster linen, I managed to ask, "Jake, honey? These sheets are a little dusty. Is there a blanket in the car?"

"Hold on. I'll go check."

I watched him try to exit through the front door, but it wouldn't open from the inside, either. This old place was cozy, rustic, and nicely private, but it was also in dire need of repair. After swirling the lock in every direction and adding a touch of brute force, he gave up and hurried out the side door. He soon returned with two blankets, thank God. He kept the tiny room's door open with the hope that a little warmth from the fireplace would find its way to us since the air in the bedroom was chilly.

"Now, where were we?" I asked playfully.

"Right about here," Jake answered as he helped me out of my sweater. "Or was it here?" He unsuccessfully tried to unhook my bra, and I whispered in his ear that he should try the front. He did, and we moved on.

"No, it was definitely here," he said smoothly.

My jeans were soon lying on the floor, and Jake removed most of his own clothing in about two seconds flat. Right away, he was done playing around and onto more serious moves. I was good with that. After all, what had it been? Six, seven, eight days since we'd last made love? I needed the physical contact as much as he did.

We slipped our almost naked bodies between the two blankets and began to kiss. I'm convinced Jake is the best kisser in the world. Before long we'd created enough of our own heat to make the top blanket unnecessary. Skipping many of our usual appetizers, we went quickly to the main course, since both of us were ready, both wanting and needing to reach the ultimate, lusty goal. We could always revisit and reignite our sweet, sensual lovemaking moves later.

Without Wendell and Malcolm nearby, I felt the freedom to make more noise than was typical for me. I don't know if Jake had the same thought, but he certainly was in tune with the action. The sounds of our breathing, our sighing, were connected by the rhythm of our bodies against the old mattress, which produced a loud rhythmic screeching, as if a dozen angry crows lay beneath us.

I'd never before experienced the sound of old bedsprings creaking beneath the movement and weight of two lovers. I found it terribly distracting. Jake must have sensed that, because before I could take another breath, he threw one of the blankets over the top of the door, closed it, and pulled me close. We leaned up against the door and continued our passionate sexual encounter in our newly invented *vertical* bed.

The sounds of passion returned, beating rhythmically against the wooden door. Our breathing eventually slowed slightly, but the noise continued. The pounding … the *pounding*?

"Jake!" I cried. "Jake!"

"Oh, Lindsey, my Lindsey!"

"No, Jake. Listen."

He slowed, his unfocused eyes trying to clear. "What?"

"Someone is knocking on the front door!"

Jake looked out the window, then looked back at me, his eyes huge. "Oh, my God. I think it's my sister. Why would Julie be here?" He frowned, puzzled. "Julie isn't … your surprise, is she?"

"My … surprise?"

We pulled on our underwear, wrapped ourselves up in the blankets, then ran to the door.

"Go around to the side," he called to Julie, so she did.

Julie was the first to ask, "What are *you* doing here?"

"Me?" Jake asked. "What am *I* doing here? I might ask you the same question."

"Yeah, but I asked you first, brother dear."

He wrapped the blanket around his waist and put his hands on his hips. "I'm here because my beautiful Lindsey invited me here. She arranged the whole thing."

"What?" I exclaimed, confused. "I didn't arrange anything. I thought you'd made all these plans and invited me to join you for a romantic evening."

He shook his head. "No, you're the one that sent me a FedEx envelope with an invitation, a plane ticket, a rental car reservation, and the driving directions to this cabin."

"No! I'm sorry, but I did not do that."

"Hold on," Julie said. She looked as confused as I felt. "I thought Sean had invited *me* here. I received an email from him stating that if I came to this cabin and arrived promptly at 7:00 p.m. he would tell me everything about his sexual transformation, the process, his feelings, his personal history, his entire life, *and* he would give his permission for me to publish his story in any of the psychiatric or mental health trades. He knew I wanted that, and he knew I'd come."

We were all speechless, our brains attempting to wrap around these inconsistencies.

"Sean inviting you here makes some sense," I said to Julie. "But let me get this straight. Jake, you did not invite me here, and I did not invite you here. So who did? Sean wouldn't want us to be here for his tell-all story, would he?"

"Someone wanted to get the three of us together, here in this remote spot. Who?" Jake asked. He frowned, thinking, then he muttered "Anthony."

"What do you mean, 'Anthony'?" I asked, completely confused now.

Jake took my hands in his. "Lindsey, do you remember when I told you I'd talked with the funeral director and the guy from the cemetery?" He glanced at Julie, then explained, "I wanted to figure out more about Anthony's death and burial because that didn't make any sense either."

228

Julie nodded. "I know. Sean told me you were all over that with your 'foul play' theories."

"Well," Jake continued, "I think I left out part of that conversation that might apply here. According to the cemetery guy, whoever arranged for Anthony's burial purchased space enough for *five* vaults and urns."

Julie's eyes grew wide, and panic fluttered through my chest. Julie had worked with troubled individuals all her adult life, and I could tell she didn't like what she was hearing.

"That's some serious stuff," she said. "I need some answers right now, or my mind is going to wander off to a place where I don't want to go."

Jake nodded. "I'm with you there. I'm not too fond of the paranoia that's hovering all around me right now. I'm beginning to think this entire situation, especially our presence at this cabin, is not just serious, it's dangerous."

I could barely breathe. "No one at the funeral home or the cemetery had a problem with that? With the unoccupied space in the plot?"

"Apparently it happens sometimes. People buy space in advance when they plan for others to be buried there sometime in the future."

"But, *four* others to be buried with Anthony?" Julie asked quietly.

Jake looked from Julie to me, and back again. "We could be three of the four. The only other person I can think of is Sean, but ..."

I blinked, unable to comprehend what any of this meant. "But if Sean is the one behind all of this, why would he include himself as one of the future burial site occupants?"

"I think," Julie added, "he did that to throw us off. That would give him more time to complete his plan, knowing he could have some fun scaring us to death. Or perhaps killing himself was part of his plan all along."

At best, we'd all been duped, lied to, and manipulated. Silent looks of trepidation clung like dried mud masks to our faces, and those masks were on the verge of cracking.

THIRTY-FIVE

Jake

Freezing. The outside temperature had reached that magic number. The cabin wasn't much warmer. We gathered closer to the small fireplace, the only heat source available, and I added three small logs to the dying coals. The night would, no doubt, be long and chilly. Lindsey brought out the last bottle of wine that had been left here—by whom?—and poured us each a glass.

"There's a chocolate cake in the fridge, if anyone wants some." My offer of dessert was declined. "Sure. We can eat it tomorrow after we figure out why the hell we are here. Hopefully we'll feel more like celebrating then." Right now, being anywhere but here would be a far better reason to celebrate.

"Maybe Sean is the mastermind of this rendezvous," Julie mused. "What if his message, his invitation to me was true, and he invited the two of you to be part of that?"

Lindsey and I looked at each other, then at Julie. Two of us shook our heads. No, that didn't seem reasonable.

"Think about it. If Sean had invited you both here, would you have come?" More head shaking. "Of course not. He would have felt the need to trick you into showing up."

We were grasping at straws; I knew that. And, as much as I liked a good mystery, I did not like being here. *We have cars; we can leave.* I suggested that as soon as we finished the contents of our glasses, we leave, drive away from this weirdness. We all agreed on that.

We were huddled by the fire, sipping the last of the wine, still trying to make sense of our situation, when the noise began. *Thud! Whack! Bang!* More pounding started up, but it was nothing like the pounding of making love against a door, or the pounding of Julie trying to get in. For a few seconds we sat paralyzed in shock, just listening until … the sudden silence set us in motion.

We all leapt to our feet at the same time. Julie was the quickest, since she had the advantage of clothing. Lindsey and I stumbled around, wrapped in our blankets. We concentrated on the locations of the pounding, and it didn't take long to discover that now, in addition to the front door being inoperable, the side door would not open. I smelled smoke and began to cough. We all did. I quickly checked to make sure the flue was opened properly and that the fireplace was not the cause of our coughing problem. The smoke thickened near the low ceiling looking like fog. My eyes stung, my throat began to burn. I knew Lindsey and Julie must have felt the same way.

"Break open as many windows as you can," I shouted.

I went to the closest window first and broke the glass, and that's when I discovered the windows were boarded up, too.

The cabin was on fire. We were trapped, and we were far from any kind of help. Someone meant for us to burn to the ground along with the building's dried out old timbers.

The three of us pounded and slammed anything and everything against the boarded up doors and windows, screaming for help.

I'd never experienced such fear. The love of my life, my sister, and I ... we were all going to burn to death. I remembered how much that one small match's flame had hurt my finger when I'd been lighting the fire, and I began to imagine what a blazing inferno engulfing my entire body would feel like. The thought was paralyzing. *Don't even go there,* I told myself. *Think. Make a plan. Solve this life-or-death problem.*

I could see an orange, flickering light glow through the cracks in the boards toward the back of the cabin. It wouldn't take long for this old pile of wood to burn down. The cabin itself was little more than a big stack of perfect kindling.

As I wallowed in fearful pity for us all, my sweet, delicate Lindsey took charge. "Well, I'm no Joan of Arc, and I'm not willing to die right now. Especially like this. Get in the bathroom and turn on the water."

We wet down the tiny room, doused ourselves, and put the two blankets, now dripping wet, under the door. It felt good to be doing something, but I couldn't help but wonder if we were only prolonging the inevitable.

THIRTY-SIX

Lindsey

Jake and his sister followed my directions and kept themselves and our tiny space soaked while I prayed for a miraculous thought, any idea that would keep us alive. My lifelong dream of having love, family, and the happily ever after was so close that I could almost reach out and touch it. I was certain it would come true someday soon … if I didn't burn to death right here in the bathroom of this cabin.

No. I must not think that way. I can survive; we *will* survive. *I think I can, I think I can* … climb out of that tiny little window up there. The window was so small the arsonist hadn't even thought it needed boarding up. Either that, or he or she hadn't noticed it.

"Jake! Julie!" I shouted. "I have an idea!"

I quickly explained my plan, ignoring the matching expressions of horror they wore.

"All you have to do is boost me up high enough, so I can break that little window and squeeze myself through it."

"But he's out there," Jake blurted. "He'll hurt you." He shook his head, looking desperate. I know he was only thinking of my safety, but we didn't have many options. As far as I could tell, we didn't have *any* options. "And all you've got on is soaking wet underwear. It's freezing outside."

I'd made up my mind. "It's our only chance," I said. "Give me your keys, Jake. I'll be careful. I can do this. Come on. Come on. Hurry!"

"The keys are in my pants, which are in the bedroom at the back of the cabin—"

"Never mind. I don't have time. Boost me up now! Yank off the showerhead. I need it to smash the window."

The brittle glass in the window broke easily, and I quickly scraped around the edges to remove as many of the broken shards as possible.

As I looked out to see what lay below the window, I heard Jake say, "Give her your pants, Julie. Or your shirt. Give her something. She's going to be running down a dirt road seeking help."

Moments later I was out, and Julie's pants dropped through the window right after me. I glanced through the dark but didn't see anyone or any cars, other than Jake's and Julie's. Still, I couldn't take the chance of being spotted by some crazy arsonist, if he was still around. Crawling like a marine, I dragged my wet body along the cold, hard ground—recalling briefly how I'd trained for this type of action in Wendell's blue agility tunnel. That helped take my mind off the cold, the pain, the fear. Once I was a good distance from the cabin, I jumped into Julie's jeans, and my bare feet raced down the rocky dirt road. All I could think about was saving Jake and his sister.

THIRTY-SEVEN

Jake

The fire warmed the bathroom walls until they were too hot to touch. Our diligent watering detail had kept the flames at bay, but we couldn't deny that smoke was a problem right now, and it wouldn't be long before the flames burned through. We both knew that.

Julie's voice shook when she tried to soothe me. "Jake, it might make you feel better to know that we'll be rendered unconscious from smoke inhalation before we are charred by the flames."

"Nope, I don't feel even the slightest bit better knowing that." For the hundredth time I looked back up at the window where Lindsey had last been seen. No way would I fit through that opening. "Julie, you should try to squeeze through the window. I'll help you."

She declined to try, insisting that she wouldn't fit through. Knowing this might well be the end for us, we held each other for a moment, creating a bond greater than we'd ever had before. Better late than never, I supposed.

We said our hellos and goodbyes, then we promptly resumed our water detail. Maybe, if the water held out—

She grabbed my arm. "Jake, listen! What is that? I think I hear a voice or voices outside."

She was right, though the voices didn't sound very close to the cabin. I was afraid it was Lindsey yelling, and that Sean—or whoever the arsonist was—had grabbed her. On the other hand, it could be help. Either way, we needed to attract their attention.

"Help! We're in here! Help! Help!" we screamed, banging on the wall with the broken showerhead and our fists.

The sounds came in earnest after that, and we listened to the yelling, pounding, and chopping—*chopping*? Yes, I could swear we heard chopping, outside the cabin wall. A firefighter? We stood back. As the sound got louder, thoughts of our rescue, our safety, our survival rose like bubbles, but they suddenly burst when the ax finally broke through. Sean stood on the other side of the broken wall, a crazed look in his eyes and an ax in his hands.

Which would be worse? Death by fire or death by ax? I had no idea. The wall fell, and our frantic voices were almost drowned out by the whooshing, roaring sounds of the fire as it reacted fiercely to the influx of additional oxygen. With the fire now upon us, burning at our backs, we had no choice but to move toward Sean. I shoved Julie out of the jagged opening the ax had created and right past the crazy SOB.

"Get to your car!" I yelled at her.

"I don't have keys! They were in my pants."

"Then run!" I shouted. "Run into the woods. Go! Go! I'll be right behind you."

Sean shouted something too, and I could swear it was, "Sorry I'm late."

We were out, and we ran for our lives. Panting, gasping for air, oblivious to the blisters forming on our backs and the smell of our singed hair. I looked over my shoulder just in time to see the cabin explode into a huge fireball. Julie and I kept moving, needing to put some distance between Sean, the fire, and us, and keeping a look out for Lindsey.

THIRTY-EIGHT

Lindsey

Lad did his best to comfort me as we emerged from his car, but we found ourselves hypnotized by the horrific, shocking sight before us. He placed his jacket around me for warmth, and I collapsed to the ground, sobbing, choking, then staring with disbelief as the flames shot toward the night sky. The cabin was unrecognizable. One fire truck—a compact tank pumper, according to Lad—had arrived just ahead of us, and the firefighters got right to work activating the hoses. I stared as they applied more water to the surrounding ground and trees than to the cabin.

"There are people in there! Two people!" I barely recognized the wailing sound coming from my throat. "You've got to save them."

I managed to pull myself up and would have run in vain toward the flames if Lad hadn't stopped me. He held me tightly in his arms, stroked my hair, and put his mouth near my ear so I could hear his words over the noise.

"Lindsey, if there was anyone still in that cabin, they're gone. It is entirely engulfed in flame."

The sound of additional emergency vehicles approaching was impossible to miss. Another rural firefighting truck, two ambulances, and three or four sheriffs' SUVs roared up the small gravel road, but I was numb with the realization that they were all too late.

Staring at the cabin's smoldering remains, hearing the sounds of charred timbers creaking, falling, and breathing in traces of acrid ash that hung in the air, I prayed for a miracle. That's what I needed, wanted, had to have—an incredibly divine miracle.

"Lindsey? Lindsey!"

I turned toward the sound of my name that was coming from a dark, wooded area. Two familiar figures rushed from the trees, and I stared, wondering if I was hallucinating—or seeing ghosts. The second I recognized Jake and Julie, Lad let go of me, let me run. Jake ran with his arms held out, and I dove into them, sobbing with relief.

"Lindsey," he said breathlessly, holding me close. "Oh, my God. Lindsey."

We didn't need words right then. We had each other. We were alive. We were *all* alive.

Julie stood next to Lad both watching the firefighters at work. He took one look at her pant-less legs and—being the take-charge kind of guy that he was—took off his sweater and tied it around her waist. There was nothing left for Jake to cover up with, well, except for my body. I did what I could.

We watched the blazing crime scene from a safe distance. Over a dozen firefighters, paramedics, and law enforcement personnel buzzed around, doing their jobs, and with the addition of the second fire truck, the fire's containment soon followed. The workers continued to douse the smoldering embers, adding to the dank, musty odor that now suffocated the usually fragrant scent of a forest in the wintertime.

Jake pointed toward a police car. "Look! Shawna—I mean Sean, is over there, next to the ambulance."

Sure enough, it was Sean. He had been detained and cuffed. *Good. They got him. And they don't even know the half of it.* We inched closer for a better view, and I noticed that Sean appeared to be arguing with the cops, shouting angrily and pointing toward the wooded area on the opposite side of the cabin's charred remains.

"Go see for yourself," he insisted. "The dead guy is over there. *He's* the one you want."

"Dead? You killed him?" asked one of the officers.

"Pfff … I wish," was Sean's sarcastic reply.

Even in the dark, we could see the perplexed expressions on the officers' faces as they glanced at each other, at Sean, then around the odd scene. We were all baffled and growing more confused with each passing moment. Still handcuffed, Sean was escorted toward the location of the 'dead guy.' He had an accomplice? And he was dead?

We followed the officer, who aimed his flashlight in the face of … of … Jake held me as I went limp with shock. Though his face was badly swollen and covered with blood, I could swear it was Anthony. It was too dark to know for sure. The thought of Anthony dying once was bad enough, but twice?

"Jake," I whispered. "He's moving. The man is moving. He's not dead."

Jake nodded, and I stared harder at the man's face. It had to be him. My gut twisted with so many emotions. "He's alive? Oh Jake! Anthony is alive and well!"

But Jake shook his head. "He may be alive, Lindsey, but he's definitely not well. And when I get to the bottom of this, everyone will know just what a sick, psychotic man he is."

I could see it in his eyes. The wheels in Jake's brain were spinning, rapidly. The difference this time was that I'd be on board with Jake every step of the way. We all wanted every detail of this bizarre puzzle put in its proper place. And though a huge puzzle piece had just been discovered, it appeared the puzzle itself was increasing in size.

"Get the bitch away from me," said the bloodied man, backing away from Sean. I stared at his cowering shape, incredulous. It was undeniably Anthony. "I want to file assault charges against her. Look what she's done to me."

Even in this dimly lit area, I could see the officers' confusion increasing. *Welcome to our lives*, I wanted to say, but I kept my mouth shut.

Turning to Sean, the officer asked, "Who is he referring to? What 'bitch' assaulted him?"

"Oh, that would be me," Sean purred, reverting back to the sultry female voice he'd used in his 'Shawna' days.

They stared at him, and I tried not to laugh at their bemused expressions. "Then can we assume *you* cuffed this guy and secured him to this old fence post?"

Obviously enjoying this brief resurrection of his past sexy, seductive ways, he answered, "Old habits are hard to break. Still don't go anywhere without my handcuffs. You never know."

Kindergarten teachers—any teachers, for that matter—see odd things all the time, but this scene, this crime, well, this went far beyond anything I'd ever seen or could imagine. It didn't feel real. Part of me was relieved that my ex-husband was not dead, but another part was in total shock at the things he had done, or at least tried to do. He *had* tried to kill me, kill us. Neither my head nor my heart was ready to wrap around that fact. And Sean had somehow ... *saved* us? Another difficult-to-grasp concept.

One of the officers brought us each a blanket. Now that the fire had been reduced to a smelly, smoldering pile of charred debris, the cold chilled me to the bone. The temperature in the mountains of Washington this December evening had to be below freezing, and frost was rapidly forming over the damp ground. Add to that our lack of clothing—Jake and I didn't even have shoes—and living through such a hellish experience, I wasn't surprised that our bodies trembled convulsively.

We were allowed to sit in Lad's car while we waited to be cleared to leave. He turned the engine on and the heat up high, but we left the car windows open, not wanting to miss any bits of information.

Sean was the first to leave. Julie noticed a paramedic helping him onto a stretcher and into one of the ambulances, so she hurried over to give him a hug along with words of encouragement. The fact that he was still cuffed and a police officer had gone along with him added to our ever-growing list of questions. Not knowing the details of the scuffle between him and Anthony, Jake and I surmised that he had sustained some injuries, though Anthony's injuries were far more obvious. We both knew that when Sean had posed as a sexy female, his punches carried quite a wallop, but since he'd been wearing pants instead of panties his strength had tripled. Jake could attest to that.

One of the officers asked the paramedics to check us out because we all had some minor injuries from our ordeal, but we declined. They took initial statements from each of us privately, and they were adamant that we not leave town since more questions would be forthcoming. Soon after that we were ordered to leave the crime scene. Luckily, Jake had found a spare key in the glove box of the rental car while Julie, Lad, and I stood talking, making plans to caravan back into Seattle.

We stared hypnotically as two officers escorted Anthony to the waiting ambulance. He turned toward us as he passed, sneering and snarling like a rabid dog.

"If the bitch hadn't been late," he informed us, "my plan would have worked. It was flawless. I'm not done, you know. Nobody messes with me and gets away with it. Nobody."

Jake's hands tightened into fists, but I was glad he used only words to express himself. "Hey, asshole," he said. "What kind of idiot plans a funeral to bury an empty box?"

Anthony's haunting reply echoed through the night air. "Who said the box was empty?" Then he threw back his head and laughed. His fiendish, maniacal cackling continued even as the ambulance pulled away.

After tonight, I was certain of just one thing. Evil does exist.

A WINTER WHITE KNIGHT

THIRTY-NINE

Jake

The cat was out of the bag. Anthony was alive and had been the mastermind of the attempted murder of Julie, Lindsey and me. Had he intended to kill Sean, too? I wasn't yet certain. Or, had his twisted mind intended to frame Sean for the arson as well as everything else? If he'd pulled that off, the mysterious Dr. Sommerfield could have remained dead and buried while getting away with anything—even murder. Hopefully, with the Seattle police on board, additional facts would soon be uncovered.

We drove back to Lindsey's hotel in silence, the air taut with introspection. What was my sister feeling about her client and all that had transpired, including the bombshell that had exploded tonight? Make that bomb*shells*. First, the odd, inexplicable gathering at the cabin, then the lockdown, the fire, Sean with his ax, and last but not least, Anthony ... in the flesh. Where had he been keeping himself all this time? How had he managed to hide from all the people in Tucson that knew him? I still felt that Sean must have played a part in the letters, the lies, for Anthony to realize his numerous nefarious deeds.

As Lindsey and I walked into the hotel's lobby, she looked up at me, her eyes pleading. "Let's stay someplace else."

"Sure. Whatever you want."

"I need a fresh start," she murmured. "I want to spend the night with you in a room that is not provided by the conference. I want a room that is *ours*."

"Do you want to go up and get some of your things?"

"No. Tonight all I need is you. We can go to my room tomorrow."

There was another hotel directly across the street. We got more than a few strange looks as we attempted to check in, probably because we had no luggage, no identification, no money, and not much clothing on our bodies in spite of the fact it was almost winter. Lindsey and I made a longtime homeless person look good.

"Put their room on my card." Lad had come up behind us, coming to the rescue once again. I didn't want his help, but I to admit that we certainly needed it right now.

"Thanks, man. I owe you one."

He nodded briefly, not showing even a flicker of emotion. He was one strange guy.

"Lindsey," he said, "I'll have some of your things sent over. And just so you know," he said, regarding my own lack of clothing—specifically my lower half, still wrapped in a blanket, "the credit card can be used for anything else either of you need tonight."

Maybe he wasn't so bad. "Thanks again," I said. "I owe you a lot more now."

Lad left without another word, and Lindsey and I went to up to our room. We were utterly exhausted, still reeling from the shock of the evening, and we reeked of smoke.

When we saw ourselves in the large closet door mirror, a whole new kind of shock set in.

"No wonder people stared at us," Lindsey said. "I'd have stared, too. Heck, I'm staring now."

We were covered head to toe in soot and dried mud, and Lindsey pointed out the burns on my back. I could deal with all that. But the sight of her scrapes, cuts, and bruises from squeezing out that tiny bathroom window, crawling over dirt, sticks, and rocks, then running down the road in her bare feet, hurt me deeply. Still, she never complained. My respect for her just kept growing.

Lindsey grabbed my hand and led me into the shower. We took turns carefully lathering each other with soap and shampoo, then we let the warm, comforting water rain down on our skin as we gently held each other.

"I guess I won't be going to the big meeting tomorrow morning with my signed contract," she said into my chest.

"Why not?"

"It was destroyed in the fire."

That didn't seem to be as big a deal as it sounded. "They can print out another copy. What did it say? We never had the opportunity to talk about it."

She shrugged. "I didn't have the opportunity to read it, so I don't know the details, but I do know Elisabeth was offering me a two year contract to continue on with the company, the conferences, and the creation of teaching products."

I let her be quiet for a while, then I asked, "Is that what you want to do?"

She shook her head, but she looked unsure. "I don't know. My priorities have changed. I need time to think, to heal, without so many distractions around."

I'd hoped she didn't consider me a distraction, though I know I had been. And she was right about needing some healing time after the unbelievable few months we'd just survived. I could only imagine how difficult and traumatic it had been for her, since all the weirdness revolved around her ex-husband.

"You, Jake, are my number one priority," she said right away, and I couldn't prevent a grin of relief from spreading across my face. "You, me, Wendell, and Malcolm—we're a family. The rest—our careers, our interests, our future—will come with time, when it's time."

I kissed her soft lips, wet from the shower, warm with love. I loved her so much. Life without Lindsey, would be no life at all.

As we dried off, my stomach began to growl. I was really hungry. "I could sure use a piece of that chocolate cake right now. Too bad it went up in smoke."

"Charred chocolate cake would not be anywhere on my list of treats, but I'll bet room service could bring up some delicious, fresh cake … and ice cream."

"I'll make the call."

That hit the spot. Once our energy was renewed, Lindsey and I continued talking about the bizarre chain of events that had monopolized our lives. Lindsey conceded that it all began the day we'd been notified of Anthony's passing. Why had it never occurred to me to consider the possibility that Anthony was not actually dead? If I had, this mystery might have been solved long before the near tragic fire occurred.

"I have a question for you, Lindsey. How did you get help from the police so fast?"

"It wasn't just me. It was Lad. He was parked down the road about a mile from the cabin, still keeping the company's investment safe, I guess. In my frantic state of panic, I accused him of stalking me."

Hmm. Great minds think alike.

"After that, he shared some information about his past just to get the 'stalking' idea out of my head. And … it was fascinating."

"Don't leave me hanging. What did he say?"

"I learned that he used to work for the Secret Service, which explains a lot about his personality. Apparently he'd been doing some investigating ever since the very first conference, when he noticed a few people in the audience who didn't seem to belong there. He increased his casual surveillance activities after the Sean incident in San Diego, but he said he found more questions than answers along the way."

"Exactly what I said," I interjected.

"I know! And the questions he found solidified the need for him to stay close to me." She shrugged lightly. "I think he misses his old government job. He confessed that he had no idea how exciting being the bodyguard for a kindergarten teacher could be."

I chuckled with her, then cocked an eyebrow. "Who were those people he kept an extra eye on?"

"I don't know. He didn't say. We were kind of distracted right then."

"I wonder why he left the Secret Service. From my perspective it seems like he could still handle the job." I frowned. "What's even more perplexing: why would he sign on to work for an *educational* company?"

A coy, mischievous twinkle sparked in Lindsey's sweet hazel eyes. "Ooh. Good question. A bit sinister. And we don't know the answer, do we?"

"Exactly! We don't know, but we *should* know. Someone should know."

"Then it seems your detective work isn't quite complete yet."

I liked knowing that she supported and encouraged me on the detective aspect now. I, too, had spotted some obvious holes which still needed filling. "You're right. You're absolutely right. And what about Anthony's *empty box* comment? Talk about sinister."

"I suppose you'd better get on that, Sherlock."

It was well after midnight, and we were both feeling drowsy. "Maybe tomorrow," I said, succumbing to my marrow-deep exhaustion. I had to admit I was relieved when Lindsey whispered, "Jake, could you just hold me tonight?"

"I'll hold you tonight and every night," I whispered back, gathering her in my arms.

FORTY

Lindsey

The delicious aroma of fresh coffee, and Jake's warm, firm body curled around me from behind was a perfect way to begin my day.

"Mmm. Good morning," I murmured. "Someone got up early."

He nuzzled the back of my neck. "Just long enough to call in our breakfast order and start the coffee maker. Now I'm back where I want to be."

With my arms above my head, I stretched from my toes to my fingertips and yawned as I transitioned from the darkness of sleep into the dawn of a new day. Memories of the night before returned though, and I wished I could make them disappear forever.

"Last night's events seem more like a nightmare than something real" I said. "At least it's over."

"Well, it's sort of over," Jake replied reluctantly. "You know, Lindsey, the questions from the police have only just begun. Once they hear about the previous months' weird happenings, we will be dealing with more investigations in Tucson, too. In my estimation, this thing is far from over."

"But we're safe, right? Anthony was responsible for everything—the fake funeral, the invitations to the funeral, the threatening letters, the cabin, the fire—"

"I *think* so. And, if that's the truth, I've got some serious apologizing to do. I was pretty tough on Sean."

"I'd say he was tough on you, too," I said, remembering his battered face and body last Thanksgiving.

He kissed my neck. "Are you ready for some coffee?"

I watched my naked man—we still had some clothes shopping to do—walk across the room to pour hot coffee into two cups. He didn't need to ask me what to add to mine, he already knew: a pinch of sweetener and a packet of creamer. I'd have to get along without my usual shot of chocolate. No problem.

The view was even better as he made the return trip to the bed. Coffee, a six-pack and ... *Hmm. Should we wait until after our breakfast arrived or take our chances? Decisions. Decisions.*

Perhaps Jake read my mind, or maybe it was my not-so-subtle tossing the covers to the side that got his attention. Anyway, we got hot and the coffee got cold. I felt safe and sexy with Jake's arms around me, and though his face was healing nicely from its encounter with Sean's fist a couple of weeks ago, we used caution when kissing on the lips. We didn't want to reopen any of his newly healed cuts. I threw caution to the wind, however, when kissing him elsewhere. *My* lips were fine.

Today Jake kissed me with his eyes. I was surprised at how my own eagerness for intimacy sprang from just a look. That was all I needed. One dreamy *I love you, I want you* look from Jake, and I was ready for him. He more than made up for the lack of lip action with his magnificent hands, which seemed constantly on a mission in search of my pleasure points. Waves of ecstasy pulsed through me, and before long … mission accomplished.

For two lovers with limited experience, we put our creativity and resourcefulness to good use. Every time we kissed, hugged, made love, or just held hands, we uncovered new secrets about each other's hearts, minds, bodies, and souls. Lifelong learning came naturally to both of us, and with intimate subjects like these we looked forward to our homework. I guess it's safe to say we even begged for extra credit assignments.

Our timing was perfect. One appetite completely satisfied, the other about to be. The hotel staffer who delivered our food apologized profusely for his lateness, and we accepted his apology while grinning at each other. His timing had been perfect, too.

Just when I thought the morning couldn't get any better, Jake got a dreamy look in his eyes. "You know I love you, right?" he asked. I nodded. "And you love me?" Another nod. "I want us to be a real couple, Linds. A family, forever."

Silence followed his words, though the dreamy look never left his eyes. He took my hands in his and asked, "Will you marry me? Will you be my wife?"

I suppose I should've been surprised, but I wasn't. In spite of all the recent, nightmare-like events, Jake's question felt exactly right. With a gentle, contented smile I said simply, "Yes."

Seconds later I was the naked one, stepping slowly across the room, feeling confident about the view, the vision on which Jake was surely focused. I wanted to gaze out at the morning sky, the low hovering clouds, a streak of sunlight breaking through, whatever might be visible on this memorable day, and just breathe. I had never been so happy to be alive.

"When?" he asked.

It occurred to me that someone had once said 'an engagement is not official without a ring and a date.' Maybe Jake had heard the same thing. Despite my surprise at his question, my answer came to me as soon as I saw the break in the dense cloud cover, allowing a peek at one of the mountain ranges.

"Jake, come look." He stood behind me, his strong arms wrapped snugly around me, and we gazed at the breathtaking sight. "It's snowing," I said gently. "It's snowing, right now, up there."

His affectionate hug and slow, tender sigh let me know that he remembered what I'd said months before about a white wedding. Thinking he might need a little time alone to mull over my response, I kissed him softly on the lips, then headed into the bathroom to take a shower. Had he hoped I would suggest a quick date, or was he sitting out there in shock, thinking me impulsive? Maybe he'd expected me to say, *How about June?* I'd soon find out.

As it turned out, my dear Jake had not only become a busy wedding planner while I'd showered, he'd also ordered a few items of clothing for each of us from the hotel's boutique.

"I need a little time to get things ready," he admitted. "How does four days sound? That would be, uh, Friday. Snow is in the forecast for the next seven days, either a little further east of Puget Sound or at elevations a bit higher. What do you think?"

What did I think? Oh, my! It was better than I'd dared to dream. "I think you're amazing. You're putting all the fairy tale princes to shame. But we'll keep it very, very simple, right?"

He nodded. "Sure. Leave it all to me. I want to take care of everything—except you'll need to go shopping for a dress. And, I insist that you splurge on it. Get something you love and that makes you feel like a princess."

"Oh, Jake. I don't need to splurge—"

Jake cut me off mid-sentence. "Yes. Yes, you do. Just this once. Don't even look at the price tag. I mean that."

I frowned. That seemed pretty extravagant. "But how—"

"Trust me, please. I insist. Buy whatever you want, but you must love it."

What on earth? "Okay, but … we're still keeping it simple, right, Jake?"

"Uh, sure. Except for your dress. So, get ready to go shopping. You won't see much of me today. Even a simple wedding takes some planning. I'll check out of here, and let's meet at your hotel room across the street for an early dinner. How does that sound?"

I laughed. "Too good to be true." I held out my arms and did a little spin, feeling dizzy with joy, and stopped just as the phone rang. "Hello?"

"Hey, are you two up and around already?"

I didn't recognize the voice. Maybe it was a wrong number. "Who is this?"

"It's Julie. Are you all right, Lindsey?"

I let out a breath, and my eyes flicked toward Jake. "Oh, sorry, Julie. How's your morning going?"

"Well, I'm afraid Lad has called us all together for a debriefing meeting. He says it's 'imperative' that we attend."

That was the last thing I wanted to hear. "Why would Lad call such a meeting?" I demanded.

"Um, could I please speak with Jake for a second?"

I handed him the phone but just shrugged when he mouthed "What is it?" I wanted to get dressed, but I didn't want to miss anything here, either. So I sat on the bed and watched his reaction to the phone call.

"Hey, Julie. What's up?"

He frowned while she spoke. "Why?" he asked. His lips pressed together, and he rolled his eyes, showing me he wasn't pleased either. "Okay, fine. We'll be there."

She spoke some more, and he lifted an apologetic hand as if she were in the room. "I know, I know. I'm sorry. You're just the messenger. But why Lad? Why is he so involved? I don't get that part. In fact, I think his butting into Lindsey's personal life is fast becoming downright inappropriate."

She said something, and Jake's posture sagged. "Fine. See you in an hour."

I'd been in this room just two days earlier for a meeting with Elisabeth, some conference participants, and members of the staff. This morning, however, it was set up with only four chairs around a small table. A rolling cart topped with water, juice, coffee, and bagels was parked beside it. Otherwise, the room was empty. I didn't want to be there, didn't want to talk about the fire, Anthony, or anything else having to do with … any of it. What could Lad possibly need to talk about?

"Grab some coffee, and let's get started," were Lad's first words.

"I've spoken with Seattle law enforcement. Everyone in this room will be questioned again with regard to the fire, but some of that will be done using FaceTime or Skype after you are back home, wherever home is. They don't have jurisdiction in other cities, let alone other states, so their only interest at this time is the fire. Arson charges are being filed against Anthony right now."

Jake and I had already determined this was far from over. Yes, the local authorities' interests lay only with the fire, but Lad said we should tell them everything we'd experienced from the time we received our invitations to the cabin up to the arrival of the firefighters, paramedics, and police.

Jake leaned closer and whispered in my ear, "Wow! He talks." I responded with a faint poker-playing smile and a small, cut-it-out kick under the table.

"The police discovered several articles of clothing and wigs—items I would call *disguises*—in Anthony's car, which was found about a half mile from the cabin in a thick grove of junipers. I got a good look at Anthony as well as some stills and video footage taken before, during, and after your keynote addresses, and I am fairly certain that he attended every one of them, Lindsey."

My brain played back some of those past creepy feelings of being watched, and it made sense, somehow, that the feeling had emanated from Anthony. But why? For what purpose? What did he stand to gain by watching me present my elementary art and writing process?

Jake interrupted. "You got to see Anthony close up as well as the contents of his car? They let you see all that?"

Before Lad could respond, I blurted out, "Well, of course. Lad used to be in the Secret Service."

Julie stared at me, obviously astonished, and from the look on Lad's face, he regretted having sharing that information with me. Apparently, that was a fact he had not wanted people to know.

"Here is what you need to know," he grumbled, moving on despite my error. "I am not yet sure how long Anthony will be in custody. It might not be very long if he can make bail, which will likely be less than $5000 here in Washington. From what I've learned so far, this guy is dangerous."

I was pretty sure Jake was rolling his eyes at that comment. His foot had begun to tap the floor.

"I need contact information from all of you," said Lad, "and I will give you a way to reach me as well. We will obtain restraining orders against Anthony, if that becomes necessary. If you should see him or receive anything from him, contact me immediately."

He passed out cards that included his first name, a phone number, and the word 'FIRE.' We were instructed to call or text that number and say or write FIRE along with the last three digits of our own callback number, and Lad would get back to us quickly.

"I also insist that you keep all information associated with Anthony to yourselves. If you feel the need to talk with someone, you may talk with each other or call me. Got it?"

I was outwardly speechless.

Jake on the other hand, spoke right up. "So I guess what happens in Seattle, stays in Seattle?"

No one chuckled. He received another kick and no smile of any kind from me. That didn't stop my Jake, though.

"I do *get it*, Lad. What I don't get is why you think he might be released from custody so soon. Yes, it was without a doubt arson, but don't the members of law enforcement here get that it was also *attempted murder*? He tried to kill Julie, Lindsey, and me. Maybe even Sean, too. Come on. He trapped us in that cabin and boarded up every possible avenue of escape before setting it on fire. It is plainly attempted murder. He should not be released under any circumstances."

"I understand what you're saying, Jake, but there is no identifiable evidence of that yet."

Poor Jake. His frustration had become indignant anger. "But they have three eyewitnesses!"

"Not really. Did you see him do anything at all? No, you didn't. You just heard pounding. Perhaps Sean saw something. That's your only hope with regard to eye witnesses."

Lad asked Julie and me to leave while he tied up a few loose ends with Jake. I didn't mind. My two alpha dogs needed a few minutes to settle their differences without my presence.

"I'll meet you back at the room, Jake. Okay?"

He calmed down long enough to give me a reassuring wink and say, "I'll be right there."

He didn't want me to worry, but I worried anyway. The seriousness of our situation was beginning to sink in. Like he'd tried to tell me earlier, it wasn't over yet.

FORTY-ONE

Jake

I wasn't all that fond of Lad, and he probably knew that. But we had a few things in common. For example, we needed to find the truth, and we needed to keep Lindsey safe. I'd try to be nice, at least cordial, and I hoped he'd do the same.

"Jake, I know you've been unofficially investigating the events surrounding Anthony, beginning with his funeral. I commend your intuition and tenacity. I want you to be aware of the fact that Sean has not yet been cleared of wrongdoing. He doesn't know that, and I don't want him to know that until after the investigations have been completed and the guilty have been incarcerated."

Listening to Lad calmly speak of the possibility of existing dangers sent chills up my spine. I'd hoped the worst had passed, and we could stop looking over our shoulders, but apparently that was not the case. At least not yet.

"There was a point when I suspected Sean of everything, including killing Anthony," I admitted. "I'm relieved to know he didn't do that and to know there are no murderers among us. But don't you think the fact that he was in San Diego when Lindsey received her threatening letter was just a little too coincidental?"

He nodded. "Yes, it was. But listen, Jake, I don't want you to let your guard down. I'm not yet convinced there are no murderers among us. Please continue with your perseverance when it comes to Lindsey's safety. To be frank, I think Anthony may be released on bail within a matter of days. And, as you probably already know, restraining orders on crazy perps are of little use. The way I see it, we're dealing with at least two crazies. Stay close, stay vigilant, stay in touch."

Did Lad know anything about Anthony's bizarre childhood behavior? Had he ever spoken with either Hank or Katie? I assumed not, but Lad was full of surprises. Oh, well. Since we were going 'stay in touch,' this could be a topic for another day. I would call Anthony's parents after this meeting, though, and give them the disturbing news about their adopted son. They'd have to resume looking over their shoulders, too, and more intently than ever.

I thanked Lad for confiding in me and for his concern about Lindsey's safety, and we walked toward the door.

"Do you have any questions?" he asked.

"Uh, yes. Why did you leave the Secret Service?"

His eyes flitted away. "That's classified."

Next on my agenda was planning Lindsey's fairytale, white wedding. This would be a challenge—not exactly up my alley, but I would handle it. I decided to approach the task by asking myself what Lindsey would do if she were in charge, and I knew the first thing she'd do would be to create a To Do List. Personally, I'm more of an Outline kind of guy.

So, after checking out, and knowing that Lindsey was busy shopping, I sat in the corner Starbucks with my new cell phone and completed my outline in about fifteen minutes, with the help of a double espresso.

1. Find Location
2. Make Guest List / Invite
3. Call Caterer / Order Flowers / Find Minister
4. Rent a Tux / Buy Rings
5. Hire Trio from Austin (call my old buddy Zack)
6. Make Travel/Hotel Arrangements

For the first time in my life, I was willing to splurge. And with the mindset that money was no object, miracles were possible.

I found and confirmed the location: a quaint, remodeled lodge about forty miles northeast of the SeaTac International Airport. They were about to shut the place down for the winter, but they agreed to stay open until after our wedding. I got real lucky on the location because we could have both the ceremony and the reception right there. I reserved it, sight unseen, except for a quick glance at their online website. There I saw a rustic, log and cedar, two-story lodge with old stone steps leading up to the double-door entrance, surrounded by mid-sized pines and a few leafless deciduous trees. Larger pines could be seen off in the distance. The lodge's owner assured me there would be snow on the ground, fire in the fireplaces, and views of the nearby hills. We'd need a break in the clouds to see the higher, snow-capped peaks, though. They could not guarantee that.

This last minute, out-of-state wedding in the month of December might prove to be difficult for some of the people I wanted to put on our guest list. I'd invite my parents, of course, and my three best friends from Austin if they were still around. The rest of the guests were Lindsey's friends or colleagues. Well, mostly. I picked up my phone and took a breath for courage.

"Hi Laura. It's Jake."

"Jake? Oh my God. What's the matter? You're supposed to be way up north in Washington right now."

"I am in Washington, and a lot *was* the matter—a fire, attempted murder, Anthony is alive—but we are all okay now. I was calling to see if—"

"Jake, back up. You're not making sense. Anthony is *alive*? What? That's not funny."

I did back up, and I explained some of the gruesome facts of our night from hell, but there wasn't time to go deep into detail. I had a wedding to plan.

"Married? You're getting *married*? Isn't that a little fast?"

Laura's voice was saturated with skepticism, but I gave her the benefit of the doubt. I supposed that hearing about the traumatic evening and her best friend's wedding in the same short conversation was a little too much to digest comfortably.

"Yes, we are getting married. And we want you to be Lindsey's Maid of Honor. Will you do it? I'll take care of all your travel and hotel arrangements."

Time was of the essence, and Laura's reply was slow in coming. "Jake, it's just that everything is happening so *fast*. These things take time to plan."

"Well, the wedding is this Friday. Will you or won't you? I've got to know because making your plans will be complicated and—"

"Yes. Yes, of course. I would love to be Lindsey's Maid of Honor. What am I supposed to wear?"

"Uh, how about something velvet?"

"I need to talk with Lindsey," she said flatly. "You're not much help."

"You can't talk with her. Do *not* call her. The wedding I'm planning is ... kind of a surprise."

She hesitated. "She does know she's getting married though, right?"

"Come on, Laura. Give me a little credit. Also, you need to call Judy Lopez ASAP and see if she can come with you. She'll need to get a sub for her class, and you will both need to leave together tomorrow. I will call you back in an hour with all the details."

"But—"

I was already inputting my next number. No time to waste. I had over a dozen calls to make just from my initial guest list. I'd ask a few folks on my list to make some additional calls. All in all, if every invited guest attended, we'd have close to forty people at our simple little wedding.

But it was going to take more than just filling a guest list. Within a couple of hours, I gave in to my unrealistic, self-imposed expectations and enlisted my sister's help.

"You're getting *married*? Here? Now? After all that's just happened? Oh, I wish you'd wait."

Julie's tone was one of surprise and disapproval, which was disappointing. I had hoped for joy and jubilation. Oh, well. She'd come around.

"Why wait?"

"Oh, I don't know. Let me see. It is way too soon, and you just experienced a true life and death situation. Those are two good reasons to start with."

"Exactly! You never know what tomorrow will bring, if it comes at all. Got to live in the present, the *now*. What do you say? Are you in?"

With obvious reluctance she sighed but asked, "How can I help?"

Though she'd never planned a wedding, she had thrown a party or two. With a little coaxing, she agreed to find and call a caterer and a florist. "What is the theme? Or at least the colors?"

I had no idea. I supposed I should, though. "You need to know that?"

"Yes, unless you want a hodge-podge of stuff that doesn't go together."

"No, I certainly don't want a hodge-podge." I had no idea what she was talking about.

"Okay. Well, I can proceed if you know the color of Lindsey's dress."

"She's shopping for her dress as we speak. Can I call you back on that?"

"Sure, if you can do that before businesses close for the day. If not, I'm going with a black and white theme. At least it won't clash with anything."

"Sounds like a plan." I shared the known details of my surprise wedding so Julie could get right to work. "Oh, just one more thing," I said. "Do know where Sean is staying? He must be somewhere nearby. I'm positive the police would have given him the same 'do not leave town' edict they gave the rest of us at the scene of the fire."

"That's easy. Sean's in the room across the hall from me. We had a long talk last night. In fact, he stayed in my room, said he was too upset to be alone. I couldn't say no." She chuckled. "I have to admit, it was really weird seeing him unwrap those voluptuous, expensive breasts he'd been so proud of, showing them off every day at work, while he was in the process of becoming a woman. He told me he wouldn't have to do that much longer. I think he really does want to revert back to total manhood, as unusual as that would be. He's had a hellish life, that's for sure."

"Hey, Julie. Do you think … do you think he would be my Best Man? Or would that be too strange for him— or for anyone else?"

"Right now, Jake, everything is strange. Everything is weird. Are you sure you want to do that?"

"To be honest, I really don't know. Maybe. What I do know is that Sean did not kill Anthony, and it appeared he tried to save us at the cabin by pummeling Anthony and chopping the hole in the wall for us to escape through. The tough part is we don't really know his motives or his intentions." I sighed. "But it is possible I've been wrong about his criminal participation all along."

Julie said she had no idea how he might respond to that request, but she'd ask him when they got together for lunch.

I gave her my credit card number to use for any of the payments or purchases, then continued with my other calls. First I called Lindsey's cell phone, forgetting momentarily that it had been destroyed in the fire. Damn. I did not like that, but what could I do? I was the one who had insisted she go shopping. Now she was out there all by herself with no way of contacting me or anyone else: the first flaw in my plans for today, and it was a big one.

FORTY-TWO

Lindsey

The morning was cool, damp, and overcast. In other words, it was a typical December day in the Seattle area, and the exact opposite of the weather in Tucson. Here my skin glistened with a soft dewiness. In the desert I'd hide from the sun and still maintain a light, unwanted tan. There I only felt dewy when sitting under a mister. The differences teased a slight giggle out of me as I dashed into another bridal wear shop—shop number four on my list.

A woman greeted me warmly, introducing herself as Betty, and asked if I was looking for anything special. "Well, yes. A wedding dress. One that a princess might wear."

"Are you looking for a white wedding dress or do you have another color in mind?"

I knew what I didn't want. "Definitely not solid white." I had trouble articulating what I *did* want, though. "But ... not too dark either."

The woman brought out a rack of pastel dresses for me to look at just as the other shops had done, but most of them looked like old-fashioned, spring prom dresses. I slumped, disappointed. What should have been a joyful and exciting time was frustrating and creeping toward depressing. I was getting nowhere. Maybe we were rushing things. I knew that some women took years to plan their weddings, and I guessed this dress shopping experience could be one of the reasons why.

The shop clerk escorted me to a comfortable sofa and handed me a warm cup of Zodiac Tea for Aquarians—how had she known my sign? On the table next to where I sat, she set a stack of bridal books and even a few fashion magazines.

"Honey, if you see anything you like even a little, show me. We can mix and match, modify, accessorize. You name it, I can do it."

"My wedding is Friday," I blurted, apologetically.

"Oh! That makes it difficult, but not impossible."

I think I sat on that sofa for almost two hours, searching through photos of long dresses. I did find a solid white dress, described in the magazine as a 'winter snow queen's taffeta ball gown' and I loved it. But I didn't want to wear a solid white dress. I showed Betty the photo, and I shared my concerns.

"That's not a problem," she assured me, her eyes riveted on the dress. "We'll just add some color accents using additional fabric. I recommend using layers of sheer tulle and a few subtle accents of velvet, considering the time of year. What color would you like?"

"I'm not sure. I love the colors of the desert, but they are mostly warm colors. That doesn't feel right to me, here in chilly Washington among so much green."

"That is a good point, and you've given me an idea."

Calling this woman a shop clerk was a terrible misnomer. She was a creative, talented, magical seamstress. After asking me a few questions about my likes and dislikes—including but not limited to clothing— she felt she knew me well enough to design the perfect dress. She was able to use one of the solid white dresses she had in stock, and I saw that with a few minor modifications it would resemble the dress in the magazine that I'd liked so much. She dashed off a sketch of the dress, adding the color I'd desired.

Tears of joy welled in my eyes as I saw the perfect gown for my wedding appear before me. To that dress she'd added fanciful layers of sheer, forest green tulle to the skirt, and a feathery looking, white, off-the-shoulder shrug with splashes of green velvet and golden chiffon. I would have a custom designed, one of a kind, winter wedding dress with rich, sheer color, revealing the beauty of the white dress. I loved it! Just looking at this drawing made me feel like a princess. Not a Cinderella princess but a… oh, I don't know… maybe a woodsy, sexy, gypsy princess. Yes, that was it. And, I knew Jake would love it, too.

The night before the wedding, Jake and I drove to the lodge he'd chosen for our tiny, private ceremony. It was absolutely perfect. He had arranged it all—well, except for the six inches of crunchy, sparkling snow on the ground. I didn't think he could take credit for that. He'd even called Laura, asking her to come up from Tucson so I'd have a friend to help me get ready and to be one of the witnesses. Every time I looked at Jake my love for him grew. I couldn't ask for a more handsome, thoughtful, wise, fun-loving man. Putting the past behind me, I felt like I was the luckiest woman in the world.

He'd rented two rooms for us. Being a somewhat traditional guy, he thought we shouldn't sleep together the night before our wedding. We did have dinner together in the dining room, though, and Laura joined us. She was staying in one of the cabins just down the lane from the main lodge.

I'd hoped he'd change his mind and be willing to take a quick look at my dress. I so wanted him to see it, in spite of the wedding dress tradition.

"No," he repeated. "I do not want to see your dress before the wedding. I want to be surprised. It's almost too much that you told me about the color."

I nudged him with my elbow. "Uh, Jake? You made me tell you about the color, remember?"

Laura had been listening to our back and forth chatter during most of the meal, and now she jumped into the conversation. "I have to remember to recharge my camera so I can snap a few photos of the newlyweds tomorrow. Also, Lindsey, we should go over every minute of your day leading up to the ceremony."

I flapped a hand at her. "Oh, Laura. You're beginning to sound like Jake. How complicated can it be? We wake up, shower, eat some breakfast, relax, maybe read, put on my dress, fix my hair, and get married."

"Okay. But remember, Jake can't see you till the ceremony. That adds an element of complexity."

Seeing my slight frown, Jake spoke up. "Lindsey, you're okay with not seeing me until tomorrow at two o'clock, right?"

It was so adorable, the way he wanted to be true to the traditional approach. "Of course, Jake, if that's what you want."

When our after dinner drinks arrived at the table, Laura and I reminisced about the winter break vacation in the Grand Canyon we'd taken almost a year before. Now it was Jake's turn to listen. He was attentive to our stories for a while, but I could see his eyelids growing heavy, almost shutting as we spoke. We knew he wasn't bored—nothing about that trip had been boring. He was simply exhausted.

"We should call it a night," I suggested. Jake and Laura nodded their approval, then I blurted out, "Wait! Who's watching Wendell and Malcolm?"

The look of uncertainty on their faces was not what I'd hoped to see, and their answers were even more troubling.

"A friend is staying with them at my place," was Laura's reply, though I thought I'd missed a word or two because Jake's answer, "Laura took them both to an excellent kennel," was spoken at the same time.

"No, Jake," Laura said quickly. "I talked you out of boarding the guys."

"Oh, yeah, that's right. I've been so busy, I forgot. Okay, you two. Just one final thing before we really call it a night. We need to make a deal to keep silent about the whole fire, Anthony, crime stuff. I do not want to hear any of those strange and gory details spoken at our wedding."

"Not a problem," I said. "I certainly don't want to think about any of that."

"You can count on me. I don't even know all the details yet."

"Thanks, Laura."

I invited Laura to stay in my room with me for the night. It had two queen-size beds, so we'd be comfortable, and it would feel like old times. Jake walked us to my room, but Laura made some lame excuse about needing to go back to her cabin for just a few minutes. She didn't fool me. I knew she was giving Jake and me a little *alone time* as we said good night on the eve of our wedding day.

In the morning, Laura handed me off to Julie, saying she needed to check on the status of the ceremony. That made me laugh, since there really wasn't anything to be done. I was ready, except for slipping into my dress, which I'd do at the last minute. With nothing to discuss, we sat in silence, gazing out the window at the lightly snow-dusted pine trees. Julie, an Oregon girl since her college days, was used to the cold. She'd come prepared. She'd left her bag of personal items in her car when she'd arrived at the infamous cabin, so none of her things had been destroyed in the fire. She had, however, purchased a new pair of black wool slacks, a lace-trimmed silk blouse, and a forest green cashmere sweater to wear to our wedding. She looked lovely, and it was nice to have at least one family member here. She would be the other witness.

Julie and I had little in common other than her brother, and even that connection felt somewhat strained. She seemed to know a different Jake from the one I knew. Maybe their terse conversations were merely sibling rivalry, or it could have been due to the lack of quality time together. I knew that family dynamics varied greatly; I'd seen that with children at school. I had little experience with my own family dynamics. My mother and father were both gone before I'd even known there was such a thing. And my foster families? They didn't count. At best, they were mistakes to which I'd been subjected.

Julie broke the silence. "I'm glad to see that Jake has given up being so cheap for a few days. It's about time."

That was unexpected. "I don't know about that, Julie. I've always admired his economizing ways. I think he's practical and sensible, not cheap."

"Hmm," was her only response. I got the impression she wanted to say more, but she chose not to. So silence reigned once again. I took slow, deep breaths trying to calm the slight jitters that tickled my chest, while Julie kept checking the clock on cell phone.

"Okay. It's time." Awestruck, witnessing the transformation of myself as I changed from my simple robe to an amazing gown, I was at a loss for words. This gown was far too fancy, far too expensive for this small ceremony, but I loved it. And I loved Jake even more for insisting I get it.

Julie walked with me to the interior wooden double doors just off the lobby of the lodge. "You'll need to walk down an aisle," she said gently. "Are you okay with doing that by yourself?"

I frowned. "Oh, Julie. Don't be silly. Of course I am."

"I was just thinking about the traumatic week you'd had, the whirlwind wedding arrangements." She grinned, looking down. "And then there's the shoes. Come on. How often do you wear high heels like that? I know *I'd* need a helping hand."

"Thanks, but I'll be fine. I've had some recent practice walking in shoes like these."

Julie stepped away, not entering through the double doors, and I assumed there was a side entrance, too. Just before she turned the corner she said, "As soon as you hear the music, walk on in."

"The music? Wait! There's music?"

But Julie was already out of sight. I smiled. My Jake, my darling Jake wanted to make this day, our sweet little wedding, as perfect as possible for me. Now I couldn't wait to hear which CDs he'd chosen to play.

The lobby was so quiet, so still, with not a soul around. I waited, alone, for my musical cue, and I had to admit to myself that I felt a touch nervous. Unwanted thoughts of my first wedding—with Anthony—snuck into my mind. That had been small, too, with just Anthony, the minister, a photographer, and me. I hadn't been nervous then, but I'd had several months to plan for that day, get used to the idea. Also, there'd been no horrific, terrifying event happening just a few days prior. I rationalized my nervousness and, at the sound of the music, was able to put those past thoughts to rest.

I took another deep, cleansing breath, then reached out to open the door. Suddenly, both doors were opened for me and I stepped into the room and gasped. Technically speaking, it wasn't just a 'room.' I'd walked into a total *environment*. Jake had created an old-fashioned, northwest winter wonderland, twinkling with tiny white lights, bows of pine branches, flowers, and … people! There were *guests* at our wedding. I froze, surveying the room, not able to comprehend what I saw. From my vantage point I couldn't see everything or everyone, but I did spot a live trio playing the music. Seated in rows of small white chairs were Mrs. Madera, Mrs. Wilson, Judy Lopez and three other teachers, Elisabeth Meriwether and several of the company's key staff members, and others I did not know. Oh, my! The dizziness. I almost lost my balance, but was immediately steadied by Lad.

He held my arm and whispered in my ear, "You look lovely. Come on. Everyone is waiting for you." He handed me a dainty, rustic, wintry bouquet made of white roses, miniature pinecones and tiny evergreen sprigs. "Ready?"

Unable to speak, I gave a nod.

The trio began playing the traditional *Bridal Chorus* by Wagner, and though it was recognizable, it sounded anything but traditional. I loved their jazzy rendition. Lad escorted me down the aisle, and I took the first few wobbly steps, chanting silently to myself, *I think I can, I think I can, I know I can.*

Then I froze again; would the surprises never end? There was Wendell standing proudly between Jake and

Sean, wearing the biggest smile I'd ever seen on his face. *Oh, Wendell. You're here at our wedding.* I couldn't hold back the tears of joy, of relief, of ... everything. Lad and I stood without moving for a moment, and he handed me a lace-trimmed handkerchief. The trio kept playing, and I focused my attention on Jake, my soon-to-be husband, then floated effortlessly toward him.

Lad left me at the altar with Jake. I'd never felt so safe, so loved, or so incredibly happy in my entire life. Laura stood to my left, Jake to my right, then Wendell and Sean to his right. The lighting in the room was dimmed just enough to allow the tiny white lights and flickering candles to create an ambiance fit for a princess's wedding. The ceremony itself, the words we spoke, were traditional, but everything else was ... unusual, unique. Exactly right.

Only one slight annoyance occurred: Laura's cell phone vibrated during the beginning of the ceremony, creating a buzzing noise. I doubted the sound traveled far, but we heard it, and probably everyone in the front row heard it, too. Too bad Malcolm wasn't with us; some of his sweet chirping right then could have camouflaged the noise. Laura's hand flew to the small pocket in her dress, and she struggled to silence the buzz.

When it was time, Sean handed Jake the wedding ring to place on my finger. It was a beautiful, narrow titanium band holding seven small, brilliant diamonds, and it was a perfect fit. Oh, no. The realization thumped me on the head. It was my turn to place a ring on Jake's finger, and I hadn't purchased one. I hadn't even thought about rings. Then Laura, looking lovely in a knee length, forest green velvet dress, handed me a ring. Except for being wider, it matched my band. Jake truly had thought of everything.

Then Jake whispered in my ear that there was another big surprise. I watched as he untied one of the velvet bows from Wendell's neck and removed something that had been attached there. "I hope you don't mind that the order of the rings is a little … extraordinary," Jake said with a knowing smile, placing a second ring on my finger. "This is your engagement ring."

I giggled a little just before the tears returned. It was the most beautiful ring I'd ever seen: a heart-shaped emerald, matching the forest green color of my dress. Sparkling diamonds surrounded the gem, adorning a band that snuggled up perfectly against the wedding ring.

Then came the words. "With the authority invested in me by the state of Washington, I now pronounce you husband and wife. I believe some kissing is called for right about now."

We were still kissing when the trio began to play Beethoven's *Ode to Joy*, Austin, Texas style. It was only when I heard the vigorous chirping behind us that our lips parted. I turned to see my little white bird, Malcolm, in his cage, a green bow tied to the top. My friend, Judy, sat in the front row with his cage on her lap, and I saw its cover folded by her feet. That explained why my little bird hadn't sung earlier, giving himself away. I turned back to Jake, and I could see that he was delighted by my unmistakable joy.

As we made our way back up the aisle—first Jake and me, then Laura and Wendell, followed by Sean—our friends tossed white rice and white rose petals in the air around us, like a beautiful, soft, fragrant snowstorm.

Finally, a day in our lives in which everything, absolutely everything, was perfect!

FORTY-THREE

Jake

Lindsey literally glowed with joy, leaving me at a loss for words worthy of describing her. She was my angel, my delicate rock, my partner, my woman—and now, my wife. I wanted to love, cherish, and protect her forever. I'd never thought I'd be capable of experiencing the feelings that possessed me today.

And to think that if I hadn't taken that job delivering Chinese food while working on my thesis, Lindsey and I never would have met. But I had taken that job, we had met, and this miraculous, incredible day was upon us. Sometimes, fate was a good thing.

When we got to the end of the aisle, Julie placed us next to the lobby's large, stone fireplace, and Laura organized the line of guests that had begun to move toward us. My parents were the first to approach. We had never been a close family, but we'd never had any huge problems, either. This would be my first face-to-face meeting with them in over a year. Mother, Father, and Lindsey had never met before, and I wondered how it would go. Would they approve? Would they think me crazy? Had they developed—or would they at least fake— a little warmth?

"Ready or not, here come your new in-laws, Lindsey." I hugged my parents when they reached us. "Lindsey, this is my mother, Evelyn, and my father, Edward."

She beamed at them both. "Evelyn, Edward, I am so happy to finally meet you. Your son is an amazing man."

I don't know why I'd bothered to worry. Lindsey charmed them, had them instantly under her spell. It was as if they'd known each other forever. They hugged, they cried, then they hugged again. I think they'd still be giving each other warm, heartfelt hugs if Laura hadn't intervened, coaxing my parents to a table filled with some pre-reception fancy finger food and punch.

Next came Lindsey's friend and colleague, Judy Lopez. "You look so beautiful, Lindsey. And this wedding? Oh, my. It's beyond belief. Thank you for inviting me. The trip, the drive was the best vacation I've ever had."

"You drove all that way? What about school?" Lindsey asked.

"School?" She cheerfully waved off Lindsey's concern. "I haven't used any of my personal days in years. It was time to use a few of them. And, yes, Laura and I drove here in that magnificent motor home." Judy looked over and winked at me. "How else would Wendell and Malcolm have gotten here?"

"Oh," Lindsey said, laughing. "I hadn't had time to think about that. I was just so glad to see them."

Lad, Elisabeth, Sarah, and three other key staff members stood in front of us. Lindsey knew all of them, so I was the one who needed introductions. Mrs. Wilson and several other teachers followed the conference crew, and they, too, gave me a wink after explaining to Lindsey that they had all flown up to the wedding together. Mrs. Madera and two of her best friends—who had also been Anthony's patients—were next. More winking. This winking had to stop! Then again, I supposed it was better than having to stall the reception and explain all the details of their travel and hotel arrangements to Lindsey.

Neither Lindsey nor I knew the names of the next seven guests, so they had to introduce themselves. They were firefighters, police, and paramedics, and the one thing we had in common with them was that we had all been at the cabin fire. That's when it dawned on me that the other guests might wonder who they were and why they were here. Those conversations I'd put a ban on would likely rise to the surface eventually.

The only guests not in line were Sean—my Best Man—and the band, who were my three friends from Austin. We'd do introductions later. I glanced around, wondering where Sean had gone. I'd hoped he'd be highly visible during the remainder of his time in Washington. Especially at the wedding festivities, since Lad's recent warnings about Sean's possible involvement with Anthony's crimes had me concerned. Sticking to the old saying: *Keep your friends close and your enemies closer*, I knew I'd feel better if I could see where Sean was and what he was doing right now. I didn't think I could take any more bombshells, and I didn't want anything to spoil this day for Lindsey. So, though I was all smiles, I remained on ultra-high alert.

While we mingled with guests in the lobby, the skeleton crew from the lodge and the caterers from town were transforming the ceremony room into the reception area. Julie and Laura opened the double doors and invited everyone but Lindsey and me to enter. The reception was almost all Julie's invention. I think she wanted me to experience a few good surprises of my own. So Lindsey and I stood by the fireplace, wrapped in each other's arms, waiting to be summoned—not a bad way to wait.

The rustic double doors opened one more time, and a deep, smooth voice with the mellow tone of a classical radio announcer said, "Ladies and gentlemen, please welcome Mr. and Mrs. Lee."

Everyone clapped as we entered the room, and the trio played a jazzy version of my favorite song, 'And the Birds Sing' by Tyrone Wells. I turned toward the announcer as he said, "Jake, Lindsey, let's get this party started."

"Linds! Check out the announcer!"

That smooth, deep voice had come from … Sean! Momentarily speechless, we both shrugged and grinned. It felt good to know where he was and what he was doing.

"I guess we'd better dance," said my new bride, laughing. "No time like the present, huh?"

We'd never danced together. In fact, we'd never danced apart. Neither of us had much experience with any type of dancing. Lindsey might have done the Hokey Pokey with the kindergarten kids, but I didn't think that technically qualified as dancing. At least this was an up-tempo tune so we could just do our own thing. I wouldn't have to lead; Lindsey wouldn't have to follow. Yep, we could do this.

Soon everyone was dancing, having a great time. The young danced with the old, the thin with the heavy, the hot with the not-so-hot. Everyone danced with everyone and had a blast.

I had notified all the guests before making their travel and hotel arrangements that they were welcome to invite a friend. Some had, some hadn't. Sean had invited two—which surprised us because we'd thought he didn't have any friends.

They hadn't come through the reception line, so two more introductions were in order. Lindsey said quietly. "I actually know one of them."

"You do?"

She nodded. "He's the custodian at my school."

I grabbed her hand, and away we went to say hello to the friends standing by the dark chocolate fountain.

Lindsey spoke first. "Hi, Tom. It's good to see you. I'm glad Sean invited you, and that you were able to come. I guess you, Judy, Mrs. Wilson, and the teachers all took personal days. What fun. I hope the school survives in your absence."

"Well, the invitation sure came as a surprise. A real nice surprise. Sean and I hadn't seen each other in quite a while. We used to live in the same apartment building up in Phoenix. I saw *her* once at school," he added in an embarrassed whisper, pointing his thumb over his shoulder toward Sean. "I've never been out of Arizona before now. So this is great. Thanks, Mr. Lee, for taking care of everything."

Then I asked Sean, who'd just joined us, about his other guest.

"Oh, this is Michelle. We knew each other in high school back in Benson."

"I'm very pleased to meet you," she said, giggling like a schoolgirl though she looked to be in her late twenties. "This is the best time I've had in my whole life." Then she looked up at Sean with big puppy eyes and confessed, "I used to have a huge crush on Sean, but he never paid any attention to me. And now I'm here. Go figure. This is so weird. But I'm lovin' it. And I love the song the band is playing. Let's go dance some more."

Tom, Michelle, and Sean all danced the rest of the upbeat, fast-paced song together and seemed to have a great time, but when the next song began—a slow song—all three headed awkwardly toward the vodka punch bowl.

"Jake, come with me. I want to ask Sean a question about the roses."

"Roses? What roses?" She gave me one of her Lindsey looks, the coy one, then she led me toward the punch bowl where Sean stood gulping his drink and watching the other guests dance.

"Hey, Sean. I just wanted to say thanks for the roses. They were from you, right?"

Sean hesitated before coming up with his answer. "That was a long time ago and for a completely different reason."

"Oh, I don't mean that single, sharp, red rose you snuck into my house last year. We're way past that." Sean seemed uneasy, and I rather hoped she'd veer away from this line of questioning. She was breaking the rule about discussing any fire, Anthony, or crime issues. "I'm talking about the three roses I received here in Seattle."

He looked blank. "I don't know what you're talking about."

I felt compelled to enter this discussion. "Uh, Lindsey. I don't know what you're talking about, either."

"I never brought you any flowers in Seattle," Sean said quickly. "Besides, nobody could get into your room with Lurch always around."

She looked surprised. "Hmm. Okay. Well, I guess I'll just have to keep searching for the flower giver." Lindsey gave Sean one of her huge, friendly smiles, but it faded as soon as we were out of his line of sight. Then she transformed into Ms. Detective right before my eyes. "How would he know that Lad—I'm assuming that's who he meant when he said Lurch—could keep him from entering my room? Huh? Answer me that. He would have had to be there to know that. So he *could* have set those roses on my bed. In fact, I think he did, or he had someone else do it. Did you see the look on his face when I asked him about that?"

I kept my voice low. "You may be on to something, Lindsey, but could we revisit this topic in a few days?"

"Yes, of course. But I think you will find the meaning of a yellow rose interesting. Trust me."

Lindsey and I moved on to talk with more of our guests, and the thought hit me. I tugged her away from the others.

"Lindsey, *she* is the one who wrote the letters to Sean. And he's kept them all this time."

"She, who?"

"Michelle. The girl he brought today."

She glanced at Michelle then looked back at me as if she thought I was crazy. "How do you know that?"

"Didn't I ever tell you about those old letters?"

"Uh, no, I don't think so. At least I don't remember you mentioning anything like that."

I'd seen and heard a lot of things back then. I guess it wasn't all that surprising that I'd forgotten to tell her some of it. She didn't look impressed with my lapse.

"Well, that was back when you were dating one of those other guys—Emmett or Marvin or I don't know. I don't remember exactly when it was, but I found the letters one day while Anthony and Sean—he was Shawna then—were in Venice, and I was searching for clues."

It seemed weird, remembering back that far. As if it was another lifetime, which I supposed it was, in a way.

She held out her hands, palms up. "Well? Don't leave me hanging, Jake. What did the letters say?"

"I didn't read any of them. I couldn't. I already felt guilty about being there in the first place, invading their privacy. I just took a photo of one of the envelopes, and I remembered seeing her name on the return address. She'd dotted the 'i' in Michelle with a heart."

We both glanced over at Michelle, who was giggling and touching Sean's arm, her eyes bright with happiness.

"I can picture that, coming from her," Lindsey murmured. "But why did he keep them all this time? And why did he invite her to our wedding?"

I shrugged. "I guess that's just more to think about—some other day."

Lindsey and I stood arm in arm, watching our wedding reception in full swing, gazing in wonder at the décor, the sparkling lights, the food, the drinks, everything. Julie had done a magnificent job of planning the reception. Of course, it hadn't hurt that the room was already rustic and woodsy, but now its white linen-covered tables were topped with pinecones, evergreen branches, gold glitter, and imitation snow. In addition to the huge punchbowl, there was a hot chocolate bar and cookies that resembled snowflakes. The best part was the crowd: old friends, new friends, and family all gathered together.

My family was few in numbers, but I planned to do my best to change that in the near future. Lindsey nudged me and pointed with her chin toward Lad, who was deep in conversation with Julie. It was interesting to see because that did not come naturally to either of them. Maybe the punch was helping them in the realm of social skills.

"Look!" Lindsey whispered, practically bouncing on her toes. "They're dancing! Julie and Lad are dancing a slow dance together."

I grinned at the sight. "Come on, Linds. I need another taste of that *Happily Ever After* vodka punch."

We took a few sips, then my mother appeared at my side. When she asked me to dance with her I almost dropped my glass from the shock. That was a first. It appeared my reputable, albeit aloof, family was coming together in ways I'd never expected. My father stepped up next and danced with Julie, who was *at last* behaving like a family member and a sister who cared about her brother. And they all welcomed Lindsey as if she were their own. I loved this. I loved all of this.

With apologies, I broke away from my mother when the trio started to play my special request: *When You Wish Upon a Star*. I needed Lindsey in my arms.

"Oh, Jake," Lindsey said, gazing up into my eyes. "You remembered."

"I will never forget that night in the Zuni Mountain Wilderness with you and Wendell and Malcolm—all singing this song."

We slow danced, nothing fancy, more like a stationary swaying. We didn't care what we looked like, and it didn't matter that all eyes were focused on us. We neglected to notice that the song had ended; we were still swaying when Lad and Elisabeth stepped over and stood at our side.

"We wanted to give you a wedding present," Elisabeth said sweetly.

That surprised me on two levels. First of all, I didn't think *sweet* was part of her repertoire. Also, I'd requested No Gifts. Oh, well.

Elisabeth smiled apologetically at me. "Actually, it's really more for Lindsey than you, Jake. We knew you would understand."

Lindsey opened the envelope, and we read its contents together. All it said was: *Please join us on next fall's Innovative Teacher Conference Tour*.

"I don't understand. What does this mean?" Lindsey asked. "There are no details, no requirements, nothing."

Lad cleared his throat. "We will keep you informed as to conference dates and locations, and you will fill in all the blanks. You will write your own contract for each conference in which you choose to participate." He finally smiled, and I thought that maybe—just maybe—he wasn't such a bad guy. "It's all up to you," he said. "It's whatever you want to do and whenever you want to do it. Think about it."

Lindsey stared at the paper, then back at the pair. "Thank you both. I really appreciate your faith in me, and also this kind of flexibility. I have a lot of things to think about, for sure."

"Our pleasure," Elisabeth said.

Then Lad turned to Elisabeth. "Let's dance one dance together before we go, Mother."

I'm positive both our jaws dropped open when we heard that. Lindsey and I looked at each other as Lad and Elisabeth walked to the center of the floor and began to dance. *Mother?* we mouthed simultaneously. After a few shock-filled seconds faded, their relationship began to make sense to me. Their mother/son partnership definitely answered the question, *Why would a retired Secret Service man go to work for an educational company?*

"One question answered, but another has just come to my attention. If Elisabeth Meriwether is Lad's mother, why isn't his last name Meriwether, too?"

I thought for a minute. "I'd be happy to check into that. I have a hunch that she has a business name and a personal name. You might want to think about that, too. They already refer to you as Lindsey Lark at the conferences."

"And Lindsey Lark was the name given to me at birth. I always loved my name, but I love being your wife even more."

"How about a compromise? You can be Lindsey Lark by day and Mrs. Lee by night—the best of both worlds." I'd managed to put a huge smile on Mrs. Lee's face, and I don't mean my mother.

We walked toward Malcolm, who had been confined to his cage for his own safety. The cage had been placed in a corner, away from cold drafts, and it gave Malcolm a decent view of the festivities. The little bird bobbed and sang, enjoying both the music and the guests' attention. Wendell had free range. We knew he'd never leave the room voluntarily as long as Lindsey was there. I kept an eye on him, anyway. I couldn't take the chance of a dog disappearance today—or any day, for that matter.

In my estimation, Wendell seemed a little anxious, glancing over his shoulder now and then with worry in his deep brown eyes. The new surroundings and people could be the cause of his concern, I figured. But whenever he and I made eye contact, his tail started wagging again, and he gave me a huge smile. He also watched Lindsey a lot. Well, Lindsey and the cake. He was very interested in the cake.

Julie led us to the table where the wedding cake and champagne awaited some attention. Laura brought the photographer over, and the guests formed a half circle around us.

Laura sidled up beside Lindsey, then whispered so we both could hear, "Sorry about my cell phone."

Lindsey wasn't angry, but she did make a comment. "What were you thinking bringing your cell phone to the wedding ceremony?"

"I'm really sorry. Old habit? Addiction?" She beamed. "Anyway, you'll never guess who the text was from."

One of Lindsey's eyebrows lifted in question. "You're right. I'll never guess."

"Brad. It was Brad."

My wife's slight annoyance suddenly turned to curious celebration. "Brad? Last winter's Grand Canyon Brad? The *same time next year* Brad? Wow! What did he write?"

"It was short and sweet. His text said: It's that time. R U coming?"

Lindsey grinned, and I handed her a glass of champagne. Now everyone's glass was filled, and Laura stepped forward to make the first toast.

"To my very best friend—who was gracious enough to overlook my occasional shortcomings—and to her wonderful new husband. May your life together always be joyful and exciting."

Everyone raised their glasses and with a rousing, *Hear! Hear!* they took a sip.

"Uh oh," I said, watching Sean step shakily up to the microphone. We were about to see a new, not improved, vodka-infused version of Sean.

"Well, I'm just pleased as Punch. That's what Anthony always said," he declared happily.

We froze, unsure of what to do. Fortunately, Sean changed the direction of his drunken toast, so rather than add conflict to this weird scene, we opted to let him continue.

"Here's to Jake," he gushed, raising his glass. "Jake the de-chec-tec-tective. You were chuggin' down the wrong track ... but on the right train. Kudos, my man, you were ... you were right, mostly. Yep! 'cept for the actual perpa-trink-trait ... " His eyes went wide with frustration. He shook his head. "Oh, hell. The bad guy."

Julie hurried toward Sean and grabbed the microphone from his hand, but he made one last statement as he stumbled away. "That's the way to do it!" he cried, punching the palm of his hand.

Several of the cabin-fire first responders placed themselves in close proximity to Sean, and Julie quickly began her toast, hoping to create thoughts and words more appropriate for a wedding reception.

She raised her own glass and grinned at both of us. "Jake, Lindsey, this is your day. And I'm honored to be here celebrating with you. Your wedding and your love for each other has brought our family and friends together for the first time, and I thank you for that. May your happiness last a lifetime."

Then someone shouted, "To the newlyweds!" and everyone swallowed the remaining champagne from their glasses. The trio took it upon itself to play an unscheduled, upbeat tune.

If I'd been in charge of the reception, we'd have cut the cake *before* taking all those sips of champagne, but here goes. I placed my hand over Lindsey's as Julie instructed me to do, and then we cut some slices and fed each other a few bites as the photographer snapped photos.

With her mouth full of cake, Lindsey asked, "How did you do all of this?"

"What do you mean?" I mumbled, knowing exactly what she meant.

She swallowed the cake and wiped her mouth with a napkin, all the while regarding me suspiciously. "I've been talking to our guests, Jake. And it seems that you arranged and paid for everyone's travel expenses, including airfare, hotel accommodations, a motor home, caterers, this lodge, flowers, clothing … should I go on?"

I glanced to the side. "My parents paid for their own expenses."

Her eyebrow shot up. "Uh huh. Good to know. Jake, I love everything you've done, but how are we supposed to pay for all of this? Are we going to need to take second jobs? My gosh, Jake. This must have cost more than my whole year's teaching salary."

"More like three years' worth." I couldn't help but grin. She looked so shocked and worried, thinking I'd racked up more debt than we could ever pay off.

The color had drained from her face. "Jake?"

I leaned close and whispered into her ear, "Trust Fund," before nibbling at her delicate lobe.

She pulled away, starting to look annoyed. "Trust who? Trust you?"

I chuckled. "No, that's not what I mean. I'm talking about a Trust Fund ... a great big one. You know," I said, reading the confusing on her face. "Family money." Her shock didn't surprise me. I'd never mentioned the fund's existence, and I'd never touched a dime of it until this week.

She looked so cute standing there in her wedding dress with her hands on her hips. "Wait just a minute. You withheld this information from me all this time?" She narrowed her eyes. "That's a lot like lying, Jake. You know honesty is *always* the best policy. Aesop illustrated that in *Mercury and the Woodman*. And you know how I feel about—"

I shook my head. "Sorry. I refuse to be fabled on my wedding day." She opened her mouth, looking uncharacteristically speechless. "Just kiss me. Kiss me, Mrs. Lee."

She scowled, but I saw happiness fighting to emerge. "I suppose I could make an exception, just this once."

"That would be nice."

"Smile," instructed the photographer. He snapped an after-the-kiss shot just before taking a few more cake-cutting photos. He was about to walk away when Lindsey spoke up.

"I need one more very special photo, please."

"I think I have shots of everything," he said gently.

Apparently not. She shook her head, looking determined. "I need a picture of my immediate family."

The photographer looked puzzled. "Sure. Whatever you want."

She turned to me. "Jake, go get Malcolm, and I'll get Wendell. Meet me on the front steps of the lodge."

"But it's snowing."

She beamed. "Yes! And it's perfect."

Click. Snap. That's a wrap!

EPILOGUE

Lindsey

Twelve months later.

I'd accepted Elisabeth's generous offer, not that we needed the money. We definitely didn't. Jake really meant it when he'd said his trust fund was a big one; there was a long line of family money there. Though neither of us would ever have to work again, we wanted to.

I took advantage of the creative freedom I'd been given, and made modifications to my participation at the conferences. I requested that any conference I attended be followed up with writing workshops within the local school districts, since as much as I loved the attention of standing in the company's spotlight, I wanted to be hands-on with more teachers and teacher trainers. More doing, less talking. I also took myself back to school, gaining knowledge in all aspects of elementary writing instruction to round out my Art Journal Writing Process.

At least for now, Sean had come to grips with the idea of returning to his original male self, and he was making incredible progress. Yes, he'd been a gorgeous woman for a while, but he seemed to be finding some contentment in the realization that he now was a good-looking guy. I still worried about him, though. Julie told me Sean was spending far too much time calling, even *visiting* Anthony, who was still locked up in a Washington prison. I could only assume they had found a tolerable way to remain in each other's lives. He still swore he had nothing to do with the fake funeral, the threatening letters, or the cabin fire. So far, no charges had been filed against him, but according to Lad, the investigation continued. Jake and I remained cautious where Sean was concerned. Too many questions were still unanswered.

Anthony was found guilty of arson, but only a Class B felony with a ten-year maximum sentence because the cabin's value had been so minimal; its owners were actually glad it was gone. Investigators expected to add more charges eventually, and an additional investigation in Tucson was on-going. Though Jake and I weren't privy to all the details, we heard bits and pieces from Lad now and then. He was still involved in the case.

Probably the greatest shock of all occurred the last time Lad made contact. He shared the newly discovered fact that he and Anthony were fraternal twins who had been adopted out separately at a young age. That made Lad my ex-brother-in-law. Sometimes the world is far too small. How would he cope with this news? Only time would tell.

Julie and Lad continued to see each other romantically after the wedding. Once their relationship was out in the open, Julie informed us that Lad planned to continue assisting Elisabeth at the conferences and also take on a few special assignments for various branches of law enforcement. Julie's psychiatric practice flourished, and whenever she found extra time she wrote articles about her experience and knowledge gained from working with her patient, Sean.

And Laura? Not much in her life has changed this past year except that she and Brad committed to meeting up not just once, but twice a year, which I suppose could be viewed as progress. It still wasn't a real relationship—at least not in my book. So Laura keeps looking.

Jake. My wonderful, loveable Jake is the best husband and pet daddy in the entire universe. He managed to convert some aspects of our year from hell into a doctoral thesis and earned his PhD in psychology with enthusiastic, unanimous approval from Wendell, Malcolm, and me. And since his passion—separate from the passion he bore for me, of course—involved mystery, crime, and investigation, he's begun an internship in Forensic Psychology.

Oh, I almost forgot to mention this fact. Jake, in his spare time, pursued his dream of writing and ended up— with a little help from me—publishing a short eBook novella entitled: *Boxing the Bones*. It's fiction ... though I happen to know he borrowed some of his story ideas from real life. Something about a plot dug deep enough to hold five bodies ...

~

Thank You!

Thank you for reading *Letters, Lovers, & Lies*. I hope you liked it.

Would you like to know when my next book is available? Sign up for my monthly NEWSLETTER for Readers and Writers and you'll receive notifications and other exclusive content.
http://www.cricketrohman.org

Reviews are helpful to readers and authors. If you enjoyed *Letters, Lovers, & Lies* please leave a REVIEW on Goodreads or your favorite online retailer.

One last thing . . .

The main characters, Jake and Lindsey, live in my head every day as I contemplate their future adventures. The dog, Wendell, is not only in my head, he's in my heart. I must admit that I had a dog just like him years ago.

Cricket Rohman grew up in Estes Park, Colorado and spent her formative years among deer, coyotes, and beautiful blue columbine. Today she is a full-time author writing women's fiction and romantic, suspense-filled mysteries about cowboys, teachers, dogs, Hollywood... even Alzheimer's.

Cricket loves to hear from readers.

Connect with her via:

Email: cricketrohman@gmail.com

Website: www.cricketrohman.org

Facebook:
https://www.facebook.com/CricketRohmanAuthor/

Twitter: https://twitter.com/CricketRohman

WANTED: AN HONEST MAN
Book 1 in The Lindsey Lark Series

With a little mystery, a little romance, and shocking twists and turns, WANTED: AN HONEST MAN captures the bittersweet growth of a young woman trying to make sense of her turbulent life.

Lindsey Lark, a beautiful, talented teacher is a fighter and a positive thinker, but after the man of her dreams betrays her, then steals her beloved dog, she struggles, and is not yet aware there is far more to her heartbreaking situation than meets the eye.

Strange, threatening phone calls begin to haunt her. A stalker, perhaps? Though she doesn't want to be alone, she isn't ready to go looking for new love, but men find her anyway.

A handsome college student involved in some tricky human research gets into trouble in more ways than one. His inherent propensity to play detective, though helpful at times, seems to attract Murphy and his darned Law far too often … and now his eyes are on Lindsey. Will his heart follow?

"Charming … unexpected … emotionally charged!"
--Amylynn Bright, author of Finish What We Started

"Ms. Rohman's entertaining novel, WANTED: AN HONEST MAN, has all the hallmarks of a bestseller including a cast of inspired characters that bring real world authenticity to her tale."
--BookViral

https://www.amazon.com/dp/B01FG5R2P4

HIT THE ROAD, JAKE!
Book 3 in The Lindsey Lark Series

Thrilling, romantic, and sprinkled with humor, HIT THE ROAD, JAKE! reinvents the 'buddy movie' concept with the written word … and a pretty woman.

Practically newlyweds, Jake and Lindsey created the perfect win-win plan. While traveling between Tucson and Estes Park in their RV, Jake would solve embarrassing mysteries schools wished to keep under wraps, and Lindsey, being the 'cover' for their presence, would conduct workshops for teachers.

They were good at finding the offenders responsible for petty theft, disappearing records, and blackmail, but when new mysteries turned personal—slashed tires, spattered blood, steamy love letters to Jake, a stolen pet … everything changed.

Who was this enemy that secretly harassed them from town to town? Jake called in some favors and managed to finagle the DNA testing of several blood samples. The results were shocking, and the dangers they faced became deadly.

"Cricket Rohman really nails it! She gives her readers a ton of depth in both the story line and character development. A great, fun read!"
---Lala Corriere, author of Bye Bye Bones: A Cassidy Clark Novel

Buy now: https://amzn.com/B01FKK8024

SAVING MADELINE

SAVING MADELINE is both heart-wrenching and humorous. In the beginning, Roxy, a naïve young actor arrives in Hollywood to follow her dream and escape from her mean-spirited family. When she finds herself coexisting in a cramped Los Angeles apartment with a wounded warrior and her German shepherd, tensions run high . . . And then her mother moves in—so much for escaping.

Along comes the well-connected acting coach, James Jonathan Jarvis, and Roxy's big break in showbiz: a part in a reality TV show with a wilderness survival theme. But a week before rehearsals begin, her mother disappears. Roxy's search leads her close to Montana where she and Madeline become trapped in a real life-and-death situation.

Though the daily obstacles that challenge these three women are paramount, they manage to find humor in their frequent calamities, and Roxy's Hollywood misadventures buffer the troubling glimpses into the world of a woman whose memory is fading.

Buy now: https://www.amazon.com/dp/B06XCDJ57B

FOREVER ISLAND
Book 1 in The Fantasy Maker Series

JD Middleton, a stressed-out chef, reluctantly embarks on a vacation offered by The Fantasy Maker. On his application, he'd requested solitude in a tropical paradise. He's shocked to be left on a desert island. It seems he'd have his solitude, but the island, though tropical, was no paradise. Nothing but ocean, sand, and jungle. No place to get a beer or a bed. What had he gotten himself into?

When a beautiful woman, Sara Sinclair, appears unexpectedly, how will he cope? She's tenacious and has a job to do. They both have secrets but join forces making good use of their opposing interests and skills as a romantic relationship builds. Will there be fireworks? When confronted with life-threatening circumstances, who will survive?

Buy now: https://www.amazon.com/dp/B076LFV38T

WINTER'S BLUSH
Book 2 in The Fantasy Maker Series

Romance, intrigue, dogs, and horses. Who could ask for more? Winn Wahlberg. She needs to get home for Christmas, but fate intervenes ... more than once.

The Fantasy Maker strikes an agreement with Clay Washington. All he needs to do is escort a young woman around Denver for five days. After that, he will receive his own fantasy vacation. What's the catch? He must pretend to be someone he's not.

Winn, a gal who's never left Yuma, Arizona, is thrilled to visit a big city and experience snow for the first time in her life. But when her escort shows up late, then gets into a fistfight, second thoughts creep in. He harbors a phobia; she hides a secret. However, they cannot deny their attraction to each other, though they try.

The Fantasy Maker mapped out an amazing week for Winn, but real life altered those plans. Their adventure is soon eclipsed by danger. Is their enemy Mother Nature or something far more evil? What do they need? A Christmas miracle.

Buy now: https://www.amazon.com/dp/B07846CCQB

COLORADO TAKEDOWN
Book 1 in The McAllister Brothers Series

Mystery, suspense, romance, a smart dog, and one intuitive horse. COLORADO TAKEDOWN has it all.

Suspense-filled and Romantic! Nothing will stop a McAllister cowboy from protecting the woman he loves.

Hannah Hudson has a distorted view of home and family due to her odd, impoverished upbringing. She longs for her own Happily Ever After, but she's willing to settle for escaping the Phoenix heat and her dreary job. Then, along comes a miracle, and her life is changed forever. With her heart filled with hope, she heads for a ranch in the cool hills of Colorado.

Shortly after arriving, her luck runs out. A tragic accident occurs—or was it a murder? A troubling reality sets her reeling. She's alone. There is no Dairy Queen, no Circle K along the winding mountain road that links the remote ranch to the nearest town. The seclusion of her new world is frightening.

Trace McAllister, a wise, local cowboy, shows up and helps her learn the ropes around the ranch and in the bedroom. Love is in the Rocky Mountain air. A brilliant cattle dog and an intuitive palomino horse add fun and excitement to their days. But their fast-blooming chemistry is fraught with conflict, secrets, and a relentless, unidentified evil.

Buy now: https://www.amazon.com/dp/B07C192G2Z

MONTANA COUNTDOWN
Book 2 in The McAllister Brothers Series

Cowboys, mountain wildlife, gunfights, love in a loft, search and rescue—*Montana Countdown* has it all.

Troy McAllister is determined to keep all the flirty, local horsewomen that frequent his ranch at a safe distance. He enjoys the attention, but a real relationship? No Way! He's too busy overseeing his ranch, the horses, and the guests — with subtle assistance from Kitchi, a wise Native American man.

Heather Holbrook, overcome with guilt ever since she stood powerless, witnessing her brother fall from the sky, begins a quest to help others — a pursuit that lands her in grave danger.

Troy and Heather are surprised when intermittent sparks fly between them, but unnamed evil forces are at work.

Nothing makes sense, and Heather turns up missing. The clock is ticking, mysteries must be solved, or people will die.

Buy now: https://www.amazon.com/dp/B07KV3PJPH

Coming Soon!
Book 3 in The McAllister Brothers Series